Forgotten and Lost

An

Exciting Spiritual and Adventure

Novel

By Deacon Patrick Kearns

Disclaimer

This book has been written with the intent of establishing fictitious characters, locations, and events. Although there may be some similarities with non-fictitious people, locations, and circumstances, the representations made in this book should be considered completely fictitious. The attitudes, actions, and convictions of the characters do not necessarily represent the same of the author or the Catholic Church and should be considered solely held by the characters.

ISBN: 9781701793583

Dedication

Forgotten and Lost
is dedicated to all those holy individuals who continually inspire me to never give up, keep fighting the good fight, to keep writing, and to see God's reflection in all those around me, especially:

My wife Liz,
Deacon Kerry,
Danny Baugh,
Mike Roberts,
Father Jonathan,
Father Uhlenkott,
Father Paul Konkler,
Jeneah, Sean, and Kenzie
Kevin, Tim, Terry, Mike, and Dan Kearns,
and so many others too numerous to mention.

Forgotten and Lost

Chapter 1

Summer had been overtaken by fall, and winter was beginning to slowly creep in for the small rural town in western Idaho. The evenings felt much cooler and each morning an icy frost covered the ground, housetops, and cars. Jonas had winterized his motorcycle by filling the gas tank full of gas and adding a fuel stabilizer. He cleaned the large cruiser and shined the chrome before covering it with a tarp and rolling it into the corner of the garage. Jonas enjoyed riding his motorcycle much more than driving his car, but with the roads now icy it would be too dangerous to ride until spring. The muted skies of winter seemed to affect Jonas. The sun had always enlivened his soul, energized him, and brought a sense of opportunity and adventure. Now, with the loss of the sunny day which would be absent for the next few months, Jonas knew he would need to find ways to combat his tendency to feel depressed.

With little to do on a quiet Saturday morning, Jonas lit a fire in the fireplace and poured a glass half full of Tullamore Dew Irish Whiskey. He opened the freezer and fetched a small velvet bag that hung from the internal shelf. After opening the bag, he grabbed and then dropped three cube-like stones into his glass. He briefly thought to himself, *I wonder if these stones are really better than ice?* He then recalled who had given him the stones as a present. The whiskey-drinking stones were a gift from his older brother, Drew, who had been shot and killed in Iraq quite a few years ago. Jonas had little detail as to how or why Drew had died. His older brother was a member of a covert military group that worked undercover and were banned from sharing any details of their missions, even with family members. All Jonas knew was that Drew enjoyed what he did and that he felt compelled to serve his country.

Jonas stood up from his recliner chair, walked to the corner of the living room, reached and opened the drawer of a side table, and retrieved a folded letter. He unfolded the letter and then began to read what was written on the official United States Air Force letterhead:

It is with great regret that we must inform you that a beloved member of our Armed Services has died in the action of service to our great country. Chief Master Sergeant Drew Kline who served selflessly and with honor was killed while on duty in Iraq. Please accept the enclosed dog-tags of the Sergeant which were recovered and know of our deepest respect for the Sergeant. Due to the special circumstances of his assignment and how he died, it was impossible to recover his remains...

Jonas' eyes filled with tears and he couldn't continue reading the letter. He instantly felt short of breath and his heart ached. He carefully folded the letter and returned it to the drawer where it was safely kept and cherished.

Needing some distraction Jonas turned the television on and began watching the news. The reporter was discussing the upcoming midterm elections, highlighting the numerous protesters and opposition rallies. There were videos of conservative groups and liberal groups each yelling and making slanderous claims against a variety of candidates. Jonas saw that no one in the videos seemed happy or content, but rather filled with anger and hatred. He turned the television off and let his mind wander. He began to question,

What has this world come to? Why are there so many unhappy people? Why am I unhappy? What is the purpose of this life? What is the point? Impulsively he stood and grabbed his car keys from on top of the counter. Within seconds he left his home, started the car, and began to drive. He had not planned a destination he was just escaping from his current state of thought and circumstance.

After driving for almost an hour Jonas came upon a small town by the name of Jordan Valley. There didn't seem to be much there; a small gas station, a restaurant, a school, and a few homes. As he entered the town, the highway became the main street for the duration of the town, which appeared to be less than a quarter-mile, and then turned back into a highway again at the far edge of the town. Continuing to drive, Jonas searched the road ahead and it appeared desolate. Rethinking his motives, he decided to turn the car around and return home. As he reversed his direction and reentered the town he saw a small weathered sign with the words "St Bernard's" and an arrow pointing to the right. Internally drawn he followed the sign's directive and turned right onto the small gravel road. Almost immediately Jonas could see a small traditional-looking church on the left side of the road a few hundred yards ahead. As he approached the church he saw that the parking lot was empty. He questioned, *I wonder if it is even open?* He stopped his car in front of the church and turned off the ignition. He felt compelled to enter the building but wasn't sure why. He had not been to Mass in quite some time. Pushing past a slight hesitation he rose from his seat in the vehicle and walked toward the front doors. He reached and took hold of the doorknob and was surprised that it opened. He was anticipating that the doors would have been locked. As he entered the church there was a small room straight ahead, an anteroom with additional doors that led into the main nave of the church. He grabbed a small prayer card from one of the side tables in the entrance room and then proceeded into the church. He sat on the most rear bench and gazed toward the darkened but beautiful sanctuary. Even though there was only scant light around the altar he could see that behind it there was a golden tabernacle and a lit red candle to its side indicating that Christ was present inside the tabernacle in the form of consecrated hosts. Jonas quietly began to pray, "Lord, I need your help. I feel worn out and seem to have lost my way. I am not sure what to do next. Please help me." He then sat in what felt to be a deafening silence. After a few minutes, he realized that he was still holding the small prayer card in his left hand. He turned the card over and written below a comforting picture of Jesus the card read:

Prayer to Know One's Vocation

Lord, my God, and my loving Father,
You have made me to know You,
to love You, to serve You,
and thereby to find and to fulfill myself.
I know that You are in all things
and that every path can lead me to You.
But of them all, there is one especially
by which You want me to come to You.
Since I will do what You want of me,
I pray You send Your Holy Spirit to me:
into my mind, to show me what You want of me;
into my heart, to give me the determination to do it,
and to do it with all my love, with all my mind,
and with all my strength right to the end.

Jonas knew that somehow the card was a sign from God and that God was speaking to him but he wasn't sure what he should do or how he should do it to be able to hear God's voice more clearly. He re-read the card six times, each time wondering how he could become more acquainted with God and how to learn to better do what God wanted him to do.

Forgotten and Lost

After spending almost an hour in contemplation, praying, and feeling a little frustrated, Jonas decided that he would return home. Just as he was about to rise from the bench a young priest entered the church. Jonas was initially startled by the abrupt entrance, and the young priest was equally surprised when he noticed Jonas. Jonas offered, "Sorry to startle you, Father." The young, handsome, dark-haired, and athletic-looking man dressed in black clerics and a roman collar responded, "No problem sir, and by the way, I am not a priest even though I look like one" as he pointed to his black clerics and white Roman collar. He added, "My name is Carter and I am a seminarian stationed here for my pastoral year." Jonas must have had a look of confusion on his face and it was noticed by Carter. The seminarian explained, "I am in my second to last year at the seminary and prior to being ordained to the diaconate and then to the priesthood we are sent to live and work in a parish as part of the ongoing discernment and formation process. I just arrived here last week." Jonas felt very comfortable with the young man and Carter must have felt the same since he sat down next to Jonas without an invitation. The men visited for the next two hours sharing aspects of their lives with each other. Even though Jonas was much older they had a lot of similarities and shared interests. They both enjoyed the outdoors, motorcycles, and had even read some of the same books. The Conferences of the Desert Fathers by John Cassian was each of their favorite spiritual books with exception to the bible.

Jonas started to feel as if he was taking too much of Carter's time, and now tired from the visit, he thanked Carter, excused himself, and then walked out of the church and back to his car. He started the engine and then drove back in the direction of his home.

Chapter 2

Carter awoke to the sound of the church bells ringing. Instinctively he rose from the bed, dressed, and began to walk toward the sound of the bells. It wasn't until he was almost halfway to the church that he fully regained his senses and realized that he wasn't back at Mount Angel Seminary, but rather in Jordan Valley. He suddenly froze when he realized that no one should be inside the church capable of ringing the bells. He had locked the doors to the church the previous night before going to bed and the small church was without a pastor, temporarily, since Father Clemens was on vacation in Rome. Now quite nervous he intensified his walking speed to investigate. As soon as he opened the door he recognized Mr. Cunningham, a local rancher and parishioner. Carter belted out, "What is it, Mr. Cunningham?" Without slowing his forceful pulling of the rope that rang the bells he responded, "The Old Hen House is on fire. We need help." Carter ran out of the church and looked in the direction of the one restaurant in town. He immediately saw smoke filling the sky above it. Mr. Cunningham was right to ring the church bells since there wasn't a local fire department and the church bells were also used for emergency notification to the other ranchers and townsfolk.

It was only a matter of a few minutes and there were dozens of people arriving to help in trucks, cars, four-wheelers, and horses.

The men and women formed a chain-line that began at the horse trough and as they filled buckets they passed them quickly hand to hand until they arrived at the end of the line and the water was heaved onto the fire. Mrs. Cunningham pumped the water pump that emptied into the trough as fast as she could, but she wasn't able to keep up with the demand. Finally, Mr. Cunningham yelled out, "Let her burn, she is too far along." You could tell these rugged ranchers were not wanting to quit but Mr. Cunningham was right to stop. He wanted to avoid anyone getting hurt especially since the fire had already consumed most of the building. Instead of trying to put out the fire, their energy and effort were now being directed to avoiding the spread of the fire to the other buildings. The bucket line broke apart and the individuals with buckets now filled them with water and walked with their buckets in different directions putting out hot spots from the floating embers.

Twelve hours later, the fire had seemed to burn all that it could burn. The Old Hen House was now a pile of ash. Luckily the fire did not spread, and no other structures were affected. At one time or another during the day, everyone from the entire town had shown up to help by either offering manual labor, use of their tools and equipment, or by bringing food and drinks for the workers. Carter spent most of the day either consoling those who felt the loss or by just being present and reminding others that life was more important than things and possessions.

All seemed to be going well, as well as could be expected for such an emergency in a small ranch town until Mrs. Cunningham screamed, "Where is Old Abe?" It was as if time stood still and the thirty-plus residents froze. Everyone seemed to have forgotten about the old homeless man who lived behind the restaurant in a makeshift hut constructed with scrap wood and cardboard. Old Abe was a military veteran and was now in his early seventies. He was polite, reclusive, and the locals always ensured that he had enough food and blankets to be comfortable. One might say that the town had adopted Old Abe.

Mr. Cunningham ran to where the hut had been and began to tug at some of the burnt structure that had fallen on top of the area. Six additional men jumped in and with the extra hands, they were able to move a tremendous amount of debris. Suddenly the men stopped as a burnt corpse was identified. Mrs. Cunningham lamented loudly, "I knew it. I just knew it. That sweet man." Carter walked up to her and put his arm around her shoulder. She immediately turned toward him and hugged him with all of her might. Tears flowed down her face and her deep emotion and reaction affected everyone else present. Carter began to cry and so did the other men and women who were nearby.

Forgotten and Lost

Chapter 3

Jonas had been struggling while trying to discern what he should be doing with his life. He felt as if he was at a crossroads and that a decision needed to be made, but what that decision was, he was unsure. He had tried talking to God but there was no discernible response. He felt alone and isolated. He turned the TV on and watched and listened to the report about the restaurant fire in Jordan Valley. He recognized Carter and could see the grief and pain in the faces of those in the video clips. Then the reporter began to describe how a homeless man was burned to death in the fire and that nobody knew who the man was other than his self-reported name of Old Abe.

Jonas turned the power off to the TV. He then began to pray for the soul of the recently departed man. His mind filled with inquisitive thoughts about the man, who he was, and what his life had been like. He wondered, did he know God? Why was he homeless? He wondered about his family and if he had been forgotten. He began to think about how the world saw this man and how God looked at him. Jonas was suddenly filled with enormous emotion, compassion, and empathy. The feeling was all-consuming and unlike anything he had ever experienced before. It was indescribable but powerful and transformative. It was as if God sent his Holy Spirit down upon him and he was now beginning to see things with greater clarity than he could have even imagined before. He immediately knew that in some way God was calling him to be His hands and feet. He knew that God had a purpose for him and although he didn't completely understand it yet he needed to respond. He grabbed his bible and car keys. With a brisk walk, he left his home and didn't even close the door behind him. Without hesitation, he drove to Jordan Valley and to the site of the restaurant fire. Remembering the footage from the news report, he walked to the alley where Old Abe had lived. Falling to his knees into a pile of ash he began to pray aloud for Old Abe, "Dear Lord, I pray that Old Abe was greeted by You at his time of need and that You comforted him. If he may be in purgatory I offer my prayers and love for him that You may pardon his past transgressions if any, and to warmly welcome him into Your loving embrace." Jonas began to cry, tears rolled down his face, and his heart felt as if it were going to explode. He could feel God's presence and it created an interior feeling of unworthiness. Jonas' mind filled with his faults, his past selfishness, his prideful actions, and the events where he had harmed others. This self-revelation was powerful and painful. The agony continued to grow, and Jonas finally yelled out, "I am sorry Lord. I am a sinner and have not been a good man. Please help me!" The pain and overwhelming anxiety intensified. Jonas wanted it to stop. He needed it to stop. Looking for some sort of relief he threw himself into the ashes face first and then began to roll in the ash and soot. He lamented in pain and disgust for almost thirty minutes with intense yelling, crying, and thrashing about, until finally curling up into a fetal position. He remained curled for the remainder of the afternoon and eventually passed out in exhaustion.

The next morning Jonas awoke, and the intense pain had subsided. He felt different, changed in some way. He felt drawn to go to the church. He arose from the ash heap, completely filthy from head to toe, and began walking towards Saint Bernard's Church. He was oblivious of how he looked, covered in soot. After a few minutes, he arrived at the doors of the church and began to enter. Carter who had been out for a morning jog caught a glimpse of a filthy man attempting to enter the church and yelled at him, "Can I help you?" Jonas did not hear him and continued into the church. Once inside Jonas felt again the presence of God and this time it wasn't painful but refreshing, honest, and pure. Recalling in his mind the stories about Saint Frances and how he stripped off his clothing in a public square, and offered his entire being to God, Jonas did the same. In an instant Jonas had removed all of his clothing and stood in front of the large crucifix and tabernacle, naked, and yelled out, "Lord, take me and use me for your work. I am a sinful man filled with shame and discontent, but I am a vessel to be filled with your love. I shed all that there is in this world for you. Please purify me, help me, I am here to serve you and those whom you love." Just then Carter entered the church and witnessed the mad man, naked, yelling at God. Somewhat frightened Carter approached the man and as he neared he recognized that it was Jonas. He asked, "Jonas, is that you?" Jonas turned toward Carter and then fell to his knees and while weeping he said, "Father, forgive me my sins. I need to be united to God." Carter gently touched Jonas' arm and in a comforting and loving voice offered, "Jonas, you are loved, please get up and have a seat." as he gestured toward the front pew. Jonas responded and did as he was asked and rose and sat down on the pew. Carter sat down beside him and said, "Jonas, you know I am not a priest yet and I cannot forgive you your sins." The explanation didn't seem to matter to Jonas and without hesitation, Jonas began, "Bless me, Father, for I have sinned…" and proceeded to voice his past sins and transgressions. Carter knew he was not allowed to give absolution but also knew that he was witnessing something important and powerful, the purging of a soul, and the bringing to light the past evils that had created such darkness and stain upon the man's soul. He listened carefully and with great attention as Jonas listed with extraordinary detail an entire life's worth of sinfulness. After twenty minutes Jonas finally ended with, "Dear Father, those are all of my sins." There was a brief pause and then Jonas continued, "Oh my God, I have offended thee, in choosing to do bad and failing to do good, I have sinned against you whom I should love above all things. I firmly intend with your help to sin no more, to do my penance, and to avoid further temptation. In the holy name of Jesus, I ask for your forgiveness, pardon, and mercy." Carter was moved by the sincerity of the confession and could see the healing effects taking place in the man who had just revealed every hidden transgression he had ever committed. Jonas looked at the seminarian awaiting absolution. Finally, Carter spoke, "Jonas, your confession was heartfelt and true. I know that God knows of your sincerity. In your contrition, I am assured that God will respond with mercy. Although I cannot give absolution, God can. In my heart, I know that you are forgiven. Go now and serve the Lord with all your heart, mind, and soul." Jonas began to cry. He knew he was forgiven and given a second chance in life. He stood and began to walk away from Carter with purpose. It was then that Carter was visually reminded that Jonas was naked and yelled out, "Stop Jonas, you need something to wear." They both looked at the pile of clothes on the floor. They were completely covered in soot and unwearable. Jonas was at least six inches taller and fifty pounds heavier than the seminarian and it was obvious that sharing clothes would not be an option. Without any other identifiable options, Carter beckoned Jonas to follow him into the sacristy. Once inside they opened a closet door and revealed a variety of albs, cassocks, and vestments. Sorting through the variety of sizes the seminarian grabbed a black cassock and handed it to Jonas. He wrapped it around his large frame and then proceeded to button each of the thirty-three buttons (one for each year of Jesus' life here on earth). The seminarian invited Jonas to have a meal with him, but Jonas declined, "Thank you but I have a mission and purpose now. God spoke to me and I must do as he commands. I will not forget your kindness, and neither will He." Jonas then turned and walked out of the church.

Chapter 4

It had been almost 2 weeks since the encounter with Jonas and Carter couldn't stop thinking about him and the holiness of the encounter. Yet, he couldn't make complete sense out of what occurred. He didn't know what exactly to think about it. Was it an act of craziness on Jonas' part, or was he a saint in the making? Not knowing what to think, and if he had acted appropriately by listening to his confession, bothered him greatly, so much that he asked to visit with his spiritual director back at the seminary to help discern the whole event.

Carter arrived at Father Mateo's office and knocked on the partially opened office door. A man's voice said, "Come in. I expect it is you, Carter." Carter responded, "Yes, Father. It is." Carter walked around the desk to embrace his director knowing that mobility was at times difficult for the priest due to his blindness. The men greeted each other with a hug. No one at the seminary knew much about the priest's history, only that he became a priest later in life and that he had become blind in an accident. He was one of the most popular professors at the seminary. He was known for applying theological ideas to practical real-life applications in such a way that even the most complex of ideas seemed simple when explained by Father Mateo.

Forgotten and Lost

Carter began to explain to his spiritual director his encounter with Jonas while trying to not miss or leave out any of the details. Father Mateo listened carefully and a few times he interrupted Carter to ask clarifying questions. Carter described meeting Jonas and instantly feeling a certain level of connection even though he didn't know why. He proceeded to explain how they reconnected after the fire tragedy and that he wasn't sure if Jonas was crazy or not. Carter noticed that during the conversation Father's eyes filled with tears a few times and he seemed to be affected greatly by the information. Carter continued to describe his encounter with Jonas as well as many other encounters during his short time in Jordan Valley. Father Mateo seemed to place the greatest amount of attention toward the events surrounding Jonas. Father then used relatable stories from the Saints to help explain some of the actions Carter witnessed regarding Jonas. Father eventually stood and grabbed for his white walking stick. He turned toward Carter and said, "Follow me." Father led Carter out of the office and down a long hallway. They entered a room that Carter had never seen before. Father sat down on a chair that rested against the wall and directed Carter, "Son, on the fourth shelf, the third book from the left, grab it." Carter did as he was asked by Father. It was an old and very thin book. Father continued, "Open the book to page six and follow with your eyes." Carter turned the page and listened as Father recited by memory word by word what was written in the book:

"Whosoever, therefore, comes and teaches you all these things that have been said before, receive him. If he teaches so as to increase righteousness and the knowledge of the Lord, receive him as the Lord. Let every apostle that comes to you be received as the Lord. But he shall not remain except one day; but if there be the need, also the next; but if he remains three days, he is a false prophet. And when the apostle goes away, let him take nothing but bread until he lodges; but if he asks for money, he is a false prophet. And every prophet that speaks in the Spirit you shall neither try nor judge; for every sin shall be forgiven, but this sin shall not be forgiven. But not everyone that speaks in the Spirit is a prophet; but only if he holds the ways of the Lord. Therefore, from their ways shall the false prophet and the prophet be known. And every prophet who teaches the truth, if he does not what he teaches, is a false prophet. And every prophet, proved true, working unto the mystery of the Church in the world, yet not teaching others to do what he himself does, shall not be judged among you, for with God he has his judgment; for so did also the ancient prophets."

Carter listened carefully trying to understand the meaning. There was a brief pause as if Father was praying for direction and guidance. He then continued, "Son, what I shared with you is from the Didache. A work that was written in the first century by the early Christians and influenced by the apostles themselves. Some even say it was written personally by the apostles. I want you to take the book and read it, pray over it, and in time your understanding of Jonas will be revealed." Carter didn't know what to say. He had always known Father Mateo to explain everything in such detail and with such clarity that there was nothing else to consider. Yet, here, he explained nothing. His sharing only led to more questions. Before Carter could ask any further questions, Father dismissed him, "Son, often less is more. Take time to heed my words. Go now and may God always keep you. I will see you again in a few months." Carter stood, briefly thanked the holy priest, and then left the building.

Chapter 5

After leaving Carter a few weeks prior, Jonas had set off on foot only wearing the donated cassock and his sandals. Instead of heading east toward his home, he set off in the direction of the west. He left his wallet, all of his belongings, and all of his past life behind.

He had only walked a few miles when a trucker by the name of Terrance pulled over and offered him a ride. Terrance lived in the small town of Marysville, California, and was a cross-country truck driver. He had previously been an executive, managing a medical equipment company for many years, but when the company decided to close its doors a few years back he decided to change careers and to live a much simpler and lower stress life. Terrance was a large man, six feet two inches tall and weighed close to three hundred pounds. His large frame and deep loud voice created an intimidating presence, yet his warm smile and kind demeanor was a contradiction.

Terrance has a soft spot for men and women who appeared to be struggling in life. He could remember all too clearly when he had gone through some tough times in the past and had prayed that someone would reach out to him in his time of need. Those memories were probably the catalyst that led to inspiring him to pull over and to extend a helping hand to Jonas.

As soon as Jonas climbed up and into the cab of the large vehicle Terrance immediately asked, “Are you hungry? Do you want something to eat?” Jonas had not eaten for two days and his stomach was empty and produced a constant rumble. Jonas replied, “Sure, any little thing would be greatly appreciated.” Terrance thought for a minute and then said, “Crawl back into the sleeper section” pointing to a bed area behind the seats “and you will see a small fridge on the left. Open it and get us two sodas and grab the thing wrapped in tinfoil.” Jonas did as he was instructed and quickly returned with the drinks and tinfoil bundle. He began to hand everything to Terrance. Terrance replied, “You keep one of the sodas and look at this” after receiving the tinfoil package he unwrapped the foil and said, “It is my wife’s specialty. I call them Little Debbi Snacks. They are squares of fudge, peanut butter, and a whole lot of goodness.” Terrance laughed and then grabbing a large piece he shoved the entire thing into his mouth and then handed the bundle to Jonas. Jonas graciously accepted and quietly bowed his head and whispered, “Dear Lord, thank you for this nourishment. Please allow it to feed my body and my soul and bless Terrance and his wife for this precious gift.” Terrance was caught off guard by the sincerity and reverence of the prayer. Something deep within him awoke, a deep emotion at the witness of Jonas’ action.

Terrance kept quiet for the next ten minutes trying to understand what was happening within him. He felt calm but restless at the same time. He felt safe but uneasy. He felt uncomfortable but comforted by Jonas’ presence. While Terrance was dealing with this internal struggle of discernment, Jonas broke apart one of the squares and slowly he placed a piece onto his tongue and savored the Little Debbi Snack. Terrance, realizing after a few minutes that Jonas had only eaten one small piece, he asked, “Don’t you like them? You only ate a small piece?” Shyly Jonas remarked, “No they are delicious. I just didn’t want to be presumptuous or greedy.” Terrance laughed out loud and then commented, “No, no brother.

They are all for you. Eat them all. Heaven knows I don't need them." Jonas ate another square and then carefully re-wrapped the package and gingerly pushed it deep into his cassock pocket.

The drive from western Idaho to Marysville was an eight-hour drive crossing the Owyhee mountains, through southern Oregon, and across a large portion of Nevada. Terrance enjoyed talking and having Jonas along. Jonas was an attentive listener and was a treat for Terrance.

During the drive, Terrance shared detailed aspects of his life beginning with his childhood. He spoke about his early life, attending school, playing sports, and even his past girlfriends. Terrance disclosed things about his life that he had never told anyone else before. He stopped a few times mid-sentence and thought, *Why am I saying these things to this man I just met?* He then realized that Jonas was not judging him but allowing him to share freely all that needed to come out into the light. A few times some rather painful memories were revealed and disclosed, and the more things that Terrance identified and revealed the more things seem to come to mind.

The sharing of personal memories continued for the next four hours until finally Terrance had a profound moment of clarity and said, "Jonas, I had always thought I was a pretty good guy. I don't drink anymore, and I have never cheated on my wife. But as I have listened to myself over the last few hundred miles I have now come to see myself for who I am. I have not been a good guy at all. I have been and am very self-centered, prideful, and inconsiderate." Terrance's voice quivered some and then became silent. Jonas knew that the Holy Spirit was working within him and felt no need to say anything. Jonas knew that the Spirit was working through the silence. Terrance had purged every sinful memory of himself for the last few hours and now the Spirit was helping him sort through all those memories. As Terrance internally struggled, he was unaware that Jonas was privately praying and asking for the intercession of his prayers and that they would be directed to Jesus, but through Mary, Saint Peter, Saint Paul, and all the holy people he could think of.

It was now seven o'clock in the morning and there had been three hours of silence in the cab. Jonas had received a directive a few hours prior while deep in prayer, and it was now time to share it. Jonas spoke, "Terrance, I have a simple request. Would you mind stopping at the Catholic church just for a minute?" Terrance was initially startled by the interrupted silence. However, he welcomed the distraction. He had worked himself into an internal frenzy hyper-analyzing all that he had shared with Jonas and had been scrutinizing all of his past transgressions. Terrance finally replied, "Sure Jonas, we are about to cross the bridge into Marysville and we can stop at Saint Joseph's parish. I don't think it will be open yet, however." Jonas smiled but didn't comment.

The large semi-truck pulled up in front of the gothic-style church and Terrance released the air brakes making a loud whooshing sound. Jonas caught a glimpse of what he thought was the rectory and asked, "Is that the rectory?" Terrance stated, "Yes, but I don't know who the priest is anymore. I haven't been to Mass for almost twenty years." Without hesitation, Jonas turned and looked Terrance directly into his eyes and with a stern, but a kind voice said, "Do you want to make things right with God again? Do you want to become whole?" Terrance wasn't offended at all. He felt something deep within him respond. He felt somehow the invitation was coming from someone much greater than the homeless man sitting next to him. He knew this was an invitation that could change his life. Terrance was filled with emotion, so much that he could not speak. All he could do to acknowledge Jonas was to nod his head in acceptance. Jonas quickly directed, "Follow me" and jumped out of the truck and began to walk toward the rectory.

As soon as Jonas arrived at the rectory door he knocked firmly. After a few seconds, the door opened and standing in the doorway was an elderly priest who commented, “Can I help you?” Jonas explained that Terrance wanted to have a confession, that it had been almost twenty years, and that he needed and wanted to become friends again with Christ. The priest seemed a little confused and hesitant, probably because of the appearance of Jonas who was unkempt and wearing a cassock. The priest eventually looked past Jonas and looked directly at Terrance who was so filled with emotion it showed on his face. Father asked, “Is that true my son, do you want to confess?” Terrance nodded in acceptance. The priest then invited both men into the rectory. Although Terrance entered, Jonas chose to remain outside.

Terrance was warmly greeted by the priest who helped him with the forgotten formalities of the ritual and then carefully and prayerfully listened as he unburdened his soul. The priest commented that Terrance must have been thinking about these things for a long time. Terrance explained that he suppressed a lot of it and it wasn’t until he had met Jonas that he remembered. The priest gave Terrance some sound advice and then absolved him of his sins. Immediately a tremendous weight had been lifted from him and he felt as if he was a new man. His entire being filled with the emotions of happiness, opportunity, hope, and love. The priest commented, “It isn’t often that a man comes to me with twenty years on sins and desires to be united with Christ.” Terrance responded, “It wasn’t my idea, Father, at least not initially. It was Jonas’. There is something very special and holy about that man. I could not put my finger on it at first but now I see that he is either my angel, or a prophet, and sure was someone sent to me by God. He saved my life.” The men stood, shook hands, and then turned toward the door. Terrance spoke, “Father, you have to spend just a minute with Jonas to see what I am talking about.” The men walked out of the front door of the rectory and looked for Jonas. The streets were clear, and he was nowhere to be found. As quickly as he entered Terrance's life, he had now disappeared.

Chapter 6

Carter had been consumed with his work at the parish. The pastor, Father Clemens, had written to Carter and stated that his vacation in Rome had been better than expected and that he was going to ask the Bishop if he could remain for an extended sabbatical. The priest explained that he had been a pastor for many years and had never taken a sabbatical. Now, finally having had taken some time off he realized that if he didn't take additional time to nourish his mind and soul that he would be doomed for burnout and a mental breakdown. The pastor was asking for Carter's support knowing that although he wasn't a priest yet he could provide spiritual support to the parishioners in his absence. He also knew that the Bishop could ask one of the retired priests to support Carter by making weekly or bi-weekly stops at the parish for Mass coverage. Initially, Carter felt as if he should decline the request, especially since the whole purpose of a seminarian year at a parish was to learn about parish life through the observing and witnessing of events from an experienced priest. Yet, he also knew that the pastor needed the rest and that God would not ask of him anything he could not handle. He eventually wrote the priest back and gave his support.

Carter had called Bishop Kerry and requested a meeting to discuss his assignment and also to discuss the needs of the community. The meeting was set for 1 p.m that day. Carter arrived a few minutes early at the diocesan offices in Boise and was greeted by Alma the receptionist. He was informed that the Bishop was expecting him and that the Bishop's secretary would be down for him in a few minutes. It wasn't long until Liz, the Bishop's secretary exited the elevators and greeted Carter with a kind voice, a smile, and a warm handshake. She escorted Carter to the fifth floor of the large building, and then down the long corridor, and into the entryway of the Bishop's office. As soon as Bishop Kerry caught the eye of Carter he stood up from behind his large desk and invited Carter to have a seat located in front of the desk. Bishop Kerry spoke in a kind and caring voice, "What can I help you with my son?" Carter began to explain the situation of Father Clemens being away and that he had received a letter from him with his desire for an extended sabbatical. As Carter spoke he could tell that the Bishop was already aware of the situation. The Bishop responded, "Yes, Carter, Father Clemens not only wrote to me. He also called me, and we spoke at great length about this. I agree he not only deserves a sabbatical, but he also needs one. He is one of our greatest priests and has done so much for our diocese."

Chapter 7

Jonas made his way across town toward the Safeway store at the edge of town. He had been told that behind the store was a levee and beyond the levee, close to the river, there was a homeless camp. Jonas' stomach began to rumble, he had not eaten for quite some time. He paused for a moment and looking up toward the sky, he prayed, "Lord, I know you care for me. If it is your will I would gladly take some nourishment." He then proceeded to the corner where a man stood holding a sign that read, HUNGRY VETERAN – WILL WORK FOR FOOD. Jonas walked toward the man and dressed the way he was, in a dirty cassock, the man holding the sign paid no attention to Jonas. Jonas stood next to him without speaking. After about five minutes the man finally spoke to Jonas, "What do you want, this is my corner?" Jonas smiled and replied, "God knows what you are doing, and He has asked me to tell you that He loves you and that there is a better way to live than this." The man holding the sign instantly began to weep. Jonas knew exactly why the man was so moved. God had instructed Jonas to say those words knowing that the man was capable of working and holding down a job but that he chose to beg for money instead. He used the money to buy drugs, and he was addicted to methamphetamine. The man wasn't a veteran and had no intention of working for food. It was a deception. Jonas continued, "Christ wants you to live an honorable life, a holy life, a life you can be proud of." The words deeply affected the man. He suddenly stopped crying and internally he felt significantly different. He had been experiencing some withdrawal symptoms, nausea, and severe anxiety since he had not injected methamphetamine for almost 24 hours. He had also felt as if he was crawling out of his skin and had severe cravings. Yet, instantly the withdrawal symptoms and cravings had vanished. He physically felt better than he had in years. The man stood speechless and in awe of what had just occurred. His encounter with Jonas and hearing the words that he spoke had transformed him. Jonas turned and while parting from the man he left him with these words, "Go to St. Joseph's parish and thank God personally for what he did for you." Without hesitation, the man dropped his sign and walked in the direction of the church.

Jonas continued toward the grocery store and as he crossed the street a woman drove her car next to him, rolled down her window, and handed Jonas a twenty-dollar bill stating, "Have a nice day and God bless you." Jonas smiled and thanked God for His generosity. Jonas entered the store and his presence immediately drew attention from the store manager. The manager approached Jonas and said, "There will be no stealing of food here. I am tired of you people coming in here and taking things. If you don't have any money I will need to ask you to leave." Jonas looked at the name badge of the manager and it read, MATTHEW, GENERAL MANAGER. Jonas replied, "Mathew was the name of the tax collector, he too thought money was the answer to everything until he met Christ." Jonas raised his hand from his pocket and revealing the twenty-dollar bill asked, "May I proceed young Mathew?" Somewhat embarrassed the manager nodded his head in approval.

Jonas walked around the store thinking and praying. He must have walked up and down every aisle and had not touched an item. Thirty minutes had passed, and Jonas still had not gathered anything.

Unknown to Jonas, Matthew had been watching him on the closed-circuit video cameras. He was curious and intrigued. Eventually, it was too much to handle, not knowing what Jonas was doing, and Matthew approached Jonas and asked this time in a much friendly manner, "Is there anything I can help you find, sir?" Jonas answered, "I am trying to find a way to feed the people behind the store who are starving. I can feel their hunger and it pains me greatly. I just don't know the best way to spend this money." Matthew was caught off guard by that response. He immediately thought of his grandmother who had raised him. As a child, Matthew would accompany his grandmother to the store and she would carefully walk up and down the isles trying to figure out how she would use the little money she had to not only feed her family but the poor family next door whose father was killed. Matthew never completely understood why his grandmother felt compelled to care and provide for people who were not family and especially when they didn't even have enough money to provide for themselves. Matthew then recalled his grandmother's words that she shared one day, "I can feel their hunger and it pains me greatly." Matthew's eyes filled with tears and he turned to Jonas and said, "You give me the twenty dollars and I will have my assistant help you." Jonas smiled, he sensed that something good was about to occur. Jonas handed Mathew the money and then waited as Matthew abruptly walked away. After a minute, two young women pushing a shopping cart approached Jonas and shared, "Our boss said to have you fill this cart with food so you can take it to the people you were talking to him about." Within minutes, and with the help of the women, the cart was filled with fruit, loaves of bread, salamis, cheeses, snacks, and enough food to feed an entire army. Jonas and the women pushed the cart to the checkout counter and one of the women proudly shared, "Mathew said that there will be no charge for these items, they are a donation." Without slowing their stride the women pushed the cart right past and through the checkout aisle and when they reached the exit door they handed the cart off to Jonas. Jonas smiled, took the cart, and thanked the women. Jonas turned and looked in the direction of Mathew and slowly raised his hand in a thankful gesture. Mathew's eyes erupted in tears and they began to stream down his face.

Chapter 8

Carter laid in bed almost all-night thinking and praying. He felt confused with what God was asking of him. He voiced aloud in a lamenting tone, "God, I just don't get it. I am still in the formation to become a priest. To become a priest. Did you hear that? I am not yet a priest. I don't know what I am doing. The whole reason for my pastoral year was to live and work with a priest so I could learn. You took my priest away and I needed him. You have me here, in a parish, and what can I do? I am not even a deacon yet. I can't celebrate a Mass. I can't baptize. I can't hear confessions. I can't do anything." He then laid in hopeful anticipation that God would speak to him and that in some way he would feel some consolation. Yet, there was noting that followed but silence. Carter felt isolated and alone. He sensed darkness surrounding him and he knew he needed to do something or he risked becoming encapsulated in the darkness. He abruptly rose from his bed, quickly showered, dressed, and grabbed the car keys, and left the rectory. Once outside, he contemplated entering the adjacent church building to spend some time in front of Jesus in the Blessed Sacrament, but instead, he entered his car and began to drive away from Jordan Valley. He had two choices, to head northwest toward the Oregon towns, or east and toward Idaho. He chose the easterly direction.

It wasn't long, and he had driven sixty miles and was approaching the town of Caldwell. During the drive, he felt remorseful for not first entering the church back in Jordan Valley, and had decided that when he came upon Caldwell he would visit Our Lady of the Valley Parish and would apologize to Jesus. After making his way through a few surface streets he eventually parked his car in the church parking lot and entered the church. He hadn't been to that parish in some time and instantly he noticed that there was a large and magnificent stained-glass mural behind the tabernacle and a heavenly angelic painting above the sacristy. The beauty of it was breathtaking, and he instantly felt a sense of awe and holiness. He continued to walk toward the tabernacle and when he arrived he dropped to his knees and began to pray, *Lord, I am sorry for not making you my primary focus in my life. I know I need to trust and to be patient. Please forgive me. I know you will not give me more than I can take but help me, please. I need some help. Please help me. I feel tired, alone, and sad.* Carter, still on his knees, praying, was startled by a voice that was directed toward him and coming from the rear of the church, "John, we are waiting for you, let's go." As soon as Carter turned to see who it was speaking to him, exposing his face to the man from whom the voice originated, he then heard from the tall slender man, "I'm sorry, I thought you were John, I apologize." Carter felt that in some way God was intervening and he stood and walked toward the man. The man was now able to see the clerics that Carter was wearing and responded, "I am sorry Father. I didn't mean to disrupt you. I should know better. My name is Mike. I am a parishioner here." Carter responded, Nice to meet you, Mike. I am Carter and a seminarian. I am currently stationed at Saint Bernard's in Jordan Valley and came here to pray. I am not doing so well right now. I know God has a plan for me, but I am just not getting it. This Catholic journey of mine is a little scary and to be honest, a little lonely and sad right now." Carter realized that he was sharing very personal thoughts and feelings with a stranger but that didn't seem to matter. He sensed that Mike was a good man, a holy man and that the encounter was inspired by God. Mike's eyes teared at hearing Carter speak with such transparency, honesty, and vulnerability. Mike instantly took Carter's hands into his massively large hands and held them and said, "Let's pray." Carter agreed and listened as Mike began aloud, "Dear Lord, creator of everything good in this world, I ask that You hear our prayer and give us direction and guidance. Your soldier is wounded and needing help, please guide us and put upon our hearts a way of healing the wounds of this seminarian."

A period of silence followed the prayer and then suddenly Mike squeezed Carter's hands even tighter and then proclaimed, "I know what it is. You are to join us on our podcast." Carter looked bewildered so Mike explained that along with a few friends they had a weekly podcast by the name of The Idaho Catholic Podcast and that they met each week and recorded a session. He further explained that the podcast had rekindled his faith in a special way by not only talking about the faith but meeting with the guys each week in a kind of fellowship. Carter liked the idea of making a few new friends. Carter smiled and agreed to participate. Mike, who must have stood at least six foot seven in height towered over Carter and upon hearing Carter's acceptance he wrapped his long arms around Carter and gave him a bear hug.

Mike and Carter made their way into the conference room that was located in the hall just outside of the main church. The room was set up with professional microphones, a mixer, and two laptop computers. It looked like a professional recording studio. Also, in the room were the men that Mike spoke about. "Hey guys, this is Carter and he is a seminarian and the newest member of the Idaho Catholic Podcast Team." The men stood and one by one greeted Carter with a handshake and words of welcome. Instantly Carter felt happy and knew that God had heard his prayers.

Chapter 9

Jonas, with a shopping cart full of food from the grocery store, pushed the cart around to the back of the store and then up, over, and then down the levee road heading toward the river bottoms. The supermarket was located on the west side of Marysville and adjacent to the Feather River. The desolate area on both sides of the river remained somewhat hidden by the elevated levees and was often populated by homeless people.

As Jonas pushed the shopping cart toward a homeless encampment it was apparent that he had gained the attention of many. There must have been at least fifty men and women who had erected tents or tent-like structures and had been without regular meals for some time. Jonas had intended to offer the food to those suffering but before he had the opportunity to voice his loving gesture he was rushed upon by at least ten of the homeless people who instantly began beating Jonas. He received numerous kicks to his body, what felt like dozens of punches to his face, and finally, he fell to the ground in agonizing pain. Three of the men grabbed the cart and while running pushed it into the encampment while one woman remained behind. She looked at Jonas with tears in her eyes and spoke, “I am so sorry. They don’t realize who you are.” She then turned and walked toward the encampment.

After a few minutes, Jonas attempted to stand but the pain in his ankle prevented him. He sat back down on the ground and looked up into the sky and prayed, *Lord God, forgive them, they do not know what they have done.* Just then, Terrance, the truck driver from their previous encounter appeared and after stopping his Ram pick-up abruptly he jumped out of the truck and yelled, "Jonas, what happened to you?" Jonas minimized the incident but explained that his ankle was injured and that he was having difficulty walking. Terrance explained that he was having a family reunion at Riverfront Park, just a few minutes' from where they were and that his cousin Len Napoli from Redding was there and could help him. Jonas smiled and accepted Terrance's help. Terrance assisted Jonas to his feet and then supporting his weight helped Jonas to slide into the tall truck.

As promised, after a three-minute drive, Terrance and Jonas arrived at a park-like setting with picnic benches, shade trees, and a large gathering of people. Terrance helped Jonas out of the truck and encouraged Jonas to wrap his arm around his neck and shoulder to off-set some of the weight from his injured ankle. The two walked side by side until they reached the group. It was apparent that some in the group were a little guarded and concerned by the appearance of Jonas. Jonas was still dressed in the back cassock that now had become quite dusty and dirty and his sandals appeared overly worn and torn. His grey beard had grown long, and he seemed unkept. Yet, as soon as Terrance shared, "This is Jonas. This is the man I told you about," instantly there were smiles and words of welcome. Debbi, Terrance's wife, had already dished up a plate of food and served it to Jonas expecting him to start eating it without delay. Clearly, he had been without food for some time, he looked emaciated. Debbi watched intensely as Jonas took the roll from the plate, blessed it, broke it, and slightly raised it he mumbled a few inaudible words. She couldn't make out what he had said but was mesmerized by what she saw. There was something very holy about this man and she recalled the words of the Bible, *they recognized him in the breaking of the bread.* After a moment she realized that she had been staring at Jonas and not wanting to make him feel uncomfortable she returned to her lawn chair back at the picnic table to ponder what she had just witnessed.

After disappearing for a few minutes Terrance returned with a tall, well-groomed, handsome man, and introduced him as Len Napoli. Terrance explained that Len attends Our Lady of Mercy parish in Redding and that he was also a physician. Len asked if he could examine Jonas' ankle and with a positive verbal confirmation from Jonas he began. He gently moved the foot in all directions while supporting the ankle with his other hand. He was careful to not hurt Jonas and after about a minute Len declared, "It doesn't seem to be broken, just a sprain. I will be right back. I have something for you." Len immediately drove his car away from the river bottoms, over the levee, and to a small medical supply store next to the medical center. He purchased their highest quality ankle brace and a walking cane for the price of $213. He quickly returned to the gathering site and with Jonas' permission applied the brace and instructed Jonas on how to properly walk using the cane. Instantly Jonas felt better and could bear weight on the ankle with the assistance of the high-quality brace. Jonas began to thank Len but before any words came out of Jonas' mouth Len said, "No need for thanks, except thankfulness from us. Terrance shared that you changed his life and we have seen a new man emerge in front of our own eyes regarding Terrance. We are indebted to you." A tear formed in each of Jonas' eyes and he simply looked up toward the sky and whispered, "Thanks be to God."

Chapter 10

Father Mateo had decided to stop teaching at the seminary due to his age. He had been finding it more and more difficult to keep up. He had the full support of his superiors and they had offered him options such as being a spiritual director for the seminarians and visiting priests or living a life of prayer for the Church. Father had taught for so many years that he didn't know how to do anything else. All he knew was how to be a priest and how to teach the faith.

Father had befriended a new seminarian who had arrived from Idaho. His name was Dylan. One day Dylan had explained to Father that there was a very small but successful movement in the Church where inspired priests would set up two chairs in busy secular areas and post a sign stating things like, "Ask a priest a question?" or "Need Confession?" Dylan stated that many of the priests felt that they were engaging with people who most likely would not visit a parish and that they inspired others to begin a process of thinking about the faith and the Church with many encounters. He also stated that there was some risk as well since many people in the secular world have disdain or even hatred for what they incorrectly believe priests and the Church stand for.

After a great deal of discernment and prayer, Father Mateo had asked and received permission from his superiors to have Dylan, or another seminarian, drive him into the town of Mount Angel daily so he could set-up a station where people could ask him questions. He decided that he would establish a spot under a shade tree in Fisher Memorial Park just off the main street. Knowing Father's plan, a group of seminarians found two nicely padded lawn chairs and created a professional-looking sign that read,

ASK FATHER MATEO

A QUESTION ABOUT LIFE.

IT'S FREE.

The sign was light blue honoring Mary and the letters were bright white representing holiness. Each corner of the sign had small crucifixes painted and the letters Q and O in the wording of the sign had the miraculous medals embedded into them. The sign was affixed onto thin metal rods and could be easily placed into the ground for stability.

As previously planned by Father, at 7:00 am before class, Dylan drove 1.5 miles down the hill from the seminary into the town and assisted Father Mateo to his designated spot in the park under the large oak tree. The chairs were placed side by side, slightly directed toward each other and separated by about 2 feet. Dylan paced off three large strides away from the chairs and then firmly pressed the metal rods at the foot-end of the sign into the ground facing in the opposite direction of the chairs. Other than the two men, the entire park was unoccupied. Dylan asked Father, "Father do you need anything else?" Father replied, "No, just come fetch me at the end of your day." Dylan thought it was quite curious that he wasn't bothered by what time he would be picked up and that he had made no arrangements for food or water. Dylan commented, "Father what about food or something to drink?" Father smiled and stated, "God will provide." Dylan was shocked by the comment and stated,

"I will come at four-thirty today to get you if that is alright?" Father replied, "Whatever fits your schedule, you know where I will be."

After Dylan drove away Father enjoyed the silence of the park. He could hear the small birds chirping and flying around. He was able to identify the scampering noises of the squirrels looking for food and their playful jumping from branch to branch. There was a slight breeze that grazed his face, Father found it delightful and cooling.

Many hours had gone by and Father had detected that some people had come and gone from the park, but no one had engaged him yet. It was now one o'clock in the afternoon and Father's stomach began to growl. Suddenly a small child had come upon him and in a sweet voice, she asked, "Do you like green beans?" Father laughed and responded, "Why yes, do you have some green beans?" the young child chuckled in the sweetest way and said, "Why no, why would I have green beans in the park." The young child then, without hesitation, climbed upon Father's lap and started petting his beard while talking about dolls, the birds, tea parties, and anything else that came to mind. Father assumed the young child must have been about three or four years old and he sensed that a parent must have been close but he didn't hear them. The two enjoyed their playful conversation for the next thirty minutes until a soft woman's voice from what seemed to be from about thirty feet away, said, "Alright Katie, time to go." The small child abruptly and innocently kissed Father on the cheek and then jumped off of his lap and ran in the direction of what Father assumed to be her mother.

Although the park had many visitors that day no one else chose to visit with Father. He remained in his designated spot the entire day, some of the time sitting and at other times standing. The solitude didn't seem to bother him. He enjoyed listening to the sounds that filled the park and he envisioned that Christ was sitting in the other chair most of the day and they had wonderful conversations about life, heaven, the soul, and the early saints.

Dylan arrived as promised at 4:30 pm and assisted Father into the vehicle. He loaded the chairs and the sign and returned Father to the seminary. During the short drive, the two shared superficial conversation but Dylan was preoccupied and that affected his ability to effectively visit with the elderly priest.

Chapter 11

After Mike had finished the introductions between the men and Carter greeted each man with a firm handshake, Mike gestured the men over to a side table where there were two pizzas, a few bottles of alcohol, and what looked to be a mini keg. Mike blessed the food and with haste, the men began piling pizza onto paper plates. While connecting a hose and CO2 cartridge to the mini-keg Nick explained that this was his newest batch of microbrew. He called it *Heavenly Bliss* with a touch of caramel. Once tapped, and with the pouring of the first glass, foam squirted into the air. Nick exclaimed, "Oh shit, way too much CO2" and turned the knob on the cartridge. He then proceeded to pour five perfect glasses of beer for the guys. John was the first to taste the creation and then Mike. Both in unison proclaimed, "That is a great beer."

The men ate and drank for the next twenty minutes while catching up on each other's lives, families, work-life, and endeavors. Mike was the natural leader of the group, but each man possessed a uniqueness that complemented each other well. Mike in his late 30's worked in finance and had seven children. John in his early 40's worked for the State, had two children, and his wife was from out of the country. Nick who was in his middle 30's was a university track and field coach, had two small children, and was in the midst of adulthood. Ryan in his late 20's worked in agricultural research and was recently married with his first child still in the womb. And now, Carter, who was in his twenties, and a seminarian, added to the eclectic Catholic group of men.

Now quite full of pizza, and each with their second glass of *Heavenly Bliss*, each man sat at the table and pulled their professional microphone close to their mouth. After flipping the record button on the computer Mike started the Podcast, "Welcome listeners, we have a wonderful program for you from the Idaho Catholic Podcast Crew. This is Mike Roberts and the usual guys are here with us today, please introduce yourselves," while gesturing to the other men at the table. Immediately each of the men shared their names, "This is Ryan Kline," "This is Nick Collins," "This is John Allen," and then Mike continued, "And we have a new addition to the crew and his name is Seminarian Carter." Mike then hit a button on one of the computers and the room filled with applause and the men chuckled into the microphones. After a few seconds, Mike explained that the topic for the episode would be on the issue of prayer and discernment.

For the next 40 minutes, each of the men contributed to the conversation about how they approached prayer and discernment in their lives and shared pertinent examples that undoubtedly resonated with many of their listeners. Mike had previously shared with the group that their weekly listener count had steadily climbed since starting the podcast the year prior and that they had almost 5000 listeners each week now. The men jokingly harassed each other at times and comforted and supported each other at other times when the conversation turned personal and sensing that emotions were raw. The charism of the podcast was about how ordinary Catholic men can live extraordinary lives when they keep their focus on God and surround themselves with other men striving to be holy. Eventually, the podcast came to an end when Mike turned on the theme music and stated, "Well, as you can hear the music, that is a reminder that this session of the Idaho Catholic Podcast is coming to a close. We would like to thank you for listening tonight and accompanying us on our journey toward holiness. Know that we here are praying for you daily, understanding the fight that we all fight to try to be a reflection of God's love and truth to the world. Please tell a friend about this podcast, that it is easily found at www.IdahoCatholicPodcast.com. Goodnight, God bless, and may He always keep you close." Mike then clicked the computer button and enthusiastically shouted, "That's a rap!"

Carter enjoyed his time immensely with the men. He needed to be with other men who although struggling at times were being successful in living authentically Catholic lives. There was a deep bond between the men and Carter was invited to be a part of that. They lived varied lives but were grounded and connected in one thing, the truth of the faith, and a relationship with those of the Trinity. The gathering was much more than just a recording of a podcast, it was a time of fellowship, comradery, prayer, and inspiration to continue living the life the men were called to live. These gatherings helped to sustain these men and Carter felt and witnessed the power of the Holy Spirit in the room as the men shared their experiences. Internally, he felt at peace knowing that God had listened to his prayer and that he was gifted with these new friends.

Chapter 12

Jonas said goodbye to Len, Terrance, Debbi, and the rest of the family, and although they offered to have Jonas stay with them for a while he declined. Earlier in prayer, he heard God instruct him to keep moving along while reminding him that he was on a mission. During the picnic, Jonas had witnessed numerous trains passing by on the tracks on top of the levee. He also noticed that often the trains would stop to add or release train cars at the interchange of tracks. He knew that he would have the perfect opportunity to catch a free ride somewhere. Walking gingerly and with a slight limp he made his way over to the levee and when the train stopped he climbed up and into the freight car. Surprisingly, he was greeted by another man as soon as he sat down. In the rear of the car was a man who appeared to be in his 30's, had long black hair that draped past his shoulders, and looked tired and life-beaten. Yet, he smiled and shared, "Greetings fellow free-loader." Jonas smiled in reply and added, "Greetings right back to you, my name is Jonas. Who might you be?" The man stood, wobbled some while an empty bottle of vodka rolled out of his lap, and then declared, "I am Cyrus, the suffering servant of God Almighty and His mother." He then became light-headed and collapsed to the ground. Jonas began to move toward him to ensure that he was alright but then stopped as soon as he heard the snoring.

Forgotten and Lost

The train was heading north and although it was making frequent stops along the way it was quite smooth and enjoyable for Jonas. The weather was tepid, and the speed of the train created a mild breeze that cooled the flesh. Jonas enjoyed the scenery of rice fields, wheat fields, fruit orchards, and distant rolling hills.

Eventually, Cyrus awoke and reintroduced himself failing to recall the previous encounter. Jonas could see that the young man, who he guessed was in his late twenties or maybe even middle thirties, was a troubled soul. Cyrus stated that he was in a band, that he played the bass guitar, but hadn't played for some time since he lost his guitar. The men visited and shared stories from each of their lives and enjoyed each other's company. Looking outward from the freight car Cyrus recognized the town of Red Bluff and stated that the next town would be Redding and that was where he would get off. Cyrus explained that there was a shelter there by the name of The Good News Rescue Mission and that he could eat there and take a shower. He also shared that he had started attending RCIA classes at Our Lady of Mercy Parish and that ever since he met Mary he wanted to become Catholic. Jonas asked about Mary, thinking it was a parishioner. Cyrus explained, "Well Mary sent me Anna who is my angel. She cares for me, brings me sandwiches, and even picks me up for RCIA classes. She is my sponsor. But it was Mary who opened my eyes." Jonas was intrigued by what Cyrus was sharing and wanted to hear more. Cyrus continued, "One day, I had been drinking and I am pretty sure I was going to die. I was in the backroom of where there was an after-hours party and I must have fallen because I was wedged in a corner and couldn't get up. I think I hit my head because there was blood and my head felt like it was going to explode. I prayed that God would put me out of my misery. It was then that Mary appeared. She was just instantly there. She was life-size but hovered above the ground. She wore this light blue dress that flowed in the air. It was transparent but you couldn't see through it. It was unlike any color I had ever seen. Her face radiated with such beauty and purity I almost couldn't look at her. Being in her presence consumed me. Instantly my pain evaporated. I completely sobered and filled with such a peace that I had never experienced before. Then she turned her head slightly to the side and gazed with her beautiful blue eyes into mine and it penetrated deep into my soul. She spoke to me, without words, but I could hear her. She said that I am her suffering servant and that my soul is beautiful. She said that her Son had a special mission for me and that I will change people's lives by just being me. She encouraged me to follow the Son and that I needed the Sacraments to help find my way. She told me that her Son had given me an angel and that her name was Anna." Cyrus paused, and his eyes filled with tears. Jonas could tell that Cyrus deeply believed every word he had shared and that the encounter had changed him forever. Jonas patiently waited until Cyrus could compose himself. After taking a few deep breaths and wiping his eyes he continued, "She then floated toward me and kissed me here" pointing to his forehead. "That kiss was the most pleasant experience I have ever had. I can't explain it. I instantly knew how much I was loved. I wish others knew just how much they were loved. If they did they wouldn't feel so alone." Jonas began to cry realizing that Cyrus had an authentic encounter with the Mother of God.

Eventually, the train arrived in the town of Redding and slowed and finally stopped in the middle of the town at what appeared to be a small rail station. About a block away there was a gathering of people and banners were hanging that read, Farmers Market. Cyrus yelled out, "Anna, Anna." Then a young beautiful woman standing about fifty years away at the market turned and when she spotted Cyrus she started running toward the train. Jonas asked, "Is that your girlfriend?" Cyrus laughed and then commented, "Oh no, I would not even think that. She is my angel. She is the one Mary said would be my help and she is. She loves me, not like a boyfriend, much deeper. She loves me as God loves me.

We are just friends, but much more than just that. Our souls are connected." Just then the train started moving and Cyrus jumped off while Jonas continued northbound.

Chapter 13

Father Mateo had now been visiting Fisher Memorial Park in the middle of Mount Angel daily, dropped off and picked up by the seminarian Dylan, for five weeks. The locals had become accustomed to seeing Father stationed under the large oak tree with his two padded lawn chairs and his blue and white sign. Initially, very few found the courage or had the desire to engage with the elderly priest, but each day more and more were now stopping by. Surprisingly, more non-Catholics spent time with Father than Catholics. Little Katie would visit almost daily for a few minutes, sitting upon his lap, and while stroking his gray beard, they would discuss important things like tea parties, stuffed animals, and Dora the Explorer.

Now it was almost two in the afternoon and as usual, Father's stomach began to growl. Each day he purposely neglected to bring any food or water knowing that God would provide and that God truly knew what and when he needed what he needed in his life. Unable to see due to his blindness Father relied upon his hearing to know when people were approaching, yet, as he aged his ability to hear progressively diminished and he often didn't discern another's presence until they were upon him. In response to their voice, he would sometimes be startled and then apologize

Forgotten and Lost

A man wearing a roman collar approached Father and asked, "May I sit down Father?" Father Mateo immediately responded, "Welcome my son, have a seat. What should we talk about?" The man didn't reveal that he was also a priest and introduced himself simply as Robert. Robert asked, "Father will you hear my confession?" After confirming that it would be an honor, Father Mateo reached into his right front pocket and pulled out a small, thin, purple stole made of silk and with gold fringes. It looked very worn but still presentable. He placed the stole around his neck and initiated the holy confession by making the sign of the cross and verbalizing the introductory prayers. He then asked, "So what are your burdens, my son?" Robert paused for a few moments and began to breathe very deeply. Father Mateo reassured him and encouraged him to bear his soul and to reunite with God. Feeling comforted Robert began, "Bless me, Father, for I have sinned. I have sinned greatly." The man paused and began to breathe very deeply. Father Mateo intuitively knew this was going to be a very difficult confession but at the same time knew it would bring healing and comfort. Quietly Father Mateo prayed that God would give the man courage, humility, and the strength to reveal what had him in such darkness and pain. Suddenly Robert began, "Dear Father, I am addicted to pornography. I watch it for hours each day and it has consumed me. I set up a special server, so I could access the dark web while at work and that my work would not be able to see what I am doing. What I am the most ashamed of is that I am attracted to child and homosexual pornography." Now that his darkest secret had been revealed Robert began to hysterically cry. Father Mateo allowed the man to cry for almost two minutes without speaking, feeling that the man had so much emotion and hurt inside of him that it needed to be purged. While the man cried Father prayed constantly for God's intervention and that He would give him the right words of instruction. Father Mateo, feeling that the man had cried sufficiently enough now asked, "Robert, have you acted upon those sins? Have you violated anyone?" Robert replied, "I have not touched anyone or anything like that. I am not proud of the things I have done to myself, making the sin worse. I feel that I am out of control and need to stop this, but I can't." Father asked and was informed by Robert that he had been sinning in this capacity for almost ten years now and that this was the first time he had ever confessed this sin and addiction. Robert added a few lesser sins to his confession and then finished by stating he had confessed all the sins that he could recall. Father gave some council regarding sexual sin and how that it not only disrespects God but how it harms society as a whole. He encouraged Robert to begin the habit of doing some type of chore or task whenever he was tempted to view pornography, to be distracted from the immediate temptation. He also encouraged him to start seeing a professional counselor who was Catholic. Father then prayed the prayers of absolution and as he touched the man's head in the healing gesture of forgiveness it was instantly revealed to him by God's grace that this man was a priest. Father Mateo could not withhold his emotion and tears began to flow from his eyes. Robert asked, "What is it, Father?" Father Mateo shared, "I know you are a priest, God just revealed it to me and my heart hurts for you. The devil is trying so hard to hurt us and he is using any weakness to destroy us." Robert was filled with embarrassment and knew he had been beaten by the devil. The men sat facing each other in silent prayer for the next ten minutes. Finally, Father Mateo said, "Brother, this is what I recommend. You have committed no crime, just sin. Like any addiction you need help. You need God's help and the help of man. I ask that you inform the Bishop of your weakness and ask for help. Trust him. He is your shepherd. I also ask that you keep a minimum of weekly confession or more often if you sin again. Never hold any sin on your soul. You and I both need the full strength of God's grace to fight against the devil. Also, I will pray the Divine Mercy Chaplet for you every day that you will be healed. You are forgiven, go in peace my son." Robert crossed himself, stood, thanked Father Mateo, and walked away internally healed and on his way to freedom.

Chapter 14

Jonas remained on the train until he reached the mountain town of Mount Shasta. He could see the majestic mountain from the freight car door and was amazed that it was still covered in snow during the summer month. As soon as the train slowed and before it had completely stopped Jonas found a way to slide down the rusted external frame of the train car and onto the ground without reinjuring his ankle. He then said another quick prayer for Len who had shown him such kindness and for purchasing for him the ankle brace and walking cane.

Following his intuition, he began to walk away from the train depot and quickly found himself on West Lake Street. He noticed that many of the vehicles were pulling motorboats and camper trailers and he thought that he must be nearing a lake. After walking for almost an hour his ankle was now beginning to ache, and he knew that he would need to stop and rest soon, or maybe even erect some sort of shelter off and away from the road before his ankle gave out on him for good. Suddenly, a man in a white pick-up truck pulled up next to him and as the passenger side window rolled down a middle-aged man wearing a polo-type shirt and a golf hat asked, "You need a ride?" Jonas knew it was a sign from God and instantly looked up toward the sky and whispered, "Thank you." He then turned to the man and replied, "I would truly enjoy that." Jonas climbed into the truck and thanked the man for his kindness. The man introduced himself as Danny and shared that he was on his way to a men's retreat in the forest. He also added, "The retreat was planned for almost a year and 22 men had signed up. That son-of-a-puddle John Evanoff and that son-of-a-good-for-almost-nothing Paul stood me up again. I have all this food, all this gear, and here I am alone. Maybe it is for the good." Danny then laughed out loud and continued, "No, I like those guys. I am just mad because I was looking forward to sharing some time with them." Jonas patiently listened as Danny shared the whole history of the *Men-In-Motion Retreats* and how one retreat, in particular, changed his life. "That year we were having a winter retreat at my cabin and during one of the activities, we decided to split into teams. Each team had seven men and we were given only a small shovel and three one-gallon buckets. We had ten minutes to build the tallest column of snow we could. It was hilarious to see the men dig with the buckets and to start piling the snow one scoop at a time. The columns quickly rose to over 10 feet and the men were trying to figure out how to outdo each other. Some of the men were digging while others climbed on top of the shoulders of other men. Men then handed the shoulder-mounted men buckets of snow as fast as they could as they tried to build the column taller and taller. The retreat leader yelled out that they had one more minute. Each team decided to start rolling the snow on the ground into elongated snowball-like beams that looked more like a cross between a bowling ball and a fat baseball bat while trying to get as much height as they could. The plan was to have the tallest man sitting on the shoulders of the second tallest man place the snow-beam-object on top of the column at the last second to gain the first prize. In a frantic crunching of snow and flinging of the beam on top of the column, they both stuck and the timer yelled that the time was up. In their hast no one initially noticed, but as the men took a few steps back from the columns that stood almost twelve feet high they saw on top of each column was a perfectly sculpted statue. Mary the mother of God was on one of them, and a Christ the King on top of the other. It was truly miraculous. What we witnessed took our breath away. We all knew what we had done, and in the brief eight seconds it took to create that final mound of snow there was no way we could have created that. The men could not have created something so beautiful if they had five days to create it. It took my breath away and convinced me on the spot that Christ was present there amongst us. To this day, that experience has changed my life. I can't describe it, but I was somehow transformed that day." Tears welled up in Danny's eyes as he finished telling the story and Jonas smiled a confirming smile knowing the truth in Danny's words.

It didn't take long, and the men arrived at the group site G-38 at the Lake Siskiyou Campground and Jonas immediately noticed the large professional-looking banner posted at the entrance of the large group site that read:

As soon as Danny pulled into the site a group of men yelled out, "Danny is here, let the games begin." Danny was immediately filled with joy and excitement. He truly loved the men and especially being with them in the forest. Danny jumped out of his truck, greeted the men with handshakes, and then turned to introduce his new friend. Instantly he realized that he did not ask the stranger his name and that he also didn't even ask him if he wanted to come to the campground. He turned in embarrassment and asked, "Sorry friend, I didn't even ask your name." Jonas smiled and shared, "My name is Jonas and I am a wandering soul." The men looked at Jonas from head to toe and were not very impressed with his presentation. He was without a doubt a homeless man, unkempt, for some reason was wearing a Catholic Cassock and extremely worn sandals. He was wearing the outfit, but he didn't look like any priest or religious brother they had ever seen before. Dennis was the first to speak in reply, "Nice to meet you, Jonas. Have you known Danny long? Are you a religious?" Jonas reacted almost instantly, "Well, as for Danny we have just met but are connected in a special way, and for being religious, wouldn't you say all of us here are in one way or another?" Jonas didn't answer the question but with his warm smile, gentle nature, and the way he carried himself, it was instantly apparent that he wasn't just a homeless man. There was a holiness about him, but it was obscure and indescribable. The men were drawn to Jonas, but most didn't know why.

Chapter 15

Carter returned to the rectory feeling peaceful, inspired, and happy. He grabbed the church keys from the key holder mounted on the wall next to the kitchen phone and walked out of the rectory to the church next door. Using his key he unlocked the weathered wooden entrance door and entered the church. He walked over to the confessional and entered through the door on the left which was the "Priest's door," unlike the confessor's door which was on the right, and sat down in the chair reserved for the holy priest. He began to fantasize about what it might be like to be a priest and hear the confessions of others, and what it might feel like to absolve people of their sins through God's saving grace. He even made the gesture a few times as if he was signing someone with the cross of the priestly blessing. It wasn't long until Carter fell asleep in the confessional. Maybe it was the long drive back from Caldwell, the stress of meeting new friends, or maybe it was even the many restless nights that recently stole away his sleep. Nevertheless, he was exhausted and now at rest.

Suddenly, Carter awoke to a voice coming from the other side of the confessional. "Bless me, Father, for I have sinned, here are my sins." He detected a faint shadow of a small woman behind the privacy screen. He didn't recognize the silhouette nor the voice. She continued, "Father, I am so ashamed. I did something so terrible

I don't know how I can ever live with myself. I just knew my husband was cheating on me and it infuriated me. He had promised to love me in good times and in bad, and that he would remain true to me forever. He knew how I felt about cheating and that I had caught my father cheating when I was ten and how that led to their divorce. He promised he would never cheat on me and I believed him." Carter knew he needed to speak up, he wasn't a priest, he wasn't even a deacon, yet there he was listening to the woman's sacred confession. Just as he was about to speak up she began to cry out loud and while speaking even faster she shared, "He started coming home later and later at night. I asked him where he was or what he was doing, and he was so secretive. After a few months, I had convinced myself that he had another woman and that he was going to leave me. Angered, I drove to my old high school boyfriend's house and began to flirt with him. We drank a few beers and before I knew it we were having sex in his pick-up truck. I knew it was wrong, but I didn't care. I wanted to hurt my cheating husband." She then began to not only cry but wailed in lamenting emotions. Her words were almost indiscernible due to the quiver in her voice, but Carter clearly heard, "Then my husband came home late that evening and shared that he had taken a second job at the livery stable to earn enough money to buy me the engagement ring he wasn't able to buy before our wedding. He stated that he had promised himself that before our first wedding anniversary he would have a ring on my finger." Carter began to panic, he knew she was wanting to hear some holy and sage advice and that she would want forgiveness, a forgiveness that he could not give. He began to deeply pray to God for help. Sweat began to roll off his forehead like a river, his palms began to cramp, he began to hyperventilate. He was in trouble and he knew it. She then added, "I ruined our lives. I did the exact thing I feared he was going to do to me. I cheated on him when he was sacrificing his time and his life for me. He was loving me, and I turned away from him. I ruined everything. I did what my parents did to each other." She then began to scream, "I hate myself. I hate myself." Carter froze, he didn't know what to say. He was in way over his head and he knew it. She continued, "I know what, I am going to go home and pack my bags and run away. I will leave a note stating what I did and run away so he will never have to see me again." Carter began to pray even more fervently and as he kneeled on top of the kneeler his right knee slid off the pad and slammed onto the ground. Without thinking and reacting in sheer pain from his knee hitting the concrete, he belted out, "Damn it!" The woman instantly reacted, "What Father, am I damned. Am I damned to hell if I do that? Yes, you are right. That was a stupid idea. What was I thinking? You are so right Father. I will go home and tell him exactly what I did and beg for forgiveness. One should always be truthful even if that means reaping what we are due to our mistakes. I knew this was where I needed to come. Thank you, Father." And without a further word she rose and ran out of the confessional. After waiting a few seconds Carter peeked out from his side of the confession booth fearing that there might be a line of people waiting for confession. He was relieved when he discerned that the coast was clear, that no one was there. He ran to the church doors, locked them from the inside, and collapsed onto the floor.

Chapter 16

Father Mateo had just returned to the seminary and after thanking Dylan for the ride back from the park he started to make his way to the priest's residence when he heard the rumbling of a motorcycle. The noise grew in intensity as the motorcycle continued to approach Father. Just as Father contemplated jumping in one direction or another to avoid being run over the motorcycle came to a screeching halt and the motor silenced. Without his vision, Father was unable to see that the man was stocky but short, bald, probably in his late fifties, and had a long dark and unkempt beard that draped to the man's mid-chest. He looked worn by a life of drugs and alcohol. He was covered in tattoos and his eyes were shielded behind dark sunglasses. He looked to be a shady character, to say the least. In a raspy smoker's voice, the man shouted, "Are you, Father Mateo?" Father replied, "Yes, that is I?" The man continued, "Can I have a minute of your time?" Father agreed, and the men made their way to the bench at the edge of the koi pond. The man introduced himself as Jimmy and stated he had been referred to him by an old family friend. Father wanted to ask who the old family friend was but being tired he instead chose to get right to the point and ask, "So what is it that I can help you with?" The man began to explain that he had been trying to find the right job but every job he had turned out to be a horrible experience. He stated that he had been in prison for stealing cars and motorcycles and he thought people in prison were better than those people outside of prison. He reported he identified as a devout Catholic but after so many failed attempts of trying to become a parishioner he was finally giving up. He stated that he had finally decided to join the church of Satan's Disciples. He reported that he was currently a minor disciple, which was what they call those who recently joined the church, and he finally felt that he had joined a church that he could really connect with. Father began to sense great darkness surrounding the man and it began to make Father feel very uneasy and anxious. Father asked, "What is it that makes you feel so strongly about this church and faith, if you can call it that, it is right for you?" The man explained, "I feel like these guys really get it. They live by a code that puts them above everyone else. They see the world as people striving for power and that there is no one outside the church that is good. These guys live by a rule that sets them apart from everyone else, they despise authority, and fight against it because all authority breeds greed." The more the man spoke the darker his words became and Father not only sensed a great evil in his midst, but he became sickened and nauseous by the man's intensity. Father stood and shouted, "This is making me sick. The evil here is too much. I can't be next to it." The man looked completely shocked and offended by the holy priest's reaction and replied with great anger, "That is exactly what Father Avery said and exactly what he did to me too. He even went so far as to say that I needed an exorcism. I knew you couldn't help. You all just don't get it. You can't see that I am right and that you all are blinded by your religion. You can't see the truth even if it hit you over the head." In disgust and while spitting in every direction the man climbed back on his motorcycle, started the engine, and sped away from Father. Immediately Father knelt on the ground, pulled a worn rosary out of his pocket, and began to pray the Divine Mercy Chaplet:

Forgotten and Lost

You expired, Jesus, but the source of life gushed forth for souls, and the ocean of mercy opened up for the whole world.

O Fount of Life, unfathomable Divine Mercy, envelop the whole world and empty Yourself out upon us.

O Blood and Water, which gushed forth from the Heart of Jesus as a fount of mercy for us, I trust in You!

O Blood and Water, which gushed forth from the Heart of Jesus as a fount of mercy for us, I trust in You!

O Blood and Water, which gushed forth from the Heart of Jesus as a fount of mercy for us, I trust in You!

And continued to pray the entire prayer for the next 10 minutes while meditating on and praying for the troubled man's soul.

After finishing his prayers he had lost his appetite so Father skipped dinner and went directly to bed. Completely drained of energy from the emotions spent during the encounter and the fervent prayers, Father fell asleep within a few minutes. Once asleep the Holy priest began to dream. He appeared to be re-experiencing the encounter with the troubled motorcycle man but this time he could actually see the man's soul. The words coming from the man's mouth seemed to mimic what he had experienced just an hour prior but Father's attention was drawn not to the words but to what he was seeing within the man's soul. He could see that there were at least three demons within the man and the darkness that entrapped them was not only without light but appeared to be something much more. The soul was not only without light, but appeared to be a place of rot, decay, and the opposite of life. He then smelled an overwhelming smell of sulfur and the stench of feces. It made him gag and he began to choke. As he choked and gasped for air he exhaled upon the man's darkened soul and as he exhaled he whispered the words, “Get away Satan and all you evil ones. Jesus Christ will heal this man.” Father then witnessed the evil spirits being expelled with such tremendous force from out of the man’s soul, across the room, and up and out through the ceiling. The man shook and trembled as if he was having a grand mal seizure. When the flailing of his extremities ceased the man’s eyes opened and he voiced in a small and quiet voice, “I was waiting for someone to do that. I came to you and you couldn’t see me underneath the darkness. I needed you and you pushed me away.” Father abruptly awoke from the disturbing dream and wondered if it were a nightmare or if God had revealed something prophetic. Unable to rest his mind after that experience he remained awake and pondered what he had just experienced for the rest of the night.

Chapter 17

Jonas helped Danny set-up a small pup-tent and then attempted to insert the newly purchased army cot into the tent. With a man at each end of the cot they tried to insert it through the door but as they pushed and guided the cot they quickly identified that the cot was at least six inches longer than the tent and that there was no way the cot could be used. Danny instantly began to lament, "I told myself the only way I would tent camp again would be with a cot. I swore I would never sleep on the ground again and here I am having to sleep on the ground, Damn it!" Jonas listened to Danny vent his frustration uninterrupted for at least a minute and then asked, "Do you have any rope?" With a puzzled look, Danny replied, "Yes, why?" Jonas said, "Just trust me, brother." Danny walked over to his pick-up and from behind the seat, he fetched some rope and delivered it to Jonas. Jonas removed the tension bars from each end of the army cot and tied a piece of rope to each end of the cot's fabric through the grommets. He then took each end of the rope and threaded it through an opening near the upper edge of each end of the pup tent and then tied the rope to a tree branch. It didn't take long and Danny could tell that he was converting the cot into a hanging hammock that would be suspended by the adjacent trees, but still housed within the tent. The design was ingenious, and Danny kicked himself for not thinking of it. In less than three minutes Jonas had turned a bad situation into something wonderful. Danny now had a bed to sleep in. Instead of it being a cot it was now a suspended hammock. Jonas instantly earned Danny's respect for thinking outside of the box and for his creativity. In appreciation, Danny offered Jonas the use of some of the camping supplies he had brought for the friends who had stood him up, but Jonas only accepted the use of the frayed wool blanket that appeared to be Army surplus.

As the afternoon turned into evening all the men had established their personal camp areas and they then gathered around the campfire. Melvin who had been a Boy Scout and Eagle Scout leader for almost 2 decades had already scoured the area for seasoned wood. With the completion of numerous trips, carrying handful after handful of branches and logs, he had stacked them into a large pile. He then started the fire by rubbing two sticks together making sure the men could see that he used no matches in creating the flame. Melvin was a very humble man but a few years prior Danny had bet that he could start a fire quicker with a flint stick than Melvin could with wooden sticks and had lost the bet. Since then it had become a tradition for Melvin to start the initial fire of the retreat with his rubbing sticks in plain view of the men to ensure that Danny would never forget the lost bet. This wasn't done in meanness but rather in masculine chiding.

Many of the men had brought different types of alcohol with them for the camping retreat and as they arrived near the fire they staggered their bottles on top of a nearby large rock that luckily had a flattened top. The collection of booze resembled a well-stocked bar that included whiskey, rum, vodka, a large box of red wine, and some other homebrew concoctions. One by one the men poured a glass of their favorite beverage and then took a seat in a folding chair that circled the fire. Dennis grabbed his guitar and began to play modern Christian melodies in the background as the men began to socialize. Dennis was quite talented and an exceptional singer. Periodically the men would be distracted from their conversations by the beauty of the music and the delightful tone of Dennis' voice and would stop talking to relish in the serenity of the moment.

Jonas felt very comfortable with the men and although he wasn't drinking any alcohol, he did feel included in the gathering. After a few hours had passed it was apparent that some of the men had frequented the bar more than others since some of their voices showed a progressive loudening with each new beverage and some social etiquettes were disappearing, mainly the restraining of shared flatulence. At one point one of the men challenged one of the other men to a tree-climbing contest and it took John, one of the men who had not over-indulged, almost an hour and an entire box of Cheezies to talk the two men out of climbing the trees in the dark and to understand that their questionable intoxication might be problematic to the challenge. Thanks to John a potential disaster was averted.

After that incident, Jonas decided to excuse himself from the group and after grabbing his borrowed blanket he quietly slipped away out of sight from the group. He nestled down under a large pine tree using both hands to scoop pine needles together and create a small mound that he rested his head upon as nature's pillow. Jonas fell asleep and was able to remain asleep while missing the further antics, pranks, and embellished stories that went on well into the night around the campfire.

Chapter 18

Carter was excited two weeks had gone by and it was already time for another meeting of the men to record The Idaho Catholic Podcast. He was especially excited he would be able to spend some quality time with his newly discovered friends. His drive from Jordan Valley to Caldwell didn't seem too boring since he had so much to think about. A few days prior Mike had sent him an email with the announcement that they would be meeting at his house for the recording and also an invitation for Carter to lead the session with a topic of his choosing. Ever since he received the email he had been pondering a variety of ideas and potential topics he thought could be interesting to the audience and to the other men as well. He thought of things such as Celibacy or Holy Orders. He thought about Friendship and Sacrifice. He had thoughts of Discernment and Discipleship, but none of his ideas seemed to satisfy him completely.

The gathering was to take place at 7:30 pm but for some reason, Carter miscalculated how long the drive would take and he arrived twenty minutes early. Mike lived on a small farm with a milk cow, goats, chickens, and a goose. He and his wife Janell grew most of their own vegetables and had three large gardens as well as two greenhouses. While parking the car Carter noticed Mike sitting on an overturned five-gallon bucket next to the small barn that housed his tractor. He had a cigar in his mouth and a beer in his hand. Carter called out, “Hey, Mike.” Mike looked up and waved for Carter to come over. Carter immediately noticed that Mike looked saddened and was not his usual chipper self. As soon as Carter came close enough to not have to shout he asked, “Are you alright Mike?” Mike looked up from staring at the beer bottle in his left hand and replied, “Not really, I just heard some devastating news.” Carter immediately thought it must have something to do with his wife or one of the children. Mike added, “I received three phone calls today, one after another from each of the guys. Ryan is moving to Washington for a new job. Nick is moving to Buffalo to be a head coach at a university, and John is having back surgery and said that he doesn’t want to continue with the podcast afterward.” A tear welled up in Mike’s eye and with a slight tremble in his voice, he said, “Everyone is leaving me, all of my closest friends who have been helping me in my journey. I feel like I have been kicked in my stomach.” Carter didn’t know what to say so he said nothing. The two men remained in quiet contemplation for the next few minutes. Suddenly a red pickup approached and slid to a dusty stop just a few yards away from the men. Mike looked up and identified the man climbing out from inside of the cab. Before Mike could say a word, the jolly-looking, slightly overweight man belted out, “Did I hear that Mike needed my help?” Mike looked over toward Carter and with a mildly irritated look explained, “That is Matt Ping. I left him a voice mail two weeks ago asking if he could come over and help me move my refrigerator. That was two weeks ago, and we did it, without Matt’s help, the same day.” Mike breaking out of his funk sarcastically replied, “Great to see you, Matt. We already moved the fridge, but we do have the podcast tonight and maybe you could shovel the cow manure while we record?” Matt laughed and without missing a beat he responded, “That would be great, not the shoveling thing, but being part of the podcast. I would love to join you guys.”

Forgotten and Lost

Matt had been trying for months to wiggle his way into becoming one of the co-hosts of the podcast." Matt had hosted a show on Salt and Light Radio, a Catholic Radio station in Boise called The Men's Room for some time and was quite capable. Now knowing there were going to be three openings, Mike hesitantly offered Matt to stay and join them. Matt was so excited to hear the invitation that he jumped up high into the air while screaming, "Yahoo." When he landed he must have twisted his ankle because as he landed he collapsed to the ground and rolled at least three full turns to his left. Mike and Carter instantly laughed out loud in reaction to the hilarious event and then realizing that Matt might actually be hurt tried to calm themselves. Mike inquired, "Are you alright, Matt?" Matt slowly rolled onto his back and then sat up. He reached for his right ankle and began to palpate all aspects of the region. He then took his shoe off, and then the sock that had a hole the size of a quarter at the site of his big toe and began to visually inspect his entire foot. He pointed his toes away and then retracted them. He then wiggled each toe, one by one, and then finally commented, "I think I am alright." Mike immediately burst into laughter and shared, "Well, that is good news, cause if you weren't, I didn't want to be the one to tell you that you rolled right on top of that big cow shit pile that I was wanting you to shovel. No need now, you smashed it into the ground and created fertilizer, except for the part that is in your hair, across your back, and stuck to your ears." Matt screamed, "Damn it!" Carter erupted in laughter and just then Nick, John, and Ryan walked up and joined in with the bellowing response.

After a few minutes, the intensity of the laughter had died down and Carter said, "I know what the topic of tonight's podcast should be." The men all looked in anticipation of what Carter would say next. Carter then added, "Shit happens." The men immediately launched back into intense laughter, all but Matt who was still trying to pick the manure out from inside his left ear.

Chapter 19

Father Mateo had not been back to the park for almost a week. He had somehow acquired what the doctors had diagnosed as influenza or the flu. His body ached down to his bones and he had no appetite. He felt nauseous and his fever had remained between 100.2 and 102 degrees for almost four days. He was taking Tylenol alternating with Motrin to help with the aches and to try to control the fever, but it didn't seem to be helping. The seminarians and the other priests at the seminary feared that they were going to lose their old friend and mentor if he didn't soon begin to show signs of improvement.

Father's illness and witnessed suffering was on the mind of so many at the seminary. Dylan had remembered listening to Father Mateo teach on suffering and felt compelled to find the notes he had received from the lecture. He specifically remembered a handout he had received, and he dug through his notebooks and folders and eventually located what he was looking for from that special day. The handout read,

Drawing from sickness and suffering he experienced in his own life and in the lives of those he served through his priestly ministry, St. Josemaria explained that, Suffering is part of God's plans. This is the truth, however difficult it may be for us to understand it. It was

difficult for Jesus Christ the man to undergo his passion: "Father, if you are willing, remove this cup from me; nevertheless not my will, but yours be done." In this tension of pleading and acceptance of the Father's will, Jesus goes calmly to his death, pardoning those who crucify him.

This supernatural acceptance of suffering was, precisely, the greatest of all conquests. By dying on the cross Jesus overcame death. God brings life from death. The attitude of a child of God is not one of resignation to a possibly tragic fate; it is the sense of achievement of someone who has a foretaste of victory. In the name of this victorious love of Christ, we Christians should go out into the world to be sowers of peace and joy through everything we say and do. We have to fight — a fight of peace — against evil, against injustice, against sin. Thus do we serve notice that the present condition of mankind is not definitive. Only the love of God, shown in the heart of Christ, will attain the glorious spiritual triumph of men" (Christ is Passing By, 168).

Dylan had convinced the other first-year seminarians they should all fast from food and begin a 24-hour around the clock prayer vigil at Father's side to accompany him either to health or to his final reward. Each of the men signed up for an hour shift and sat at Father's bedside praying unceasingly. Some of the men prayed rosaries and others their liturgy of the hours. Some of the men prayed novenas and some just sat and talked to Father even though he did not respond. Father had not awakened for the first two days of the vigil, but eventually, his fever did break and he slowly regained consciousness. It was almost 2 a.m. when he first spoke, "Anthony, thank you and all the boys for tending to me." It was the seminarian Anthony that was at his side when he did finally wake and he was shocked that the blind priest would have known that, especially since he had not said a word for the entire hour he had been with the ailing priest. Anthony was speechless and didn't know how to respond. Eventually, he was able to mutter out the words, "You are welcome, Father," but he seemed to fall back to sleep before hearing them. Or, at least that is what Anthony thought.

At the top of the hour, Anthony was relieved by Mark, who an hour later was relieved by Paul, who was then relieved by Phillip, and then Jimmy, Scott, Juan, and so on until morning came and Dylan opened wide the curtains and allowed the beaming morning sunshine to enter the room. As soon as the light hit Father's face he awoke and belted out, "I have seen it. I have seen it." Dylan inquired, "What is it, Father, that you have seen?" Father added, "I have seen our destination and our Lord." Excited beyond belief Dylan asked, "Can you describe it to me Father?" Father took a deep breath and then paused as if he needed to quickly pray before reacting to Dylan's request. Then he spoke, "My dear Dylan, I do want to share what beauty and love and brilliance and honesty and truth He has revealed to me, but He said it is only my personal revelation and not to be shared with anyone else at this time. He said that I am not to speak of it anymore but that it was a consolation to strengthen me for what I must still do here on earth. He said He is not quite ready for me yet, and that I am to fulfill my purpose here first before He will take me home." Father smiled a deep and authentic smile and then remained silent. Dylan, although extremely let down, understood.

Chapter 20

Jonas was the first to wake up and wandered over to the site of the previous night's campfire. After taking a stick and probing into the ashes he was able to detect a few coals. Crouching down he blew onto the coals and with a little effort they began to glow a fiery orange-red color showing there was still energy awaiting additional fuel. He then reached over and grabbed a few branches from the woodpile and snapped a few creating small twigs. He placed the twigs on top of the coals and with only one puff of air they ignited. Patiently he added slightly larger twigs and branches to the fire and in a matter of minutes, there was a roaring morning campfire. Melvin was the next to awaken and he approached Jonas, smiled, and commented, "Good morning, I'll be right back. Have my morning constitution and then time for coffee." Jonas watched as Melvin grabbed a roll of toilet paper from a box sitting on top of the picnic bench and a small plastic shovel and disappeared behind a few bushes. Jonas suddenly felt the urge as well but instead of mimicking Melvin he identified a campground restroom only fifty yards away and decided to use it.

By the time Jonas returned to the campsite six additional men had awakened and three large pots of coffee were brewing on camp stoves. Each man had an empty cup in their hands and was awaiting the coffee pots to start percolating. It was as if they were still half asleep and in a semi-trance knowing that it was coffee that would start their engines.

As soon as Mark joined the group it was as if new energy had arrived and he began cracking jokes, harassing the men, and commenting on just about everything. The laughing must have been enough to either wake up the other guys or motivate them to climb out of their warm sleeping bags. It might have also been the idea that if that many guys were already awake and up then there would be a fire and coffee for the taking.

It wasn't long until the men were drinking black coffee and awaiting the arrival of Father Mario for Mass. Dennis had informed the group that Father Mario from the town of Weed would be coming to celebrate morning Mass with them.

The previous night many of the men had acquired nicknames from others in the group. Some of the most memorable names were Aqua man, Eddie Haskell, the Beaver, and the Green Monster just to mention a few. The only names that appeared to have made it to morning and appeared to stick were Aqua man and Eddie Haskell since almost all the men continued to use those names when speaking to the man it was ascribed to the night before.

Father Mario arrived accompanied by an elderly man who introduced himself as Butch. Some of the guys thought he might be a Deacon from Father's parish, but it didn't appear to be so, just a man choosing to help and serve Father. It didn't take long for Jonas to identify that most of the men knew Father quite well and Jonas found out that Father Mario had been the pastor at Our Lady of Mercy parish in Redding, the parish most of the men attended for many years and that was why they knew him so well. Jonas noticed that Father appeared quite shy as he would greet each of the men authentically but then would disengage quite rapidly. Jonas studied Father as he made his way across the campsite and witnessed at least three occasions of Father looking back at Jonas with an inquisitive expression on his face. It didn't surprise Jonas that after Father set his Mass gear on top of a table the men had prepared to be used as an altar, that Father waved and beckoned Jonas to approach him. Jonas did as he was directed and when he arrived in front of Father, Father asked, "Do I know you?" Jonas responded, "No Father, I don't feel that we have had the pleasure." Jonas could tell that by him wearing a cassock it must have initially confused Father. He assumed that Father must have thought that he was some sort of religious or religious nut, to say the least. Jonas sensed something within Father and asked, "Father, do you need to talk to me about something? Many have said I am a good listener." Father appeared worried but at ease, both emotions at the same time and without much hesitation, he asked, "Do you have a few minutes?" Jonas smiled a warm and loving smile and the two men turned away from the crowd behind them and started walking into the forest on the hiking trail. Father began to discuss many things that he carried close to his heart. Jonas listened carefully and at times asked some clarifying questions. He gave reassurance and at times offered some mildly confrontational responses, however, done in love. But, most of all he tried to be a reflection of God's love and be understanding of this holy priest. The more time the men spent together, the seemingly more relaxed Father appeared to become. He started to smile and laugh. It was as if he needed to be with someone who he felt was his equal, at least spiritually, and that he didn't feel would judge him. The two walked and talked as if they had known each other for a lifetime and by the time they had circled back to the camp, 45 minutes later, Father almost looked like a new man. He was relaxed, social, warm, and engaging. It was as if his guard had been lowered and something within him had been transformed.

Knowing that the men were now starving because they had been fasting for Mass, except for black coffee, Father wasted no time beginning Mass. Father began Mass in the usual way, except it was anything but usual. They had cleared a site under a large oak tree and were surrounded by picturesque views of the mountains and were encircled by God's creation that included birds, deer, and many of nature's other animals. John read the first reading and Dennis sang the psalm. Father proclaimed the Gospel and immediately began to share his homily. He started by sharing how so many have been let down by the scandals in the Church and how many of the priests involved had assisted in worsening the public view and reputation of the Church and pushed away so many from the faith. Then he turned his attention away from the sinful molesters and back to the Church. He shared the idea that we are not Christians because of what a priest does or doesn't do. We are Christians because of Christ and what we believe about Christ and the truth He has shared and the truth we have come to know. He then began to share some of what Jonas and he had talked about on the trail and he commented, "This man Jonas has opened my eyes in ways you cannot believe. He is not an ordinary man. I hope you get to know him better while you can." He then asked if Jonas would share a few thoughts with the men.

Jonas stood and walked to the altar and just before arriving he turned to the men and began to speak. Instantly the men were mesmerized not only by the words, but his tone, his heartfelt delivery, and how the Lord's Spirit appeared to have overtaken him. Jonas spoke about love, pride, secrets, gluttony of food and alcohol, laziness, and so many things. It was as if he knew each man's sinful secret and was speaking to them directly. It was as if he had read their souls and was confronting them right then and there about how they have chosen to walk away from God. His words pierced the men's hearts and souls, and many began to tear up and cry. Something was happening and the men knew it. God must have sent an angel or maybe was it Christ himself in the body of Jonas. This was not an ordinary man that could do what he was doing to these men. It was as if Jonas spoke for hours, but at the same time, it was as if it were only a minute. No one wanted him to stop because the men knew they were in the presence of truth. Even Father Mario was weeping with great intensity. Then abruptly he stopped and said, "Father, give them the heavenly host." Father instantly stood and obeyed Jonas' command. He directly began the liturgy of the Eucharist and the men began experiencing the celebration more deeply than they had ever before. As Father raised the host and began, "This is my body…" Melvin, Danny, John, Mark, and Dennis had all noticed, at the same time, that Jonas had disappeared. They visually scanned the area and he was nowhere in sight. In reverence for the holiness of the Mass, they tried to keep focused on the celebration, but their minds constantly wandered with thoughts about Jonas.

At the end of the Mass, everyone thanked Father as he packed up his gear. The men invited Father to stay for breakfast, but he stated that he had a meeting to attend and that he needed to go. Father asked the men if they had seen Jonas since he wanted to thank him. The men all reported that they had not seen Jonas since he shared at the Mass. Father smiled as if he knew something the men did not, and then with a joyful wave, he parted from the men and away from the campsite.

Chapter 21

Mike and Carter had become close friends over the last three weeks. Something clicked during the visit at Mike's home a few weeks earlier and the men felt drawn to each other, drawn in a Christian manly way, not sexually. The two men were well-grounded in their sexuality and the thought of acting on homosexual inclinations sickened each of them. Mike felt nourished and inspired by the way Carter could connect life's events to something greater, something supernatural. Carter felt encouraged by Mike's love of the faith, his respect for the Church and clergy, and how authentically he lived his life. Mike had asked Carter if he wanted to join him, Janelle, and the kids at the rodeo. Carter had welcomed the invitation and even agreed to volunteer to work with Mike during one of the mornings serving breakfast with the asphalt cowboys. This was something Mike did every year on the opening day of the rodeo.

As instructed, Carter arrived at the large community hall on the rodeo grounds at 4:45 a.m. He looked for Mike but discerned that Mike must have overslept. Carter introduced himself to many of the other volunteers and since he was wearing his Roman collar and his clerics he was treated with great respect from those of faith. Most called him "Father" thinking that he was a priest. Some he gently corrected but for the most part he let the misunderstanding go ignored. Just before it was time to start serving the public Mike arrived and apologized stating that his youngest was sick with the flu and he had been up most of the night cleaning up vomit and diarrhea. When the head cook overheard Mike sharing his events of the previous night he insisted that Mike leave and not participate in the serving of the food in fear that he might be contagious. The cook did not want to take a chance that Mike might make others sick and didn't want to take any blame for the possibility of tainted food. Quite disappointed Mike left the breakfast service line, but he also understood.

Carter was given the task of serving the hash browns. The order of the food line began with plates and utensils, then servers for scrambled eggs, sausage, hash browns, and the finally humongous pancakes. There were syrup and butter already on the tables and a coffee and juice bar for beverages. It was quite the spread with at least thirty-five servers and as soon as the gates were opened people began to flood the area. Instantly there must have been three hundred people lining up and more and more arrived each minute. Carter was shoveling the cooked spuds as fast as he could and even a few times he missed the consumer's plate and flung the food helping onto the ground.

Stationed next to Carter was officer Martin who stood almost seven feet tall and appeared very intimidating in his police uniform. He was polite to the customers but never broke a smile and had his officer game face on. Almost immediately Carter noted the contrast from the external presence of the man and his words and demeanor. Carter and Officer Martin visited while they worked, and Carter was surprised at the level of compassion and empathy shown in the officer's remarks. Officer Martin had shared that he had been with the police force for almost twenty years and now was assigned to the gang task force. He shared that he had found his time with the task force to be very stressful due to him being a child of a mother who was sexually assaulted by a local gang. He shared that he was adopted but had later found his birth mother who informed him that the reason why she gave him up for adoption was that she had been gang-raped by one of the local gangs and he was the product of that incident. She shared the trauma was so much that she needed to ensure he went to a good home and she needed to find a way to heal from the abuse. Officer Martin shared with Carter that he understood, but it was what she said next in reply to his question at the time that changed his life. He said that he had asked her why she didn't just get an abortion. He added that she said, "Because even though that event was unimaginable, I had no control over it. I did have control over my actions related to the baby. I chose to not be as equally violent and cruel. I chose to not kill but to allow life to live. That is what God would want. I know I didn't have the strength to care for you, but I certainly did not want to kill you." The affectless and emotionless giant of a man suddenly became tearful and said, "She taught me that day that there are some things we have control over and other things we do not, but the things we can control we need to take seriously and to include God in the making of those decisions."

Just as Carter and Officer Martin thought they were having a slowing of customers a belligerent man approached the line demanding to be served without paying. It didn't take a scientist to discern that the man was intoxicated, and Officer Martin immediately snapped back into police mode. He scanned the situation and called for back-up while noticing that the man was wearing a weapon. The weapon by itself in Idaho wasn't unusual since no permit is needed for concealed carry in the state and many of the residents also carried weapons. It was the man's erratic behavior and aggressiveness that troubled the officer. Suddenly, the disturbed man locked eyes on Carter, and yelled out, "You damn pedophile. I am going to clean the streets with you right now." The man lunged in the direction of Carter and without hesitation Officer

Martin jumped over the serving table and tackled the man. The officer's brute strength was too much for the man and within seconds Officer Martin had flipped the man onto his stomach, spread his feet apart, and had him handcuffed. The officer kneeled on top of the man placing his right knee into the center of the man's back and warned the man that if he moved he would make the rest of his day more than uncomfortable. Carter was shocked at how quickly the officer could change gears from having a compassionate and mild-mannered conversation with him to becoming a responsive and powerful force of protective energy that would have frightened anyone to the point of wetting themselves. He was in awe of the officer and tried to imagine what his life must be like day-to-day and the sacrifices that he willingly gives for the protection of others. Carter thought about how many police officers there must be in the United States that were similar to Office Martin and just how many were not only unappreciated but often also treated poorly by the community they are trying to protect. He thought about what a thankless job an officer must be and that being a priest wasn't nearly as difficult as an officer must be. He immediately began to pray for officer Martin:

O my God, I adore Thee and I love Thee with all my heart. I thank Thee for having created Officer Martin, for having made him a good man, and for having watched over us this day. Pardon us for any evil that we have done this day; and if we have done any good, deign to accept it. Watch over us today while we work, while we take our rest, and deliver us from danger. May Thy grace be always with us, especially Officer Martin.

Amen

Chapter 22

It was as if Father Mateo had never fallen ill. He had snapped back and was more joyful, energetic, and optimistic than ever before. He had been asking Dylan to drive him back to the park for a few days now, yet Father had only received medical clearance from his physician and the approval of his supervisor to return to the park the prior day.

Dylan had noticed a change in Father's demeanor. He was often seen whistling joyful tunes, smiling to himself as if he was having delightful conversations with someone who wasn't there, and had a contagious laugh when one did converse with him. On the way to the park, Father asked Dylan if he could stop at the printer's office. Once there, Father jumped out of the car and using his white walking cane he navigated into the place of business. Father had asked Dylan to remain in the car while he completed his errand. Dylan was curious about what the elderly priest was doing. It was very unlike him to engage with local businesses. Father had always been more of a recluse, academic, and hermit-like man. Dylan watched as Father pulled a large envelope out of his satchel and handed it to the man working behind the counter. Dylan could see Father giving the man instructions and then they shook hands. Father briskly returned to the car and said, "Alright, off we go to the park." Dylan wanted to know what had just occurred at the printers but he didn't feel comfortable asking. He thought that if Father wanted him to know he would have offered to share.

Father and Dylan arrived at the park and within a few minutes the chairs were set-up, the sign was stuck into the ground, and Father sat in the shade of the large oak tree patiently waiting for his first visitor. It had only been a few minutes and Katie, the young, sweet child ran to Father and jumped up and onto his lap. She gave him a quick peck of a kiss on his left cheek and said, "I missed you, where have you been?" Father explained that he had become ill and that he ended up in the hospital. Katie asked, "Did you eat too much birthday cake?" Father laughed and said, "No, it was a little more serious than that, but I am all better now." Katie shared that her cat, Maxie, had died and was wondering if she would see her cat in heaven. Father paused for a moment to think about how he would respond to such a young child. If he were to respond as to one of his previous students, he would have gone into detail of what a cat is and how it doesn't have a soul like a human, and that it is the soul that has eternal life, and only a soul that has an opportunity for heaven. Yet, this was a young child without the ability to reason like someone older. He simply replied, "What do you think, Katie?" She immediately belted out, "Yup, he will be there." Father smiled a comforting smile. She then said, "I have to go. Mommy said I could only say hi and ask my question since we have a lot of things to do today." She then gave him another peck of a kiss on his right cheek and jumped off his lap and ran away.

Over the next few hours, a variety of people approached Father for conversations, some seeking advice, and some were just curious where Father had been and why they had not seen him in a few weeks. One of the visitors announced his name was Chuck from Oklahoma. He said he was on a cross-country vacation in his motorhome and was hoping to travel through at least 28 states. He shared he was a Christian and wandered from denomination to denomination depending on the skill and holiness of the pastor and also the friendliness of the community. He also shared the quality of the band was important since the element of being entertained was important to him at Sunday service. He did disclose that he had been curious about the Catholic Church from time to time but didn't understand it more than what he had been told by various pastors, that the Church was a cult that worshiped Mary instead of God or Jesus. Father Mateo laughed when he heard that. In response to the reactive laugh, Chuck began to ask Father questions and with a professor-like skill, Father began to catechize him. They spoke about apostolic succession, where the bible came from, the authority of the Church, the difference between reverence and adoration, and so much more. Chuck was astounded with what he was hearing and how it was nothing like what he had heard about the Catholic Church in the past.

The men visited for half of the afternoon and Chuck even prepared from his motor home ham sandwiches for them to eat. Chuck found Father to be wise, holy, patient, loving, and honest. He delighted in their time together and relished each minute. It wasn't until Dylan showed up that Chuck realized that he had occupied most of Father's Day. Chuck felt that he owed something for consuming so much of the priest's time, so he took out his wallet and grabbed a hundred-dollar-bill and placed it in Father's hand. Father asked, "What is this?" Chuck responded, "It is a small gift for you." Dylan clarified, "Father, he just handed you a one-hundred-dollar bill." Father instantly returned the money to Chuck and said, "My son, I don't do this for money. I am who I am because this is who God made me. I love Him and am here to do His will. In turn, my love for Him is also my love for you." Chuck took the money back and felt a little ashamed that he had tried to pay the holy man. Chuck gave Father a sincere and heartfelt hug and then departed from the two men. As he walked away from Father his mind filled with a variety of thoughts. He thought about how deeply affected he was from his time spent with Father. He thought about how peaceful he felt at that moment. He thought about the truth in the words that he had heard about the Holy Catholic Church. He thought about Father not accepting the money and how he couldn't imagine any of his previous pastors rejecting the money. He felt inspired to look more deeply into the faith of the Catholic Church and wondered if the reason why he had been wandering from church to church for so many years was that he had never approached the Catholic Church.

On the way home Father asked Dylan to stop back by the printer's office. Dylan did as he was asked and in a blink of an eye, Father was in and out of the shop. He returned with a small box in his left hand. Before Dylan had time to restart the engine Father opened the small box and retrieved one of the business cards and handed it to Dylan. Father asked, "What do you think?" The card was printed on a lovely light blue paper with a background of heavenly clouds. The print read,

Want to know about happiness?

The answers can be found daily

under the large oak tree in

Fisher Memorial Park, Mount Angel, OR

Knowing that Father couldn't see the card Dylan began to describe how it looked with great detail. Father listened intently to Dylan's voice and smiled greatly. It was as if Father was as happy as a child on Christmas morning with the creation of those simple cards. Dylan eventually asked, 'What are you going to do with those cards?" Father smiled and said, "Oh, those cards are for you and the other boys. I need you to disburse them to the other seminarians and ask them to hand them out to people when the Holy Spirit urges them to do so." Dylan laughed and replied, "Sure Father." Dylan knew that his peers were going to give him a hard time about the cards but he also knew how much they all loved and respected Father Mateo and that they would do what he was asking of them.

Chapter 23

Jonas was walking down the freeway when suddenly a motorcycle came upon him and skid to a halting stop. A short, bearded man dismounted the motorcycle and aggressively walked up to Jonas and said, "I need to talk to you?" Jonas ignored the comment and kept walking at his moderate pace. The agitated man ran around Jonas, and stopped right in Jonas' path and said, "Really man, I need to talk to you." Jonas ignored the request and altered his path slightly to be able to walk around the man. Once again the man persisted and ran in front of Jonas this time with a less aggressive attitude and tone he said, "Please, I need to talk to you." This time Jonas stopped and asked, "What is your name and what can I do for you?" The man disclosed that his name was Jimmy and stated that his head was all messed up and didn't know where to turn. He shared that he had seen Jonas walking on the side of the road and that something inside of him urged him to go and talk to Jonas. Jonas listened to the man ramble on and on about various nonsensical things and how the entire world is full of greedy and dishonest people. Jonas could tell the man was mentally troubled and he was trying to make some sense out of the disordered and complicated life that he had created. Jonas could sense deep darkness within the man and also a small glimpse of goodness still left there too. Jonas paused for a moment and asked God for advice and direction. Then suddenly he spoke, "Jimmy, I know everything about you. How you have treated your wife, your children, and your parents…" and then Jonas gave specific examples of the many sinful and secretive things that he had done over the past twenty years. Jimmy was shocked at hearing all the evil that he had done. He was even more shocked that Jonas seemed to know in great detail everything about him. Jonas was sharing things that Jimmy had never disclosed to anyone, not even to a priest in confession. Jimmy instantly knew that he was in the presence of an angel, or a prophet, or maybe even Christ himself.

Jimmy fell to his knees and began to weep forcefully. The tears fell upon Jonas' feet and each drop that came in contact with the dust on his feet liquified it. Within a few moments, Jonas' feet were covered in a dirty mud-like mess. Jimmy noticed what he had caused and used his long grey beard to try and soak up the mess. Jonas reached down and with a gentle touch on the top of Jimmy's head said, "Through your humility and contrite heart your sins have been forgiven. You have not been forgotten and you are no longer lost. You are healed. Go and sin no more." Instantly, upon being touched and hearing those words of forgiveness it was as if everything dark, angry, and hateful that had lived within Jimmy for so long had vanished and was replaced by God's loving grace. The feeling was so foreign to Jimmy that he didn't know how to accept it. He remained frozen on his knees while Jonas turned and began to walk away. Jimmy wanted to yell out, "Don't go my Lord" but nothing came out of his mouth. Eventually, Jonas walked out of sight and Jimmy then sat down upon the ground and pondered his life-changing experience. He knew in his heart that his life was now not the same.

Chapter 24

Carter had received an invitation from the local ranchers to participate in the branding week festivities. It has been a tradition for over a hundred years in Jordan Valley that the local ranchers all come together for a week each year and help each other, one ranch at a time, brand all their new cattle. It was and is a massive undertaking and everyone in the community participated including the wives and the children. Each day the women would cook and feed the men while the men and older boys worked from sunup to sundown. Carter thought it would be a good opportunity to not only socialize and be a Catholic witness but to also give some of those Catholic ranchers a hard time for working on Sundays and not going to Mass.

Carter had coordinated a plan with Sean Cunningham to arrive at the ranch a few hours earlier than the other ranchers so he could be outfitted with a horse and tack. Carter had learned how to ride when he was younger, but it had been many years since he had mounted a horse and he was a little nervous and had shared his concern with Sean. Sean ensured Carter that he would be fine and that he would give him Betsy, one of his most tame and experienced horses.

As promised, when Carter arrived, Sean had Betsy ready for him and helped Carter relearn how to apply the tack, how to mount and dismount, and even how to rope a calf. The lessons took less than an hour, due to Carter being a quick learner, and they finished just as the trucks and horse trailers began to arrive. Within an hour fifteen trucks and trailers had arrived with over seventy people and forty horses. Carter felt as if he had gone back in time and was in the wild wild west. The ranchers wasted no time mounting their horses and heading out toward the cattle. Many of the men brought their ranch dogs to help with the rounding up of the calves.

The men were divided into groups of five with one being the lead roper, three others tasked with capturing and securing the animal by laying it down and tying its legs together, and the last man oversaw the branding iron. Carter was assigned as one of the 'group of three' support men and personally tasked with slipping the rope around the legs of the calf once it had been flipped. He needed to act quickly and precisely, or the calf would attempt to stand back up and could injure itself or the ranchers. Carter was quite intimidated by what he perceived as being in the company of a huge group of rugged Marlboro-looking men who had been ranching from the time they could breathe. Just about when he felt a panic attack beginning to start Sean rode up next to him and offered him a swig of whiskey from his flask stating, "Take a sip, it will clear the throat, ease the nerves, and wash down the trail dust." Carter flipped the lid and gulped down a double shot.

The leader of Carter's group, Butch, yelled out, "Let's get 'em guys" and began to ride hard and fast toward a group of young calves. Carter and the team followed close by and as the leader approached the calves the animals began to run in all directions. Butch focused on a brown spotted calf and began to whip his rope around in circles. After a few twists of the rope, he let it fly in the air and with great precision and skill if perfectly wrapped around the neck of the calf. Butch wrapped his end of the rope to the horn of his saddle and halted his horse. Carter and the other men rode as quickly as they could to the calf and dismounted. The two men flipped the calf onto its side and Carter slipped the knotted rope around the legs binding them all together. The fifth man, Manny, came with the branding iron and jabbed it onto the left flank and burned the ranch logo into the hide of the animal. As soon as Manny yelled out, "Done," Carter released the rope and the calf ran away from the men with great speed. Seeing that the calf endured the branding well, Butch yelled out, "Well done, now let's get another" and quickly rode to find another calf needing a brand. Carter felt quite proud of his effort and said a quick prayer, "Thank you Lord for guiding my hand and especially for not allowing me to look like a fool."

The men worked nonstop until noon and then returned to the ranch house where the women had cooked and laid out a spread of hamburgers, corn on the cob, beans, potatoes, rolls, and green beans. There were jugs of iced tea on each of the nine tables and three apple pies for each table. The men ate with as much fervor as they had shown while working on the range and filled their bellies within minutes. There was laughing, joking, and even a few burping contests occurring at each of the tables. Carter enjoyed the work and the comradery with the men but also knew that his body was not used to such strenuous labor, at least not in the recent years, and he knew that he would be paying for it the next day with stiffness and sore muscles.

Suddenly a cowbell rang and the men directed their attention to the source of the sound. Sean had already mounted his horse and yelled out, "Let's get back to work everyone, lots more to do." The men jumped to their feet and followed Sean back out onto the range.

The men worked tirelessly until the sun began to set. Carter counted that his team alone had branded at least fifty-two calves and were finding it almost impossible to locate a calf without a brand. Sean rang the cowbell again and gathered the men together. He yelled out, "I think we got 'em all. Let's go get some dinner." Sean led the men back to the ranch house where the women had once again prepared a spread of food that included grilled steaks, baked potatoes, barbeque beans, rolls, and ice-cold beer. Sean's father, Cunningham Senor, was on the porch playing a banjo and Sean's wife, Liz, who had a delightful voice, sang a variety of songs making the occasion quite festive and joyful. Many chose to sing along to the tunes and some even decided to dance a jig or two.

Chapter 25

Father Mateo had received a phone call from a reporter at the Oregon Tribune asking if he would mind being interviewed. When asked what the topic would be the reporter stated that he was interested in doing a piece on religious life and what it was like to teach seminarians. Father initially declined but decided to inform his superior, Monsignor Abbot Jefferies to see what he thought. Father was quite sure that the Abbot would say that it was a bad idea and that he should decline the invitation. However, when presented with the request, the Abbot liked the idea and thought that it might help young men with their discernment to the priesthood. He encouraged Father to call the reporter back and arrange the interview. Father had elicited the help of Dylan to make the call to the Tribune and was able to schedule the interview at three in the afternoon on Friday with reporter Roberto Hernandez.

Knowing that the interview would be before the usual return time from the park Father chose to remain home on that day. That Friday morning was uneventful apart from a few scattered thundershowers outside and a fire drill at the seminary.

A tall, casually dressed Hispanic man arrived promptly at three o'clock in a silver Toyota Prius. Father was unable to notice but the car was covered in bumper stickers supporting a variety of ultra-liberal political candidates. It also had affixed to the rear window a few coexist stickers, a 'God is Dead' sticker, and numerous rainbow stickers of various sizes and shapes.

The man approached Father Mateo who had been waiting on the bench outside of the chapel since two o'clock and said, "Good afternoon Mateo, how are you?" Father responded, "Very well, you must be Mr. Roberto Hernandez?" The man responded, "Yes, Mateo, that I am." Father smiled and commented, "After so many years of being a priest I do prefer to be called Father Mateo." Roberto snickered and said, "Sure."

Just then it began to rain and after a loud rumble of thunder, the downpour intensified. Father stood and as he turned to walk inside the chapel he said, "Please follow me, Mr. Hernandez, let's get out of the rain." Once inside the chapel, and now realizing that they were in a small church, Roberto asked, "Do we need to meet in here? I really would be much more comfortable somewhere else." Father started to feel a little irritated and commented, "Son, I am an old man. Let's just get on with this." Father sat down on the pew furthest from the altar. Roberto sighed a long and deep sigh and then sat down about three feet away from Father on the same pew. Roberto reached into his pocket and pulled out an audio recorder and turned it on without telling Father what he had done. He then began, "Mateo, how many priests have you come to know that are homosexual and are not pedophiles?" Father, quite shocked by the initial question responded, "What are you talking about?" Roberto continued, "Mateo, it is common knowledge that the Catholic Church is full of homosexuals and that having them is a good thing. It is also a proven fact that being homosexual doesn't make you a pedophile. I just want my readers to know that you support the idea that having homosexual priests is not only a good thing but something that will decrease the number of pedophiles in the Church. Additionally, what do you think about women lesbian priests?" Attempting to be polite Father reacted, "Mr. Hernandez, I was told that you wanted to interview me about religious life and what it was like to teach seminarians. Is that not correct?" Roberto laughed and said, "Yes that is true. I want to know exactly that, along with how it relates to the LGBTQ community." Father, now feeling angry and having discovered he had been tricked and that he was being manipulated by more of an activist than a reporter, stood up and shouted, "Get away from me, get away from me" and he swung his white walking stick in the direction of the dishonest man. As he swung his walking stick he felt a thump at its end confirming that he had connected with something. Just as he felt the connection, he also heard a high-pitched squeal of a voice say, "He hit me, he attacked me. I am going to sue." What Father didn't see was that the man had been out of reach from Father's swing and that he had run toward Father to ensure that the cane would strike him. Additionally, Father didn't see that the man had forcefully thrown himself onto the pew slicing his eyebrow open and that his blood was dripping down the front of his face. The man continued to squeal and pant and eventually ran out of the chapel. Once outside a cameraman was standing there with his camera rolling. Roberto yelled, "That horrible priest attacked me. I told him that I was gay and that I wanted to be married in the Church and he began to beat me. I tried to get away and he kept beating me. I was afraid for my life. This old white man thinks he can flaunt his 'white privilege' on all of us people of color. I am going to sue the Church for millions. This is going all the way to the supreme court. We must do away with the Catholic Church. They are prejudiced, immoral, and irrelevant more so today than ever before."

The dishonest man might have concocted a semi-believable story if it wasn't for Dylan who had been on the balcony inside the chapel cleaning the organ pipes. As soon as he heard the direction the interview was going, almost from the very beginning, he had turned his iPhone video recorder on and captured the entire incident on video, especially how the man had self-inflicted the wounds. Dylan quickly sent a copy of the video into his cloud storage, and to three of his brother seminarians. By the time Dylan had descended the stairs and walked out of the chapel, Roberto and his co-conspirator were preparing to leave. Roberto had not stopped yelling and threatening, anyone within earshot could hear. It wasn't until Dylan had walked up to the car door with his outstretched hand holding his phone, and when he hit the play button, Roberto finally shut up. Roberto watched intently as the video revealed the true story. Feeling panicked and trapped Roberto grabbed the phone out of Dylan's hand and shouted to the cameramen accomplice, "Drive away, drive away now." The car spun its wheels and drove away with great speed.

Father Mateo asked, "Dylan did you witness what had occurred?" Dylan assured Father that he had watched the whole encounter and that the man self-injured himself in an attempt to falsely accuse him. Dylan also informed Father that he had videotaped the whole incident and that he had copies of the video. Father didn't completely understand the technical aspects of what Dylan was explaining but found relief in the confirmation that he had a credible witness.

Dylan immediately notified Monsignor Abbot about what had occurred and who in turn contacted a local attorney by the name of Paul Cravats. In order to squash any bad publicity and to avoid the false story from hitting the papers, Paul contacted the local television station and along with giving a full account of the story, he also supplied them with a copy of Dylan's video that he had downloaded from the cloud. That evening the top story on the local news headlined, "Local reporter gets what he deserves from a Blind Monk." The story was so damning and outrageous that it was picked up by numerous national syndicated networks and repeatedly shown across the nation for the next three days. Roberto Hernandez's reputation was damaged beyond repair and his career as a reporter was gone forever.

Chapter 26

Jonas had been walking along the I-5 freeway when a small sedan stopped and the man inside the vehicle offered him a ride. Jonas happily accepted, especially since it was almost 115 degrees outside. He had walked many miles down the mountain from Mount Shasta almost reaching Redding and with each mile, the temperature outside increased. It felt like an oven outside, dry and dangerously hot. Once inside the vehicle, the man inside identified himself as Sam and he shared he was a salesman for a large banking chain. He stated that he sold merchandise and services for telebanking that included credit card machines, smart registers, and credit card adapters for smartphones and tablets. Sam was nearing fifty years of age but looked much younger. His hair was light brown, mildly receding, but with very few wrinkles. He smiled and laughed, and Jonas could tell that internally Sam was a happy man.

Sam shared that he had recently become engaged and this was to be his second marriage. He added that he had divorced his first wife years ago and received an annulment due to her having a longstanding gambling problem, an existing problem even before their marriage and that she had hidden it from him for many years. He explained that the annulment was granted by the Church on the grounds of deception before the marriage and that he was not aware of what he was agreeing to at the time of the marriage.

During the drive, Sam did become emotional at one point and shared that he was very concerned for his step-son Bryan. Bryan was the child of his ex-wife's that she had birthed before she had met Sam. Sam explained that he had become a real father figure for Bryan during their marriage and that he had raised Bryan during the ages of 7-12 years old. Sam reported that Bryan had taken the divorce very hard and afterward Sam said that he had tried to keep in contact, but Bryan had shut down and refused his calls and visits. He had heard rumors that Bryan had become addicted to marijuana and probably other drugs, and that he had attempted suicide a few times. Sam shared that he was on his way to Sacramento to visit him at Sierra Oaks Hospital. His ex-wife had informed him that Bryan had been admitted to the psychiatric hospital the prior night.

During the drive and talking to Jonas, Sam realized that Jonas wasn't a typical homeless man. He was intelligent, well-spoken, worldly, and very insightful. Sam had offered him a beer and Jonas respectfully declined while stating that he didn't drink. Sam felt compelled to help Jonas in some way. He offered him some money, but Jonas declined that as well. Sam did notice that Jonas' clothing, the long black cassock, was quite dirty and that he also had serious body odor.

Just as Sam crossed the fifth street bridge in Marysville, he remembered that his good friend, a Catholic priest, lived in the adjacent town of Yuba City. Feeling a little nervous, and not wanting to offend Jonas, Sam timidly asked, "Would you like to take a shower? I have a good friend, a priest, that we could use his rectory for a quick stop." Jonas immediately responded, "That would be great." He proceeded to tell Sam that he had been wanting to shower and possibly wash his clothes for weeks now but that he didn't have a chance. He also shared that due to the filth and the sweat from the high temperatures he had developed a rash on his inner thighs that were bothering him tremendously. Jonas lifted his cassock to show

Sam the rash, attempting to shield his private groin area from view, and Sam identified a serious rash that looks infected. He also identified, although unintended from Jonas' part, that Jonas wasn't wearing any underwear. Instantly the reality of Jonas having nothing other than the old cassock on his back, and two worn sandals, affected Sam greatly. Sam asked, "I just don't get it, Jonas? You have nothing but what I see on you. Why? You are not an alcoholic. You are not a druggie. You are educated, I can tell. Why are you living like this? You don't seem mentally ill. Can you help me to understand?" Sam sincerely wanted to understand why Jonas was suffering when it didn't appear that he needed to be. Jonas smiled and said, "Sam, I am on a journey guided by God. He has asked me to travel and to meet people along the way and to be a holy reflection of His love and kindness to those He chooses to place in my path. He allows my hands and feet to become His. He allows His words to become mine. He allows others to be affected by our encounters and I cherish those opportunities." Sam listened with great intensity to the words that Jonas was speaking. Jonas continued, "Sam, look at us. You saw me on the road and showed kindness. You shared your story with me and now you are going out of your way to help me clean up. I have a feeling that even if you don't realize it, you saw something in me that drew you to me. I can truthfully say that you didn't see me, you saw Him, the One who created us both." Sam reflected deeply on the words that Jonas had just shared and the men sat in silence for the next twenty minutes.

Eventually, the men arrived at Saint Isidore's Parish in Yuba City. Sam drove to the rear of the parking lot and parked in front of the rectory. Having called ahead he knew Father Avery was there and he was expecting them. Sam led the way and walked into the rectory without knocking. Inside, Father Avery was sitting on a barstool next to the kitchen island drinking espresso and praying his liturgy of the hours. Sam announced, "Hey Padre, we are here. I would like to introduce you to Jonas." Father stood, walked up to

Jonas, gave him a brotherly hug, and immediately said, "Brother, you need a shower." Looking him up and down added, "And some new clothes." Jonas laughed and responded, "You think so?" Father showed Jonas to the master bedroom and set him up with shampoo, soap, towels, and a scrub brush. He instructed Jonas to take as long as he liked and encouraged him to not put back on his old clothing. Father had sized up Jonas and identified that they were nearly the same size. Father offered to have a new set of clothing for him when he finished.

Sam and Father Avery visited for almost an hour while Jonas showered and scrubbed himself. The men didn't mind since it had been some time since they had visited and used the opportunity to catch up with each other's lives. They had become close friends years ago when they both lived in Redding and Father was the pastor at Our Lady of Mercy parish. During his time there, almost three years in duration, Father would come over to Sam's house each morning and they would lift weights together in the garage. But when Father was reassigned to a new parish and Sam had gone through the divorce, they hadn't kept in contact. Yet, now back together it was as if they had never parted. They harassed each other, joked, and taunted each other like siblings.

Suddenly Jonas' voice was heard from the bathroom, "Father, Father, can you hear me?" Father Avery responded and while walking toward the bathroom he said, "Be right there." The bathroom door was open and inside was Jonas standing with the towel wrapped around his waist. Jonas spoke, "I hope it is alright, I used some of your antibiotic cream from the medicine cabinet on my rash?" Father instantly responded, "No problem, take as much as you need." Knowing that Jonas had nothing to wear he asked, "You mind following me to the closet?" He then led the way to the large walk-in closet where there were a few ordinary pants and shirts but mostly clerical outfits and three black cassocks. Father asked,

"Is there something here that would be of interest to you?" Jonas scanned the closed with his eyes and after almost a minute he kindly asked, "Would it be alright if I had one of your cassocks? They are warm on those cold nights and they protect me from the sun." Father laughed and then handed him his newest one. He also handed him new underwear and two wool socks. He asked Jonas, "What size sandal do you wear?" When Jonas responded with a size twelve Father handed him a relativity new pair of Keen sandals. Jonas immediately responded, "My sandals still have some life in them." Father looked over toward the bathroom and saw that the sandals that Jonas had been wearing had as much duct tape on them as there was leather left and responded, "Jonas, I think you got your monies worth out of them." The men both laughed in response to the joke. Just then Father noticed that it was already past four o'clock in the afternoon and in a panic, he shouted loud enough from Sam to hear as well as Jonas, "I must run, I have confessions. Let yourselves out" as he ran out the front door.

Jonas finished dressing and felt like a new man. The cassock fit him perfectly, as well as the new sandals. Now having socks and underwear he felt quite spoiled. The men locked the rectory door and then exited the home. Sam invited Jonas to accompany him to the hospital to see his step-son. Jonas agreed and the men departed the church parking lot and began heading in the direction of Sacramento.

Chapter 27

Carter awoke from a deep sleep. He instantly remembered his dream in which he was a married man with six children, happily married to a beautiful and holy woman, and worked as a teacher in a Catholic school. He thought about the dream and began to wonder if he had made the wrong choice in pursuing religious life. He wondered if the dream had something to do with his recent thoughts of self-doubt and witnessing how happy his new friend Mike appeared to be as a married man. Without further hesitation, he called the seminary and asked if he could schedule an appointment to see his spiritual director, Father Mateo. The receptionist stated that Father Mateo wasn't scheduling any further appointments for spiritual direction but that he could be found at the local park every day.

Carter wasted no time and immediately posted a sign on the entrance doors to the church that read, "Seminarian Carter is out of town until further notice." He packed a few items and then began driving towards Mount Angel. He needed to see his spiritual director. He knew he was in the midst of a spiritual crisis and needed help navigating through it. He trusted Father Mateo and although he felt called to become a priest, he was now also feeling called to be a married man. He was confused and honestly a little scared.

As Carter drove, he connected his iPhone to his stereo and then to his podcast app. He saw that there was another podcast posted from *The Idaho Catholic Podcast* and decided to listen. As soon as Carter pushed the play button, he recognized Mike's voice as he introduced the Podcast and the topic on discernment. Carter listened intently as Mike explained different methods of discerning God's will in one's life but what resonated the most was when Mike explained the difference between recognizing if it was God working in your life or was it the devil. He proceeded to identify the contrast between the two. He shared that one would know it is God's voice when it calms, comforts, convicts, encourages, enlightens, leads, reassures, and stills. He also shared that one would know it is the devil's voice when it obsesses, worries, condemns, discourages, confuses, pushes, frightens, and rushes. He then taught how important it is to have a spiritual director and that if one truly wanted to grow spiritually, they couldn't rely on themselves for that. He quoted Proverbs 12:15, "A fool is ever right to his own thinking; the wise listen to advice" and from Saint John of the Cross, "The virtuous soul that is alone and without a master (a spiritual director) is like a burning coal; it will grow colder rather than hotter." The more Carter listened to Mike the more his heart began to settle. Mike's word reassured him that he might be reacting to temptations from the devil and that Father Mateo would help him see with much more clarity. Carter continued to listen thinking that this podcast was one of the best he had heard in a while. Mike introduced a guest to the podcast, Sister Brenda, who talked about some of the most influential people who had helped her over the years. She identified St. Josemaria Escrivà as a person who had great wisdom in the area of spiritual direction. She then shared a few quotes from the holy man,

"You wouldn't think of building a good house to live in here on earth without an architect."

"How can you ever hope, without a director, to build the castle of your sanctification in order to live forever in heaven?"

"...You think you are really somebody: your studies — your research, your publications, your social position, your name, your political accomplishments — the offices you hold, your wealth, your age ... no longer a child."

"Precisely because of all of this, you - more than others - need a director for your soul."

Carter had absorbed as much of the spiritual advice as he could for the moment, and he turned the podcast off. He pondered all that he had listened to and although he felt justified in leaving the parish to drive to the seminary, he also felt inadequate and that he might be letting down the people of Jordan Valley by running away. He contemplated stopping the car and turning around. Suddenly he felt overwhelmingly confused again. He did stop the car and got out to stretch his legs and to hopefully clear his head. He looked up toward heaven and prayed, *Dear God, help me to understand. I am so confused right now. I want to serve you, but I am not sure what you are wanting for me. Help me*. He then began to cry, and sadness overtook him. He sat down on the ground, on the side of the freeway. He felt paralyzed by his grief.

It wasn't long until a large semi pulled up behind Carter. A tall man jumped out of the rig and walked up to Carter, "You alright man?" Carter looked up and toward the man, a middle-aged man with a caring smile and appeared authentically concerned. Carter, feeling quite vulnerable let his guard down and responded, "I am not ok right now, I have so much on my mind." The man smiled and said, "Wait one minute, I know what will help." He then briskly walked back to his truck and returned with something in his hands. It appeared to be something wrapped in tin foil. The man introduced himself as Terrance and said, "These are made from my wife, we call them 'Little Debbi Snacks' and they always make you feel better." Terrance unwrapped the tin foil and Carter grabbed two of the chocolate treats. Terrance then sat down upon the ground alongside Carter and began a conversation. Terrance was easy to talk to and shared that he had gone through a reconversion to the Catholic Church not too long ago. He explained his encounter with a man that was the catalyst to his reconversion and when he mentioned the name Jonas, Carter immediately took note. Carter asked Terrance to describe the man and when he mentioned the man wore a priest's cassock, Carter knew that it was the Jonas he also knew. Carter shared the story of how Jonas had stripped down naked in his church and that it was him who gave Jonas the cassock and Jonas had inspired him greatly. Terrance was blown away and couldn't believe that they both knew Jonas and how he had touched each of their lives so greatly.

After talking to Terrance for an hour and a half, and eating two packages of the special snacks, Carter felt much better. Terrance eventually parted while stating that he had a load he was delivering to Washington State. He wished Carter the best and then started up his rig and drove away. Carter turned his gaze again upward and prayed, *Thank you Lord for sending me Terrance to reassure me and to calm my heart. I know you love me and will never be far away, especially when I need you.* He then returned to his car and continued driving toward Oregon.

Chapter 28

Jonas and Sam arrived at the psychiatric hospital, Sierra Oaks. They approached the building and then used the intercom to communicate with the receptionist since the facility doors were locked. After announcing they were there to visit Bryan and gave the patient-specific security code, they were buzzed in and asked to wait for a staff person who could escort them back to one of the units. Both Sam and Jonas watched as more and more visitors arrived. Eventually, a young African-American woman entered the lobby and said, "Hello everyone. My name is Ashley, and, in a few moments, I will be escorting you all back to the units for visitation. I will need to know the name of the patient that you are visiting as we visit each unit to identify if this is the unit you will be visiting. We have eight separate units and over 170 patients here. Also, there are a few rules that you will need to adhere to. First of all, you are not allowed to give the patients anything. You might think it is harmless, but I promise you, even the most benign object can be used for self-harm. So, no hairpins, pencils, pens, gum, nothing. Also, other than a quick hug there should not be any kissing, caressing, fondling, you get the idea. We do not want to watch you get down and dirty in the middle of the visitation room." Sam looked at Jonas and laughed.

Once Ashley finished with her marching orders, she led the group unit to unit and dropped the appropriate visitors off at the correct unit. The first units were unit A, then B, then, C and D, and Sam and Jonas were left on unit D. Instantly Sam recognized Bryan but was surprised by the clothing he was wearing. Sam asked, "Bryan, what is with the suit?" Bryan explained that since he had attempted to harm himself the doctor had ordered a safety vest, which was a special garment that covered him but due to the thickness and inflexibility of the material it couldn't be used to hang himself. He also disclosed that they even took his underwear away. Sam introduced Jonas to Bryan and Bryan responded, "I thought you were a patient too. Sorry, nice to meet you." Just then Sam's stomach churned, and he instantly knew he needed a bathroom and needed it badly. He asked a staff person if there was a bathroom available that he could use, and he was told that he would have to be escorted back to the lobby. Sam hesitated for a minute but when his stomach rumbled again, he immediately agreed and was taken off the unit. Bryan and Jonas sat quietly for a few moments feeling somewhat awkward since they had just met. Jonas finally broke the since, "You know, I tried to kill myself once." Bryan responded, "Were you successful?" Then realizing that if he had been successful, he would have died. He then added, "That was pretty stupid." Both men laughed. Jonas then asked Bryan a few questions about how he was feeling and if he had a relationship with God. Bryan replied, "God, who is this God? I wish I knew him if he even exists." Jonas asked permission to touch Bryan's forehead and when Bryan nodded Jonas gently took his finger and held it against Bryan's right temple. As soon as the finger made contact Bryan's eyes closed and he could see in his mind Jesus's face as clearly as if he was watching a movie. Jesus then began to speak, "Bryan, my name is Jesus and I am the son of God. You have been sick and filled with sadness for many years now but if you follow me, I will take that pain away. I am the way and the truth and the life. No one comes to the Father except through me. If you know me, then you will also know my Father. From now on you do know him and have seen him." Jonas removed his finger from Bryan's forehead and Jesus immediately disappeared. Bryan opened his eyes and as he looked at Jonas he began to cry. Jonas remained quiet, he knew what Bryan was feeling. Bryan had an encounter with Christ just as Saint Paul had on the road to Damascus so many centuries ago. Jonas knew that from that moment on Bryan's life would never be the same and Bryan knew it also. Bryan stood and walked around the table and then kneeled. He wrapped his arms around Jonas' waist and hugged him with all his might. Just then Sam returned and was surprised at what he was witnessing. Unsure of what was occurring two staff members came and assisted Bryan back onto his feet and had him sit back down on his chair. Jonas turned to Sam and said, "My work is done now, it is time for me to go. Sam, you stay, but I need to continue my journey." He then asked the staff worker to escort him off the unit. Sam asked Bryan, "What was that all about?" Bryan with tears in his eyes and almost unable to speak due to the overwhelming emotions replied, "Dad, I am not able to explain what he did for me right now, but I do know that for the first time in my life I can honestly say that I am going to be alright. I think I was broken but have now been healed. He healed me with a simple touch." He then started to cry and couldn't speak further. Sam internally filled with peace and joy hearing such positive and comforting words coming from his step-son. After regaining his composure, Bryan asked, "Dad, thank you for coming, but I do need to rest right now and to think about what just happened. I want to make sure I don't forget any of it. Do you mind?" Sam completely understood. He stood, hugged Bryan and then requested that he be escorted off the unit. When Sam reached the parking lot he searched for Jonas. He looked in all directions but could not see him. He had disappeared.

Chapter 29

Carter arrived at the park where he was told Father Mateo would be, and it didn't take long to identify where the holy priest was located. Carter spotted a large group of young adults surrounding him and listening to him give what appeared to be a catechism lesson. Carter overheard Father explaining the concept of redemptive suffering, "Redemptive suffering is the Christian belief that human suffering, when accepted and offered up in union with the Passion of Jesus, can remit the just punishment for one's sins or for the sins of another, or for the other physical or spiritual needs of oneself or another. Like an indulgence, redemptive suffering does not gain the individual forgiveness for the sin; forgiveness results from God's grace, freely given through Christ, which cannot be earned. After one's sins are forgiven, the individual's suffering can reduce the penalty due to their sin." Instantly upon hearing Father's words, Carter was taken back a few years to when he would listen so intently in the classroom when Father was his instructor.

Carter waited patiently for Father to complete the lesson and for the group to leave before announcing his arrival. Carter did eventually figure out that the group of young adults were students from a protestant bible college that had been returning to meet with Father every week.

As soon as the group of young adults left, Carter spoke aloud, "Father" and before he could say another word Father must have recognized his voice and replied, "Carter, I somehow knew you were coming. I had a dream about you last night." Father didn't share the specifics that he had dreamt that Carter had married and had numerous children. Carter asked, "Father do you have time for some spiritual direction?" Father laughed and said, "When do I not have time."

Carter explained what had been going on in his life and how he had recently begun to question his calling. Father proceeded to guide Carter through a series of questions and examinations. The process was quite painful at times since so many deep emotions were being identified and revealed from within Carter. Father was a master at helping others to see themselves with such clarity and at times that microscopic look not only revealed the good but the not so good as well. Eventually, Carter asked, "Father how will I ever know for sure what God wants from me?" Father responded, "Well, there are many ways to know but the most important is that when you are doing God's will there will be peacefulness. I don't mean life will always be wonderful and pleasant, it most certainly will not, especially when you are doing God's work, but there will always be an underlying peacefulness that confirms that you are on the right track." Carter began to cry. As the tears streamed down his cheeks he said, "Father, I am not at peace right now." Father asked, "What is it you think you want to do?" Carter explained that he thought he should try living for a while away from the parish, away from the seminary too, and to see if his peace would return." Father asked, "What is keeping you from doing that?" Carter explained that he didn't want to let anyone down. He didn't want to let the Bishop down. Father explained that the Bishop didn't want anyone to be a priest if they are not called to be a priest. He also explained that it was becoming more and more common for Bishops to ask seminarians to take a year or two off and to live in the secular world and to have a secular job when there was a concern regarding the authenticity of the call. Carter felt some relief in hearing that. Father asked, "Ok, what is the next step?" Carter said, "Well, I guess I should go see the Bishop." Father responded, "Well, son, what is keeping you. Go, go now." Carter asked, "Why the push Father? Do you think I shouldn't be a priest too?" Father explained, "That is not it at all. To be a priest, or not be a priest, that is a question for you and God. I, like God, just want you to grow in holiness and to do God's will. Discerning that will is a process and a journey and one that takes time and attention. Being a priest, or a married man or a single chaste man are all equal in the eyes of God, equal if it follows His will. Hearing Father's words gave great comfort to Carter. He was not just looking at the issue as a pass or fail grade but more of a discerning journey where no choice is a bad choice if it is what God wanted for him.

Carter left Father Mateo and drove all evening and night toward the pastoral center except for a few gas and coffee stops and a short three-hour sleep at the truckers' rest stop. Arriving at eight in the morning he was extremely lucky that the Bishop was in and that he was able to see him without an appointment. Carter didn't know that Father Mateo had already called the Bishop to fill him in on Carter's current state of mind and his situation.

After greeting the Bishop and sitting down Carter began to share his thoughts, recent struggles, and how he had thoughts that maybe the religious life was not in God's plan for him. The Bishop listened carefully and lovingly as a father would to one of his sons. He asked quite a few questions that Carter answered honestly and then proposed that Carter take a leave for not less than 2 years, but not more than 3 years and suggested that while on leave he obtains a secular job, explore the possibility of a relationship, and to live as a faithful Catholic. He explained that if during that time he discerned that he wanted to become a priest he would be welcomed back, but that if during that time he discerned a vocation to married life then that would be honored as well. Carter felt relieved and accepted the generous proposal. The two men shook hands and Carter left the office.

As Carter approached his car, he caught a glimpse of his reflection in the window. He instantly thought *I can't wear these clerics anymore.* Carter had worn clerics almost every day for the last few years. He didn't own many secular shirts and pants. He also began to think of such things as *Where will I live? How will I earn money? How will I feed himself?*

Chapter 30

Jonas had walked all evening while praying his rosary. He began with the joyful mysteries, then the sorrowful, then the glorious, and with each decade of the rosary, he specifically prayed for someone who had crossed his path over the last few months. He repeated the prayers throughout the night until to sun began to rise. He gave little thought to where he was going, or which direction. He knew God would lead him to where he needed to be. Looking up he read a sign "Fulksome Blvd," and then another that read "Welcome to Havengreens." The neighborhood was well established with mature trees, and large homes, dated, but in good repair. There were no homeless, the streets were clean, and very little traffic. He reached into his pocket and there was a small piece of paper. He unfolded the paper and he noticed wrapped inside was a five-dollar bill and written on the paper was, *Have a coffee and biscuit.*

Jonas pondered how that had gotten into his pocket and then realized that as he left the home of Father Avery, Father hugged him and must have slipped it into his pocket. Feeling very blessed Jonas scanned the immediate area and identified a grocery store. He crossed the street and entered the market. Just inside there was a small coffee corner. He approached the clerk and asked, "Can I get a coffee and biscuit with this?" as he revealed the five-dollar bill.

The young woman chuckled and then replied, “Haven’t heard that before. A coffee for sure, but as for the biscuit, not quite sure.” Jonas smiled but didn’t really understand what she meant. He stood not sure of what to do next as she looked at him. A more senior worker must have heard the exchange and felt compelled to intervene. He briskly walked to the counter, stood beside the young lady, and said, “I am sure we can take care of you, Sir. What kind of coffee would you like?” Jonas replied, “Just a plain black coffee would be great.” The man quickly went to work to grind the coffee beans and pack them into the espresso machine. While the machine created a variety of sounds, steaming, and whistling, the man asked, “Did you say you wanted something to eat as well?” Jonas held the five-dollar bill up and said, “The coffee looks like it might be a little expensive. If I have enough that would be great, but if not, that is alright too.” The man poured the freshly made coffee into a large foam-like cup, and then used a pair of tongs to reach into the display window and pulled out a large cinnamon crumb cake and placed it on a plate. As he handed the coffee and the plate to Jonas the young woman stood at the cash register and began punching keys. She then said, “That will be nine dollars and ninety-five cents.” Before Jonas could say a word, the senior worker shared, “No that is not the correct price. We have a new special today, and with the discount, it comes to exactly five dollars.” The young woman looked towards her co-worker and rolled her eyes. Jonas handed her the five-dollar bill and thanked them both. As he walked away from the counter holding his coffee and cinnamon creation, he heard the young woman say to her co-worker just loud enough so he could hear, “You are going to pay for that.”

Jonas decided to drink his coffee and eat his breakfast while walking. It didn’t take long, and he noticed a large church. He wondered if it was a Catholic church or some protestant denomination church. The church building had an unusual design and it wasn't until he came right upon it that he identified a few statues in the courtyard. He discerned that it must be a Catholic church. He approached the doors of the church and just as he was about to pull on the door he was startled by a loud voice, "What are you doing? The free dinner for the homeless was last night. You shouldn't be here." He turned around and standing ten feet away was an elderly man, grey-haired, wearing a black shirt, tan shorts, and sandals. Just as Jonas was about to speak the man added, "I know you are probably looking for a place to sleep but we just can't have that around here. We are an affluent parish and a lot of people would be scared off by you." Jonas looked at the banner hanging above the man's head that read, **Welcome to Saint Mathew's – Where Social Justice is achieved.** Jonas pointed toward the sign and asked, "What does that mean?" The man softened and said, 'Well, we pride ourselves here in all that we do for others. We have thirty-six programs for the poor and we help more people than any other parish in the valley. We have been here for almost fifty years and no one does social justice as we do." Jonas asked, "But, what is social justice." The man now seemed irritated, "I just told you, we do things for others. We do good for those who can't do it for themselves. We feed the homeless each month. We donate clothing. We have meetings about how we can help people. We talk about how people should get off the streets, get an education, not use drugs. We counsel people and try to teach them a better way of life." Jonas said, "Do you talk to them about Christ, the Good News, the Kingdom of God, Heaven?" The man reacted, "That is not social justice, that is old religion stuff. Haven't you heard a thing I have said? We are a proud social justice parish. We serve those who can't take care of themselves." Jonas began to weep, tears streamed down his face. After a few moments, he spoke, "You are not a parish, you have become a social service agency. There is no love in your actions, nor your words, just self-serving behaviors that make you feel good about yourself. God is not pleased." As soon as the man heard those words his heart was pierced. He knew what Jonas had shared was the truth, yet he had never realized it before. The man fell to his knees. Jonas stood over him and as he gently laid his hand upon the man's head and looked up into the sky and prayed aloud, "Father, this man's heart had hardened like stone. He has mistreated so many while disguised as being a Christian. He has driven many away from you and is the cause of sending so many to hell. Please forgive him, he did not know what he had done. But now he does." The man yelled out in lament, "Forgive me, Father." He ached such a powerful ache deep inside. The ache was crushing and relentless. His abrupt self-awareness of his soullessness, awful pride, disdain for others while calling himself a Christian, and his now revealed life of being a hypocrite was too much to endure. Jonas continued, "Abba, Father, drive out the demon inside and heal him." Suddenly the man fell completely onto the ground and laid there for what appeared to be an eternity with his eyes closed. It wasn't until Father Pablo, the church pastor arrived and shook the man's arm that he awoke. Father Pablo asked, "Henry, are you alright? Do you want me to call an ambulance?" Henry sat up and looked around for Jonas but didn't see him. Father Pablo asked, "What are you looking for Henry?" Henry explained the encounter with Jonas without skipping anything. Henry eventually said, "I think that man was Jesus and I treated him just as bad as the Romans had. He opened my soul and had me look at that darkness. I wanted to die but then I realized that if I did, I would be going to hell. It scared me so much that I couldn't stand it. Then he asked God to forgive me and my soul burned as if it was being purified and then he asked his Father to take the demons out of me. I can't explain it. He healed me. He has given me a second chance." Father Pablo couldn't believe what he was hearing. Henry was the most influential man at the parish and had run off the last four pastors for trying to be too religious. Father Pablo was an orthodox priest in the most unchristian, progressive, liberal parish in the city and each day he was in fear of the parishioners making false accusations and trying to run him off just like they had done to so many others before him.

Chapter 31

Father Mateo felt surprisingly energetic and had awakened to feeling quite adventurous. He remembered that he had dreamed of climbing a mountain as Moses did having an encounter with God at the burning bush. He even heard God tell him to take off his sandals since he was standing on holy ground, but then God made a joke about the poor condition of Father's feet, the fungus on his nails, and the smell of athlete's feet. As he recalled that part of the dream, he laughed out loud. Before putting on his socks he felt his nails to see if he could feel any fungus and then he curled down his upper torso nearing his feet and inhaled a long slow breath through his nose to smell his feet. There was no smell. He laughed again at God's humor.

After dressing Father made his way to the dining room and was served a pancake, oatmeal, and a bowl of fruit by one of the seminarians. As Father usually did, he internally prayed his usual morning prayers in solitude as he ate his breakfast.

After breakfast, Dylan arrived and asked, "Father are you ready to go to the park?" Father turned toward Dylan and responded, "Yes." Dylan drove Father down the hill from the seminary and they had arrived at the park in less than twenty minutes. Dylan carried the sign and the chair and placed them in the usual place and just as he was about to leave Father, Father Mateo asked, "Dylan, can you help me with something?" Dylan responded with a cautious, "Yes." Father then said, "I have been thinking a lot recently about the Dendrites, the hermits who lived in the trees and remained there in prayer and isolation from the world. I think I would like to try that." Dylan did not know how to respond to what he just heard. He was hoping that Father was kidding since he couldn't imagine the blind, elderly priest climbing a tree, nor trying to live in it. Father must have sensed Dylan's uncomfortableness and clarified, "I know I can't live in a tree, but I do want to have an experience of it. Will you help me climb one of the trees?" Everything inside of Dylan told him that this was not a good idea and somehow if he helped, he would be an accomplice to something not good. Father asked again, "Come on Dylan, just help boost me up to a branch and I will do the rest." Feeling compelled to be obedient to his former professor, an elder, and a priest, he did as asked. He took Father's arm and led him to a nearby tree with fairly low branches. Dylan lowered down upon the ground and rested on his knees and arms. He used his body to create a step that Father could stand upon. Dylan said, "Father, I am ready. Just step upon my back and you should be able to climb into the tree and feel your way up a few branches. There is a large branch about ten feet off the ground and three branches that you could use to make your way. First, climb into the tree and I will guide you."

Without hesitation, Father stepped on Dylan's back with his left foot and then his right. After wobbling there for a few seconds, he then lifted his right foot and used it to feel the branches. When he felt that his foot was secure, he then forcefully thrust his body up and forward and elevated himself into the tree. It was remarkable that such an elderly man could complete such a maneuver. Now free from the weight of Father's body Dylan stood and voiced step by step guiding directions helping Father to navigate the branches until he arrived at the large branch with a large depression in it just next to the center of the tree that was perfectly sized for Father to securely sit upon. Once Father sat down Dylan inhaled and then exhaled a huge sigh of relief. Father immediately ordered, "Alright Dylan, I am all set. Go ahead and load up my sign and my chair and take them back to the seminary. I won't be needing them today. I am going to pray and be alone with God and be in unified-spirit with the Dendrites." Dylan felt very uneasy about leaving Father but did as he was directed and after loading the items he drove away and returned to the seminary.

Father began to pray with active contemplation, where he tried to imagine that he was a monk in the early 4th century in Palestine and had been living in the tree for years. It didn't take long, and he was not only imagining the experience, but he had been consumed in prayer. No longer was his prayerful state something of his doing, but through God's grace something had taken over and he was mystically there in the 4th century. As he sat in the tree a variety of people would approach the tree and while speaking Aramaic would ask him questions about life. Surprisingly, Father could understand the people even though he didn't speak Aramaic. The first man approached and from below asked, "Dear Prophet, How am I to treat my brother who has stolen from our Father?" Father Mateo responded, "You are to confront your brother and tell him that he needs to make restitution and if he does not, the God of Abraham, Isaac, and Moses will not only curse him but will curse his children for 100 years." The man was completely satisfied with the answer and abruptly left. The next man to approach the tree inquired, "Dear Rabbi, I have twelve goats and my neighbor has only one. He has asked to have six of mine and said that he will pay me back in one year with double. What should I do?" Father Mateo asked, "Do you have more than you need?" The man answered, "Yes." Father immediately replied, "Do as the man has asked of you and your generosity and faith will bring great joy to our God and you will be rewarded with protection and health in your life. The man will do what he says, but when he delivers the goats back to you only take what you first gave him. The rest should not be accepted because when one gives not seeking anything in return he is blessed, and God will not forsake him." The man was satisfied with the answer and immediately departed. One by one Palestinians came for advice and Father Mateo gave it. This lasted almost six hours until Father fell fast asleep.

During afternoon prayers back at the seminary Dylan shared that he wanted to pray for Father Mateo who was sitting in a tree at the park. As the prayers concluded one of the more senior seminarians approached Dylan and asked, "What did you say about Father Mateo?" Dylan explained what had occurred and as he heard himself speaking, he realized just how stupid that it was to not only help an elderly, blind man into a tree but to leave him there. Instantly Dylan felt sick to his stomach. He asked a few of his fellow seminarians to accompany him and to retrieve Father from the park. They hopped into the car and drove as fast as they could toward town.

In the meantime, Father must have startled himself while dreaming and jerked. Forgetting that he was resting high in a tree he shifted his body and suddenly slid off the branch and fell downward. Bouncing off a few branches on his way down he eventually hit the ground and his neck forcefully whipped backward and slammed against the tree trunk. He heard a snap and knew he had broken his neck. Dazed from the fall he didn't know if he was alive or dead. He prayed, *God, is this it? Is this my time? I am ready God, come get me*. Just then Dylan and the crew of Seminarians arrived and seeing Father on the ground Dylan vomited. The other men ran past Dylan and his vomit and upon arriving asked, "Father are you alright?" Father responded, "Well there is my answer, I am not dead." Surprisingly calm Father said, "I think I broke my neck so don't try to move me. Call the ambulance." As instructed, the ambulance was called and once the paramedics arrived they wrapped a stabilizing collar around Father's neck and then rushed him off to the emergency room.

Chapter 32

Carter arrived in Jordan Valley just after the sun had set and it was now dark outside. He entered the rectory and after grabbing a large backpack, he packed it with his belongings leaving behind his clerics. He had a pair of jeans, three shirts, some socks and underwear, and a pair of tennis shoes. It was all the secular clothes that he owned. He grabbed his bible and his breviary and then locked the rectory door as he exited the home. Taking the rectory key off from his key chain he slid it under the door and inside the house. His heart hurt and he began to cry. He knew he was walking away from something very special and it pained him greatly. He hesitated for a minute and then entered his car, started the engine, and then suddenly realized he had nowhere to go. He had no plan. His grief swelled inside and his shedding of tears intensified. He was in an emotional crisis due to the walking away from religious life, the only life he had known since he had become an adult. He felt as if he had no one to turn to for help or support. All of his friends were either seminarians, priests, or fervent Catholics living lives of surrender and sacrifice, and he didn't feel he could face any of them right now.

As he drove away from the church and rectory and came to the main road, he needed to make a decision. He needed to turn either right toward Boise or left in the direction of the west. He closed his eyes and prayed, *Dear Lord, I place my life into your hands. Please show me where I should go. Please, I need you.* Just then a large semi raced by in front of him and blasted its horn. The abruptness of the noise and image of the large vehicle shocked Carter and he screamed an embarrassing girly-scream. After a few seconds and regaining his composure, he looked up into the night sky and said, "Thanks a lot Lord. You could have just whispered into my ear, turn left."

Carter drove almost six hours and now feeling quite hungry he stopped in Truckee, California. The sun was just beginning to show itself over the mountains. It was morning. He scanned the area and finally identified a restaurant by the name of Donner Lake Kitchen. He remembered the story he had heard years ago about the settlers traveling to California from the Midwest in the 1800s. Delayed by a series of mishaps, they spent the winter of 1846-47 snowbound in the Sierra Nevada mountains. Some of the settlers resorted to cannibalism to survive, eating the bodies of those who had succumbed to starvation and sickness.

Carter chuckled wondering what type of meat the restaurant might serve. Despite a mild questioning spirit, he proceeded and drove to the parking lot. Just as he opened his car door to exit his vehicle a white Jeep Compass sped into the parking space next to him and almost hit Carter's car door. The driver of the vehicle jumped out and ran to Carter and asked in a caring but frightened tone, "Are you alright? I almost took your car door off." The man was a Filipino, wearing a white collar and obviously a priest, then ran toward the restaurant while yelling, "I will be right back. I am Father Vance and I am going to pee my pants. I will be right back." Carter laughed and thought, *Really Lord.*

Carter waited for almost five minutes and just as he was about to lose hope that the frantic priest would return, Father Vance appeared and said, "I am so glad you are still here. I want to buy you breakfast. Do you have the time?" Carter smiled and accepted.

Father reintroduced himself and disclosed that he was the pastor at the local parish. He also shared that he has high blood pressure and that he takes diuretic medication and that the medication suddenly kicks in and then he needs to pee like a racehorse. Father added, "It kicks in at the worst times. One day I was celebrating Mass and I had just consecrated the bread and as I was getting ready to consecrate the wine I had to go." Carter asked, "What did you do?" Father laughed and said, "There was nothing else I could do. I stopped what I was doing, excused myself from the parishioners and said 'nature calls' and then ran to the bathroom. I returned as quickly as I could after doing my business and then I made sure to share that I did wash my hands," Father then erupted in laughter and commented, "True story I swear." Father added, "That is nothing, I once knew a priest with I.B.S., irritable bowel syndrome, and he actually pooped his pants during the celebration of the Mass. That must have been horrible. He took a leave of absence after that. Can you imagine the smell?" Carter listened attentively and couldn't help but notice how happy and joyful the priest was. He was lively and personable. He also appeared to be very honest, transparent, and authentic.

Carter and Father ordered the same breakfast after Father repeatedly swore that this particular breakfast was the very best in the whole restaurant. They ordered the Mary Murphy extra meat scramble with biscuits and gravy. They also ordered coffee and orange juice. While waiting for their food the men shared a little about each other while taking turns asking each other questions. When Carter disclosed that he was a seminarian but that he was taking a discernment leave, Father exclaimed, "I knew it, I knew it. I knew you were a godly man. I could see it. It must have been the halo." And then he exploded in laughter. Carter also laughed seeing how joyful Father was and how he was enjoying every minute of his life.

The food eventually arrived and after a quick blessing of the food the men dug in. Carter wasn't sure if it was how hungry he was, or if the food was as good as Father had promised, but it was delicious. The food arrived in a sizzling hot iron skillet. The concoction contained scrambled eggs with an enormous amount of chopped bacon, ham, steak, chorizo, potatoes, and hamburger meat mixed in. It also contained onions, bell peppers, jalapeno peppers, mushrooms, cheese, and bacon bits sprinkled on the top. On a separate plate, they each had an extremely large homemade biscuit the size of a pancake, sliced in half with a serious portion of sausage gravy smoothing it. The men ceased speaking and devoted their full attention to the process of devouring their meals. Each man shoveled their food nonstop into their mouths for ten minutes without speaking a word. It wasn't until Father released a large burp that Carter laughed, and they resumed their conversation.

Suddenly Father's demeanor changed, and he became serious and asked Carter what his plans were. Carter was quick to share that he wasn't sure and that he was a little scared of what the future might entail. Father asked, "Do you mind if we stop and just pray for a moment?" Carter nodded confirmation and Father began, "Lord God, in this moment of distress and uncertainty, I ask for Your wisdom and guidance to shine down on Carter. Help him to understand what Your plans are for his life and how to make it happen. God, I ask You to give him peace as he moves forward in this world. Amen." Carter was instantly filled with peace as he listened to the prayer and his anxiety disappeared. Father, returning to his joyful nature and with a huge smile on his face said, "I think you should go to Camp Pendola, the Catholic summer camp for the Sacramento diocese and work as a camp counselor for the summer. I can make that happen if you like?" The idea of spending the summer in the mountains and camping sounded wonderful to Carter. He then asked, "Really Father, you could make it happen?" Father replied, "I was one of the canon lawyers for the diocese for a few years before returning to the parish and I helped them in a variety of ways. They owe me. Let me make a few calls." Carter felt very optimistic and knew that God had placed Father Vance in his life as a sort of sign that God was still very near and watching out for him as he began this discerning journey.

Father paid the bill and then led the way out of the restaurant and into the parking lot. He handed Carter his gas station credit card and instructed him to fill both cars with gas as he made the calls. He tossed his set of keys to Carter and then sat down on the bench in front of the restaurant while Carter did as he was directed. Once Carter was out of earshot, he called the Bishop, "Hello Bishop Santo, it is Father Vance. I have a huge favor to ask. I just met a remarkable young man, actually a seminarian who is taking a leave to discern his vocation, and I think he would be perfect for Camp Pendola." The Bishop and Father spoke back and forth for a few minutes and then the call ended. Father waited for Carter to return with the cars and then shared, "Alright, it is done. They are expecting you. You begin work today. Well, you are to arrive today to settle in and start work tomorrow as the lead counselor for the high school boys' program. What do you think?" Carter filled with happy emotion and with tears forming in the corners of his eyes he wrapped his arms around the priest's small frame and hugged him with all his might. The tight squeeze must have been a little too tight because it triggered a loud escape of flatulence from Father. Father laughed and Carter gagged at the smell. Carter commented, "That is awful, you really need more fiber in your diet. That smells like sulfur." Both men erupted in laughter.

Chapter 33

After leaving the parish Jonas traveled west on the main street for about a mile until he reached the end of the road. He did notice a sign that read 'Welcome to the Delta.' Curious to what the Delta was, he asked a woman who in her car had pulled up next to him on the side of the road as she prepared to make a right turn, "What is the Delta?" She smiled and responded, "It is the large waterway just over the levee." and she pointed in the direction in front of Jonas. He thanked her and then directly began to walk in the direction of the levee.

Once Jonas arrived at the levee he climbed up and over and then he identified what the Delta was. At first glance, it looked to be a beautiful large river. Then he remembered learning in school many years ago that when rivers approached an ocean, their current slowed down, and not being able to carry its sediment with the slowing water current, the sediment was dropped, and over years, decades, and centuries, that sediment created layers. At times these layers were so large people could live on them or they could be used as fertile farmland. As he scanned the area, he noticed that on each side of the river there were grape vineyards.

Jonas made his way down to the water, removed his sandals, sat down, and laid his feet upon the cool waters. At first, the water burned slightly due to his feet being dry and cracked, but eventually the coldness of the water numbed his feet and it felt refreshing. Still with his feet submerged he reclined backward and rested his head upon a small dirt pile. Almost instantly he fell asleep.

Unknown to Jonas, there was a group of adolescent Hispanic and Black boys who had spotted him while walking on the levee and they began to plot. The leader of the group, Trevon had challenged three of the younger boys, "Hey Demetrious, Tyrone, and DeShawn, if you want to join our gang there is an initiation. The initiation is that you beat the shit out of a homeless cracker." Trevon then pointed to Jonas sleeping on the side of the river. Desperate to be included in the gang the three boys without hesitation began to sneak up on Jonas. Two of the young boys, who were quite muscular, and probably around sixteen years of age picked up branches to use as weapons, and the third, Demetrious grabbed a long thin metal bar that had been discarded in the bushes.

The boys made it within five feet of Jonas when Tyrone stepped on a twig and breaking it created a loud snapping sound. Jonas instantly awoke and sat up. He looked directly into the eyes of the boys and he could see fear. DeShawn lunged toward Jonas and struck him with the hefty branch on top of his head. The blow dazed Jonas and before he could regain his senses Tyrone repeated the action but struck Jonas across the left side of his face. Now Jonas was knocked semi-unconscious but that didn't stop the young boys from beating him. In fact, the blows intensified. Now all three boys were striking Jonas with their weapons hitting in the head, face, legs, arms, and torso with tremendous might. The attack continued for more than two minutes until the earth began to shake. Suddenly the earth shook back and forth and there was a tremendous rumble heard across the land. It was an earthquake and nothing like the adolescents had ever experienced before. It freighted them and they dropped their weapons and ran away as fast as they could.

Jonas was alive but barely. He was now completely unconscious and probably in a coma. He laid there in the dirt, covered in blood, his body twisted, and one foot still submerged in the river. He looked as if he had been placed in a clothes dryer and then flung out upon the ground. He looked pitiful.

Scared from the earthquake and not wanting to be caught, the adolescent boys agreed to separate and to make their way home. Before departing, they swore an oath that they would tell no one of what they did, especially if the old white man died.

DeShawn felt sick by what he had done. By the time he arrived home he had relived the incident in his mind so many times that it was driving him crazy. He had been raised in a staunchly Baptist household and it wasn't until his father left his mom and four sisters a year ago that they had stopped going to church twice a week. He had never wanted to be part of a gang before but now without his father and feeling neglected by his mother who now worked three jobs to try to make ends meet, compounded by his anger and resentment from being abandoned, he wanted to be a part of a family. The family he had chosen was the local gang. Yet, this act of unprovoked violence didn't sit well with him. As he relived what he had done in his mind it began to terrorize him. He couldn't stop thinking about all those bible lessons and stories he had heard at church. The stories of the prophets, Jesus, the apostles, and how they were beaten and killed for no reason. He began to think that maybe he had killed the old white man, or worse yet, that he was still alive and laying there waiting to be saved. DeShawn started to panic. He didn't know what to do. He ran into his bedroom and locked the door. He raced to his closet and dug around until he found his old bible. Opening it in haste he turned to Matthew 13:42 *They will throw them into the blazing furnace, where there will be weeping and gnashing of teeth.* Just then there was a knock on the bedroom door and a voice, "DeShawn, you in there?" It was his mother. He didn't want to speak but he heard it again, "DeShawn, you in there?" He couldn't lie to his mother. He opened the door and she instantly could read on his face that he had done something wrong, and it was something terrible, "What did you do?" Without hesitation, DeShawn spilled the beans. He told of everything they had done and how when they beat the old white man the earth began to shake and that he might be dead. As she reached for the phone she shouted, "You damn boy, don't you know God was shaking the earth to stop you from earning your way right into hell." She called the emergency number, 911, and reported that there was a severely beaten man on the side of the river and gave specifics as to where he could be found. After she hung up the phone she walked over to DeShawn and hugged him but with a stern voice said, "You messed up son and there will be consequences, but these consequences you will be able to handle. If you didn't tell me then there would have been an even greater consequence related to God, and that my son might just have been too much to handle. You think about this and what you have done. I am not sure what will come next, but you take responsibility, be truthful, and accept any punishment you deserve. We might be many things, but we have integrity and honor. No more lies, no more gangster stuff. That is for the weak, idiots, for bums. You are no bum, my son." DeShawn knew what his mom was preaching was the truth and that he had screwed up. He also knew that he would accept full responsibility even if that meant going to prison. He was not a gangster. He was not an evil person.

Both DeShawn and his mother anxiously waited for the police to arrive to arrest DeShawn. Six hours had passed, and they began to wonder what was happening. Finally, an officer arrived at the house and asked to speak to them. Officer Boyd explained that they responded to the 911 call, as did the ambulance and the paramedics, but that they could not find a body. DeShawn offered to show the officer where the incident had occurred and then the three of them drove to where Jonas was severely beaten. DeShawn led the way up and over the levee and then to the side of the river where everything occurred. There wasn't a body there. There was no sign of a scuffle, no blood, no nothing. DeShawn knew without a doubt that he had taken them to the correct spot. After walking the site back and forth for twenty minutes the officer decided that the investigation was useless and returned them to their home.

After the officer left, DeShawn and his mother sat down at the kitchen table. She reached out and grabbed both of his hands and squeezed them tight as she said, "I don't know what happened, but I know God is involved in this. You came so close to going to prison but for some reason, you have been given a second chance. Don't screw this up, son." Tears poured from his eyes and he almost couldn't speak. After a few attempts to clear his throat, DeShawn said, "I know mom, you will never have to worry about me again. Just before we hit him, he looked right into our eyes and I knew that he wasn't just a homeless man. He saw right into me. He saw my soul. I think that man was Jesus. I think I killed him." Just then DeShawn broke down and began to sob so powerfully that he crunched his torso forward and his head laid upon his knees as he wept. His mother hugged him and tried to hold him in her arms and comfort him. He cried for almost an hour until finally, he stopped. The two talked for the rest of the evening about the occurrence, their feelings, how life had changed so much over the past year, feeling lonely and hurt, how he missed his dad, how he missed his mom, how he missed his old life, and how he could start to live his life now in a more meaningful way.

Chapter 34

Father Mateo eventually woke up while in the I.C.U. and Dylan was at his side, "Where am I?" asked Father. Dylan explained that he had broken his neck. Just then the neurosurgeon walked into the room and introduced himself, "I am doctor Ephrem Abelman, your neurosurgeon. I have good news and not so good news. The good news is that you are alive and that none of the spinal nerves or cord seem to be damaged. That means that you are not paralyzed, and due to the location of the injury if you would have severed the cord you would be on a respirator right now. So, that is good news. The not so good news is that due to your age and your not so good health, you are not a surgical candidate for a bone graft surgery or repair. So, what this means is that you will be sent home with a neck brace that you will have to wear twenty-four hours a day for at least six to ten weeks to allow the bone to calcify and hopefully bond back together. I do have to say that there is a risk due to your age that the bones might not heal, and you will need to wear the brace indefinitely. However, let's not go there yet. Let's just be thankful you are alive for now." He then abruptly turned and walked out of the room. Father looked at Dylan and said, "Lucky, he must not be Catholic, Jewish I bet with a name like Abelman. Lucky would mean that I died and that I was already through purgatory and now in heaven." They both laughed.

Forgotten and Lost

It took almost three hours for the nurses and the social workers to complete the discharge paperwork that allowed Father to leave the hospital and then be driven home by Dylan. Father appeared more frail than usual and the large neck brace made Father clumsy. Still feeling responsible for the accident Dylan made sure that Father had everything he needed in his room and even gave Father a small bell that he could ring if he needed help and didn't think he could get out of bed. As independent as Father was, he disregarded the bell idea. Dylan did offer to spend extra time with Father and surprisingly Father accepted. Unknown to Dylan, Father had been pondering an idea for some time and he felt that this was the perfect time to complete the task at hand. He wanted to write down what he called his confession. Not a confession in the sense of the Holy Sacrament, but rather his life story as it related to God, like the famous book, *The Confession of Saint Augustine.* When Father asked Dylan if he would be willing to be his scribe and assist him with creating the book. Dylan instantly accepted.

Dylan deeply respected Father and in many ways related to him as if he was his father and he was the son. He desired deeply to know this spiritual father much better but that was difficult due to Father's reserved nature and the fact that he rarely spoke about himself. Dylan asked, "When do we begin?" Father replied, "There is no time like the present." He asked Dylan if he owned a computer and when Dylan confirmed that he did, Father then directed Dylan to retrieve his computer.

Dylan ran to his room, grabbed his computer, and returned just as quickly as he could. He booted up the computer and while the computer was running through the start-up systems check, Dylan commented, "I am so glad that you asked me to do this Father, you could have just as easily used the Dragon program to dictate this yourself, but I feel honored that you chose me." Father asked, "What is that Dragon program you mentioned? I have never heard of it."

Dylan explained that technology had advanced so much that now loaded on all new computers was a voice to type software program called Dragon. He then demonstrated how it worked. Dylan activated the program and then spoke a few sentences. As he spoke the computer typed the spoken words onto a word document. After a minute Dylan clicked a few keys and the computer read back the typed document with perfect accuracy. Father was amazed not only what the program could do, but how easy it was to operate. Father asked Dylan if the program could be installed on a special braille computer and without hesitation, Dylan confirmed that it could. Just then Dylan realized what he had done. He had just talked his way right out of being the scribe for Father. Dylan's mood saddened and he softly asked, "Father, I get the sense that maybe you have changed your mind about me helping you?" Father Mateo responded with great enthusiasm, "Absolutely not, I just need your help in a different way. I need you to load that program on my braille keyboard computer and teach me how to use it." It was exactly what Dylan had thought, he lost the opportunity to learn first hand about the man he admired so much.

Over the next three days, Dylan was able to do just what Father Mateo had asked. The program was now installed onto the special laptop and Father was able to use it. Father did need help setting it up on the front end each day, but once logged on he could operate the system and get it to do what he wanted it to do. Dylan agreed to help Father each day, for the first few minutes to ensure that the program was operational, and then excuse himself so Father could work in private. They agreed that seven o'clock in the evening each day would be the book dictating/writing time.

Chapter 35

Carter arrived at the summer camp and was surprised to see that they had made a welcome sign and hung it outside the main hall. The sign read, WELCOME TO CAMP - CARTER. Instantly he felt a little special and welcomed. As soon as he had parked his car in the gravel parking area a young, attractive, brunette woman started walking toward him from the hall. As she came closer Carter could tell that she was quite petite and probably about the same or similar age as he was, maybe 25ish. She had a radiating smile and said, "You must be Carter? We have been expecting you. My name is Brooklyn, really Brook, and I am the lead counselor this year. Can you believe that? Anyway, that is a discussion for another time. Let me show you to your cabin." Carter immediately liked her. She was friendly, nice, sweet, warm, and personable. She was also naturally joyful, a trait that Carter wished he had. He had often thought of himself as maybe a little melancholy and wished that he had more of a joyful spirit. It used to bother him more in his adolescence but in his late teens and early twenties, he decided that being melancholy was what God had chosen to make him and that it would be his cross to bear and somehow would assist him in his journey toward becoming a saint. At least that thought helped him from becoming depressed about it.

As soon as Carter grabbed his backpack, Brook led the way down a dirt trail east of the hall. She traveled with a light skip in her step. They arrived at the first of many cabins that Carter could see while looking down the trail. The log cabin was rustic and appeared to be slightly larger than the others further down the trail. It had a nice covered porch with a porch swing and a sign mounted above the entrance door that read KING COUNSELOR. Carter pointed to the sign and Brook laughed while explaining, "When I saw that I laughed too. King counselor, what is that? It was what the kids from last year decided to call the cabin for the boys' lead counselor. Don't worry, you are not alone. Mine is called SUPREME QUEEN OF THE CAMP." They both laughed out loud. She opened the door and instantly jumped back as three squirrels ran out and scampered past her feet. She commented, "You better lock up any food if you brought some." She then showed Carter the light switch and the heater knob. Then she stretched out her hand as if she was a model on a gameshow displaying a new car and said, "And here is your lovely bed and living quarters that comes abundantly equipped with a desk, a chair, and not one but two, completely new and never have been used rolls of toilet paper." Carter laughed. He loved her personality and playfulness. She then gave a polite curtsy and as she began to leave Carter to unpack, she said, "Come find me after you have settled in. I will give you a tour of the grounds." Carter didn't want her to leave. He was intrigued by her and just as he was about to say something, he caught himself and let her walk away while giving her an affirming smile.

Carter laid down upon his bed and stared up at the ceiling. He noticed a round black object in the corner, wedged in close to a beam. He squinted his eyes to try to discern what it was but due to the darkness in the corner of the ceiling, he couldn't make it out. Then suddenly he thought he saw it move a little. He blinked his eyes a few times and then convinced himself that it hadn't moved. But now obsessed with finding out what it was that had captured his attention, he scanned the room to see if there was something that he could throw at it to try to dislodge it from whatever it was stuck to. He eventually found a few rocks that had been left on the window seal and stacked upon each other in some sort of rock stacking art attempt.

He threw the first stone and completely missed the object by at least five feet. He commented to himself under his breath, “Great shot nimrod, been playing baseball long?” He then threw the second stone and it missed the object but hit the beam and bounced back and almost struck him on top of his head. He then took the third and last stone and pointed it at the object and with a calculating posture he reared back and thrust the stone into the air. It was a dead-on hit. As soon as the stone connected with the object it unraveled and stretched out its wings and then came flying down toward Carter while screeching the most awful and loud high-pitched sound. Instantly Carter sprung up from his bed and dove out of the cabin and onto the porch in a frantic attempt to escape the bat that was coming after him. He initially landed on the porch floor and then spastically rolled down the steps until he plopped down on top of the dirt. It was then that he noticed Brook standing there with her arms folded across her chest. With a jokingly stern attitude, she commented, “I guess I didn’t need to come back to warm you about the bats, you figured it out for yourself.” They both laughed for a minute and then she proceeded to show Carter how they shooed them out of the cabins using a broom. It was quite an easy task once shown what to do. She added, “The bats settle in over the winter and part of opening up for the summer is getting them out of the cabins. I realized when I got back to the office that we forgot to clear your cabin. A good intention a little late I guess.” Carter smiled and then commented, “I appreciate the thought.”

Brook began brushing the dirt from Carter’s shirt as he brushed it off from his jeans. The process took a few minutes since he had rolled a few times in the powdery dirt during his freighted panic. Carter felt very comfortable with Brook and that surprised him. He had always been awkward around girls, especially extremely pretty ones like Brook, but there was something special about her, unintimidating, unshowy, and down to earth.

Chapter 36

Jonas had been walking for almost three hours in the hot sun and he had become quite dehydrated. He had been looking for a drinking fountain, or a residential garden hose, or anything that he could wet his lips with. He had passed a few stores, but he was without any money so he couldn't buy anything. He eventually decided that he would ask the next person that passed by if they could help him get something to drink. As he continued to walk, he noticed a middle-aged woman dressed in a jogging outfit, walking her poodle, coming toward him on the sidewalk from the opposite direction. As soon as she was within three feet he asked, "Can you help me to get something to drink?" She immediately responded, "You need to go to the shelter. It's drinking that got you where you are now" and passed right by him without even making eye contact. Jonas continued to walk but also quietly said a prayer, "Dear Lord, please bless her. She is so angry, and she cannot see beyond her assumptions." He continued to walk with the sun beating down upon him. It was an unusually warm day for the south Sacramento area and there wasn't even the slightest breeze. Jonas had not eaten or had anything to drink for over two days and he had no reserve to draw from. He was now starting to stagger, and heat stroke was setting in. Just then a beaten-up old Ford pickup towing a trailer filled with lawn maintenance equipment pulled up alongside him and a Mexican man asked, "¿Necesitas ayuda hermano?" (You need help brother?) Jonas' mind began to spin, and he looked toward the man, they made eye contact for just a moment, and then Jonas collapsed to the ground. The man abruptly stopped his truck and jumped out. He ran to Jonas and said, "No te preocupes hermano, te ayudaré." (Don't worry brother, I will help you.) He drug Jonas' large body over to the passenger side of the truck and then lifted and pushed until Jonas was safely inside. While lifting Jonas, the man felt how incredibly hot Jonas was so as soon as Jonas was inside the cab, he poured a water bottle over his head in an attempt to cool him down. Jonas arose and the men began speaking to each other in Spanish. The man introduced himself as Mario and said that he was on his way to his church where they were having their festival. He explained that his wife had a booth there where she was selling tamales and beans, and horchata to drink and that they would get him feeling better.

It didn't take long, and the men arrived at the church parking lot where the festival was underway. There must have been almost three hundred people attending and dozens of food booths. Mario drove his truck across the lot and right up to a Mexican food booth. Although awake, Jonas was still quite dazed from the malnutrition and dehydration. Mario exited the vehicle and walked up to what appeared to be his wife. He kissed her on the cheek and then loud enough for Jonas to hear he began explaining that he had finished work and was praying his rosary while coming to meet her. He said that as he was praying and meditating on the sorrowful mystery, Jesus falling as he carried his cross, he heard a voice say, "Help me, Mario, it is too heavy for me to carry." He explained that he thought he was imagining it, but the words kept repeating. The voice was loud and clear. He then explained that as he looked up, he saw Jonas and knew that God wanted him to stop. Mario's eyes began to tear up and he explained that as soon as he looked into Jonas' eyes, he knew that he was a holy man. Mario's wife crossed herself and said in Spanish, "Go get him. Bring him here." Mario urgently gained the assistance of his brother who was helping in the booth and they lifted Jonas onto his feet and out of the cab of the truck and into a reclining lawn chair under the shade of the booth. They served him a large glass of Horchata as well as a plate of tamales with beans and tortillas. As soon as Jonas downed the delicious cinnamon and rice drink, he began to think more clearly. He slowly ate the plate of beans and the three pork tamales. As soon as he took the last bite of food from the plate Mario's wife served him another plate of beans, tortillas, and tamales. Jonas felt stuffed already but could tell that they wanted him to eat more. Now feeling much better he felt that he could communicate and began speaking to Mario's wife and brother in Spanish. They talked about a variety of things but especially about family, church life, and living their life of faith.

Mario's wife was named Hilda and his brother, Raymond. Quickly Jonas identified that they were a very holy family with remarkable faith and possessed a servant's heart. He also learned that they had a young daughter with Spina Bifida, a spinal cord condition in which the cord didn't form correctly and that because of the congenital condition she would never be able to walk. She was confined to a wheelchair and had extensive medical issues. He also learned that they had been praying for a miracle for almost six years, but their daughter's condition had only worsened. The daughter's name is Gracia, Grace in English.

Now after eating, drinking, and resting for quite some time Jonas stood up and asked if he could see Gracia. Hilda was happy to introduce the two of them. She led Jonas across the parking lot to another Mexican booth serving Tacos. After introducing him to her sister Emelina, she introduced him to Gracia. The young girl had a beautiful face, an innocent smile, a pure complexion, but her body was very twisted and looked deformed. She sat in a specialized wheelchair with padded supports for her torso, hips, and thighs. Jonas asked her how she liked the festival and Hilda explained, "She is not able to talk, but she does hear you, and I can tell that she likes you. Look at her smile."

Jonas asked Hilda if he could pray over Gracia. Instantly Hilda gave permission. Jonas bent down and with both hands, he reached around to her back while he whispered in Spanish, "Almighty Father, please remove from this child all that is broken. Heal her with Your power, and due to her parents' faith and belief in You make it so she will live a holy and lively life." Tears began to stream down the face of Hilda as she listened to the sweet and comforting words spoken. Jonas continued to pray but the additional words were too soft to be overheard. The prayer lasted almost four minutes and then suddenly Jonas rose. He turned to Hilda and said, "Your faith has healed her." Hilda was beside herself and somehow she knew that something remarkable had occurred, but wasn't sure to what extent. She needed to know if her child had been healed of the Spina Bifida.

Gracia had always had a large bulge on her back where the spine had coiled and not formed correctly. Hilda politely asked if Jonas could excuse them so she could close the curtain that separated the tent into two halves, and so she could examine her child. Jonas smiled and Hilda proceeded to close the curtain. She then loosened the straps that held Gracia firmly into the chair. Once the straps were loose, she leaned her child forward and lifted her blouse. Inspecting her skin, instantly it was amazingly apparent that the enormous bulge that had always been there had disappeared and Gracia's body was no longer twisted and deformed. Gracia then spoke in a soft and angelic voice, "Mamá, mi espalda no está rota." (Mom, my back is not broken.) Hilda screamed aloud and began to weep while yelling that a miracle had occurred. She hugged her daughter with all her might as dozens of people quickly came to see what had happened. Before she could explain, she needed to thank Jonas. She threw open the curtain and looked for him, but he had already disappeared. She fell to her knees and praised God for the miracle.

Chapter 37

` It had been three days since Father Mateo had returned from the hospital and to Dylan's surprise, he hadn't mentioned anything about the writing of his book. It was driving Dylan crazy how a man could be so excited to do something and then drop it so quickly. He needed to find out what happened. He knocked on Father's bedroom door and instantly he heard, "Come in." Dylan walked into the room and saw Father sitting at his small desk and propped up in front of him was his laptop. Father asked, "Who is it?" Dylan announced himself and looking over Father's shoulder he could see that Father must have figured out how to use the Dragon program since there was what appeared to be the writings of a book on the laptop computer screen. Dylan asked, "I just came by to see how you are feeling." Father laughed and then commented, "Really Dylan? You came by to see why I hadn't asked you to help me with my computer. Am I right?" Dylan had no intention of lying and replied, "That is exactly true Father." Father laughed and added, "I know you so well, you are just like a son to me. You must know me just as well and you probably know that I don't like to ask for help if I don't need it." Dylan smiled. Father continued, "I was able to figure out the dictation program so I didn't want to bother you, especially since you have so much to study. Theology is not an easy degree." Dylan felt like saying that he didn't know him well and that was why he was so excited to be his scribe and to learn more about the man he looked up to and respected. Yet, he held his tongue and only said, "Yes, Father. I do have a lot on my plate." He then excused himself and exited the room.

Dylan never had the opportunity to know his father. When Dylan was five years old his parents divorced, and his father left. During the years of being raised by his mother, he yearned for a relationship with his father, but he never heard from him again. His father completely abandoned them. He still felt hurt, guilty, and wounded by the abandonment. He often thought that if he was somehow a more handsome boy, or more athletic, or funnier, his dad wouldn't have wanted to never see him again. Those feelings of inadequacy tormented him at times.

It wasn't until his teenage years when Dylan was invited to attend Mass with a friend that he learned about prayer and the person of Jesus Christ that brought comfort. Before that, he had been agnostic, at least that was what his mother was. After that first encounter with the Mass, even though he wasn't Catholic at the time, he returned to church every Sunday by himself for Mass. He felt incredible peace when he sat in the church.

One day, after attending Mass for almost three months of Sundays a young Irish priest by the name of Father Kierney approached Dylan and asked him to wait after Mass so he could ask him a few questions. It was that day that Dylan began a relationship that would change his life forever. Father asked him many questions and Dylan revealed his naïve and wounded soul to the holy priest. Father instantly identified something special in Dylan and Dylan was immediately attracted to the charism of the priest. He was tough but kind. He was funny but serious. He was smart but down to earth.

Not knowing how his mother would react to the idea of attending Mass, Dylan chose to keep that a secret from his mother.

He continued to attend the Sunday 9:00 am Mass and then met with Father after Mass for almost two years until he mustered up enough courage to tell his mother. During those two years, Father Kierney had progressively taught Dylan the fundamentals of the faith. It was then that Father asked if Dylan wanted to become Catholic and to receive Baptism, Confirmation, and the Holy Eucharist. Initially, Dylan felt extremely unworthy, probably related to his inadequacy issues, but Father assured him that he was ready. However, since he was still a minor, he would need his mother's permission to enter the Church. It was that issue of needing to receive his mother's permission that was the catalyst for Dylan finally disclosing to his mother what he had been doing every Sunday morning for the past few years. Surprisingly, when Dylan presented the idea of becoming Catholic to his mother she didn't object. She wasn't even angry, but contrastingly supportive and agreed to attend the celebration.

Now, having his secret revealed that he had been routinely attending Mass, he felt free. Wasting no time, and with Father's assistance, he received all three Sacraments and was fully initiated into the Catholic Church. His involvement in the parish grew. He became active in the high school youth group and even led a teen bible study with some of his peers.

Feeling that the Church was calling him towards a vocation, even though he was still quite young, he learned of a minor seminary and applied to Sacred Heart Apostolic School for acceptance. The school was an all-male boarding school in the diocese of Gary, Indiana, and operated by the Legionaries of Christ. It was a very small school, serving 20-35 students in grades seven through twelve. To his surprise, within three weeks of mailing off his application, they accepted him and within just one additional week he had traveled to Indiana by plane and was enrolled as a freshman in the minor seminary.

Forgotten and Lost

The academics at the seminary were quite difficult but Dylan was smart, self-driven, and embraced the challenge. The curriculum was much different than that of the public schools he had attended. The seminary program followed a classical liberal arts model with particular attention to classical Latin, Greek, and modern Spanish language. He studied British and American literature, mathematics, the natural sciences, history, theology, cultural studies, and fine arts that included vocal music, theater, and communication. He learned how to read Greek and Latin, and even learned to play the trombone and flute.

The years at the seminary flew by and he not only made many friends, but he grew emotionally and spiritually. Eventually, he fulfilled the senior requirement of translating the Gospel of John from the original Greek, as well as many other competency-related tasks, and graduated with honors. He assumed that he would continue with the Legionaries, obtaining post-high school formation, until he received a phone call that his mother was seriously ill and he needed to return home. Finding out his mother had breast cancer which had metastasized, he knew he needed to be with her, especially since she had no one else in the world. Dylan was an only child and she had never remarried after the divorce.

His mother's disease advanced quickly, and she died within a week. Feeling quite lost and honestly maybe a little desperate, he wasted no time and made an appointment with the local bishop. Finding out that Dylan was a graduate of the Legionnaire minor seminary, Bishop Kerry agreed to meet with him. Bishop Kerry immediately liked Dylan and sensed that there was something very special about him. The Bishop referred Dylan to the vocation's director, Father Uhlenkott, who scheduled numerous interviews, some individual and some panel, a variety of psychological tests, and a medical evaluation. He must have passed all the tests because after a few days he was formally accepted by Bishop Kerry and the diocese as a seminarian student and sent to Mount Angel Theological Seminary to complete a philosophy degree and then to further his studies in theology and formation.

Chapter 38

Camp life was now in full swing at Camp Pendola, and there was 125 youth at the camp ranging from the ages of eight to seventeen. Brook had a cabin of third graders (eight-year-olds) while Carter had twelve young adolescent boys (sixteen and seventeen-year-olds) who quickly learned how to strut the grounds with a royalty-like attitude. The energy of camp life was positive, festive, and friendly. Carter, probably due to being a little older than most of the other counselors, and maybe from his experience at the seminary, was asked to take the lead for the morning, midday, and evening prayer. The first day of camp he had planned a very elaborate and thoughtful prayer to start the day and when he began, he quickly realized that any prayer lasting more than twenty seconds would lose the attention of the younger campers. At the thirty second mark, most of the third-graders had already begun playing soccer and the fourth-graders were leg wrestling. His next prayer was twelve seconds and right to the point.

Surprisingly the afternoon brought thunderstorms and necessitated a change in the program plans. Instead of wilderness hikes, they moved indoors and planned an afternoon of square dancing in the hall. It so happened that the camp cook, Delbert, was a professional square dance caller and loved being asked to guide the kids with lessons and directions. He even carried his square dance music tapes with him just in case he was asked. The counselors divided the kids into boy and girl groups of similar ages and placed them into small circles of eight. Delbert then asked for an adult volunteer couple to demonstrate a few of standard dance steps. Initially, none of the counselors showed an interest so feeling a little pressured Brook and Carter raised their hands. Delbert jumped down from the stage and helped Carter to put his right hand on Brook's shoulder and his left on her hip. He then proceeded to walk them through a variety of square dance steps including the Promenade, Do si do, and the Allemande left. Brook was much more of a natural talent than Carter but they both complemented each other. The kids laughed as they witnessed many mistakes and stepping on feet.

After a few minutes, Delbert climbed back onto the stage and with a flick of the switch he activated the cassette player and the room filled with lively music. With the microphone held firmly in Delbert's right hand, he began his rhythmic square dance directives and calls. Delbert knew just how to motivate the kids and his simple instructions included a progressive adding of moves, and in less than ten minutes the kids were dancing in what appeared to be a cohesive group. Brook and Carter remained a dancing couple and as the only couple not attached to a circular group they floated across the floor, back and forth, with great freedom. Both of their faces were smiling ear to ear and they gazed into each other's eyes almost the entire time as they danced. Carter was mesmerized by Brook's natural beauty. The inadvertent but frequent bodily touches as he held her, spun her and guided her with his hand on her hip, enlivened special feelings within him. He had never touched a girl, never had been kissed, or even held a girl's hand before that day. His mind now filled with thoughts wondering if God wanted him to become a married man.

As they continued to dance, he began to daydream of courting Brook as a girlfriend and imagined walking with a sunset behind them while holding hands, laughing, and joking. He even imagined them sitting on a porch swing with her caressing his face softly and him responding with a perfect slight kiss on her cheek. Suddenly there was a scream. Delbert abruptly stopped the music and drew everyone's attention to the far-left corner of the hall. A skunk had entered the room and three of the eight-year-old boys began to chase it. Before Carter could speak out, the small critter turned, raised its tail, and launched an enormous dose of skunk spray that covered at least twenty of the kids, but especially the three chasing boys from head to toe. Delbert, knowing just what to do, grabbed a cowbell and began to ring it as he walked toward the animal while staying a safe distance away and escorted it out of the building. The skunk did not like the noise. Carter dismissed all the non-sprayed kids to their cabins under the care and supervision of their counselors and instructed the others to report to the main showers. Delbert ran to the kitchen storage area and grabbed all the cans of tomato juice, tomato paste, and even ketchup bottles that he could find and delivered them to Brook and Carter.

Carter took the affected boys and Brook took the girls. After having them undress in the appropriate shower rooms both Brook and Carter began to spread the juice, paste, and ketchup over their entire bodies. Some of the kids began to cry due to the stench being so intense while others laughed. Brook and Carter found very little humor in the work and dreaded the accusations and phone calls that were sure to come from angry parents as soon as they heard what had occurred.

After almost two hours, the time required to cover the kids with the deactivating concoction and shower it off, everyone returned to their cabins for quiet time. The younger kids took naps while older kids were instructed to write in their journals.

Five o'clock eventually arrived and upon hearing the cowbell ring most knew that it was dinnertime. Some of the smaller kids however related the bell to the skunk incident and feared being sprayed again. After some reassurance, everyone made their way to the dining hall. Once all were inside sitting down Delbert climbed on top of the center table and said, “Hey kids, you know what’s for dinner?” A few of the kids yelled out, “Hot dogs,” others, “Hamburgers,” and some “Pizza.” Delbert laughed and then holding up a creatively disguised skunk-skin hat, that looked like the skunk from earlier in the day, he said, “We are having skunk stew.” The room filled with boos and some cheers. Carter and Brook laughed and then Delbert added, “Just kidding” and he placed the hat upon his head and said, “Not really, its pizza night.” All the kids cheered.

Chapter 39

Jonas had accepted a ride from a friendly trucker he met at a rest stop and was now heading south on the interstate five freeway toward Los Angeles. Bruce, the truck driver, was an elderly man, probably in his early seventies. He couldn't have stood over five feet five inches and weighed under 150 pounds. He was a slight man and looked weathered and worn out. Jonas noticed him fueling his rig at the truck stop and felt compelled to meet him. As soon as Jonas walked up to the side of the rig Bruce smiled and greeted him with a welcoming smile. Jonas noticed his saddened eyes.

Jonas asked a few questions about the rig and Bruce took over from there. He was a talker and instantly began to share things about his life. He explained that he recently became a widower and his dog companion of the last eighteen years had suddenly died. Jonas sensed a great need for Bruce to tell his story and to also have someone to connect with. Jonas asked, "I don't mean to be a trouble in any way, but would it be possible to catch a ride with you?" Bruce's eyes lit up and he instantly said, "Sure." Bruce then asked, "Wait, you don't even know where I am going. Where are you wanting to go?" Jonas replied, "Well, I am on a mission and I believe that where I am to go is exactly where you are going." Bruce didn't understand what Jonas meant but because of his polite nature, he smiled and agreed.

Bruce finished with the filling of his massive fuel tanks, washed his windows, checked the air pressure of all sixteen tires, and ensured that he had plenty of window wash fluid before saying, "Alright, I think I'm ready." Jonas climbed up into the passenger seat of the rig and Bruce did the same but into the driver's chair. With a turn of the key, the powerful engine rumbled and after placing the transmission into first gear the large truck and trailer jerked and then began to roll. Jonas noticed the CB radio and asked, "Do you use this?" while pointing to the receiver. Bruce laughed and then replied, "You haven't been in too many big rigs, have you?" Jonas confirmed, "Only one with my friend Terrance a few months back. I can't remember if he had a CB radio or not." Bruce reached down and grabbed the handset with his right hand and without hesitation he spoke, "Breaker-Breaker, this is old Bucky in the beast and just picked up a thumber and heading west. Just left the chicken coup and hoping to avoid any Christmas cards. Just far enough out to be out of reach of the city kitty but any news of any cub scouts, fender benders, flap downs, girly bears, or any sneaky skippers hiding in the strip?" Almost instantly there was a reply on the CB radio. The man speaking used similar coded talk and Jonas had no idea what was being said, yet Bruce knew exactly. It was clear that Bruce used the CB often to communicate and to socialize.

Jonas looked around the front of the cabin and noticed a small crucifix wedged between the trim and headliner just above Bruce's head. Jonas asked, "Are you, Catholic, Bruce?" Bruce turned toward Jonas and his smile disappeared, his eyes teared, and with his lower lip quivering he said, "No, but my wife, Lani was." Jonas asked if Bruce felt comfortable talking about her. He immediately said "Yes" and then proceeded to share over the next two hours stories about how they had met, their dating, and detailed descriptions of many things they had done together over the years. The more he spoke about his recently departed wife the more peaceful he appeared. It was obvious that he cherished his wife and that she had meant the world to him.

Things seemed to be going well and the men had covered a lot of ground. It wasn't until they hit a huge pothole and the cab bounced up and down with quite a lot of force that Bruce yelled out, "Oh me knickers, there it is again." He screamed a painful and lamenting scream and clenched his teeth together and started to grind them in agonizing pain. Jonas asked, "What is it, Bruce? Is there anything I can do?" Bruce attempted to regain his composure, but the pain was excruciating. He took a few deep breaths, panted a few times as if he was practicing Lamaze child-birth breathing, and just as he was about to respond to Jonas, he burst out again in a troubling scream, "Oh my freaking heaven, this damn thing is going to kill me yet." He then began to pant but this time he took his foot off the accelerator, let the rig coast, and steered it to the side of the highway. Once it stopped he opened his door and tried to step down, he must have missed the step, and he fell upon the ground. He screamed again, "This damn kidney stone feels like it is tearing me up inside." Finally, Jonas knew what was happening. Bruce had kidney stones and the jarring of the cab must have dislodged it and that was what was causing the tremendous pain. The pain must have been seriously intense since Bruce had now curled up in a ball and continued to pant like a female dog in heat. Jonas couldn't stand to see Bruce suffer and said, "Don't worry Bruce, I know what I'm doing." He then reached down placed the palm of his hand upon the site where Bruce's right kidney would be and the said with absolute conviction, "You are healed." Bruce felt a blast of heat and pressure that lasted for only an instant and then the pain vanished. With a bewildered look Bruce stared at Jonas. Jonas calmly directed Bruce, "Now go to a private place, maybe in that little cove area between the cab and the trailer and urinate." Still in shock, Bruce did as he had been instructed, stood, walked to the area behind the cab where he was shielded from view of the traffic and from Jonas, and he began to urinate onto the ground. He initially hesitated thinking that he might re-experience the unbearable pain but instead, the urine flowed freely and as it fell upon the ground, he could see by the light of the full moon tiny particles of what must have been the stone. Unobstructed, the urine flowed and flowed. He must have had almost two liters of fluid stored in his bladder. After almost two minutes the urine flow ceased, and Bruce was overjoyed from the miraculous healing. He zipped up his pants and planned to hug Jonas for what he had done. Returning to the cab he looked for Jonas. First in the cab, then on either side of the rig, and even up and down the freeway. He was nowhere in sight. He had completely disappeared.

Chapter 40

Dylan had just finished taking a mid-term exam from his Christology and Pneumatology course and was pretty sure he had failed. Feeling quite down emotionally he made his way to the seminary chapel and planned to spend some time in adoration of the Holy Eucharist. He often found that when he was struggling and needed to be uplifted, sitting in the presence of Christ always seemed to do the trick. Luckily when he arrived at the adoration chapel the adorer there was just preparing to leave. That meant he had the opportunity to be alone with Christ. As soon as the person left the room, Dylan walked up to the Monstrance that housed the consecrated host and kneeled. After a moment he slightly raised his head so that Jesus was in view, and he spoke, "Lord, I am feeling a little down today. I feel that I am in the right place and my vocational call is real and true, but I just need some inspiration. I am feeling worn out and tired." He then sat back upon his heels and awaited a response.

After almost an hour of complete silence, Dylan finally received a mild impulse. He felt the urge to visit the sacristy in the church. He crossed himself, thanked Jesus, and exited the side-chapel. Walking over to the church he wondered what it was that Jesus wanted him to do over there. After entering the church, he proceeded toward the altar and after genuflecting in reverence to

Christ housed in the tabernacle, he made his way to the rear of the sanctuary into the sacristy. The sacristy is where the clergy vestments are stored as well as the liturgy books, candles, altar cloths, the unconsecrated wine and hosts, and the vessels used for the Holy Mass. It is also where the priests and deacons vest and prayerfully prepare before the Mass.

Dylan stood in the middle of the room unsure of what he was to do next. He looked toward the crucifix mounted on the wall and asked, "OK Lord, I am here. What do I do now?" His request was followed by a deafening silence. Dylan looked around the room and noticed a closet door slightly ajar. He walked over and opened the door and revealed a vast variety of priestly vestments. Without hesitation, he placed the amice around his neck and tied it in place.

He then donned a white alb and then tied a cincture around his waist. He had never worn holy vestments before, and it felt a little like a dress-up day at elementary school. He then wrapped the stole around his neck and tucked the ends underneath the cincture. He browsed through the closet looking for the perfect chasable and then finally locating one of beautiful white and golden silk, he removed it from the hanger and draped it over his torso. Chills radiated across his body. He then placed the maniple on his left arm and spotting a biretta on the shelf he gently placed it on his head. He walked over to the full-length mirror that was mounted on the inside of the closet door and gazed at his appearance. His initial reaction was that the person he was looking at appeared to be an entirely different person than who he was. Instead of the thought being troubling, it brought comfort. He discerned his reaction to represent that after ordination he would be transformed into a slightly different but better version of himself. Now only a seminarian, he would eventually be ordained a transitional deacon and then a holy priest. That anointing and the Sacramental effect received with each ordination would, in fact, change his soul indefinitely.

He slightly turned to his right, and then his left, while looking at the mirror. He wanted to get a comprehensive look at himself. Internally he was filled with joy and delight. He then lifted his right arm as if he was giving a blessing, practicing the priestly gesture, and giving it to an imaginary congregation. Glancing over to the shelf area by the sink he noticed a tray with the sacred vessels sitting upon it. He walked over to the counter and began to set out each piece in its proper location as if he was preparing the altar at Mass. He laid down a corporal, placed a paten and chalice upon it. He reached for the Roman Missal that was stored on the shelf and laid it down to the left of the vessels. He opened the drawer and taking one of the unconsecrated hosts he placed it on the paten. He then opened the lower cabinet that was in front of his knees and took the large bottle of communion wine and poured a small amount into the chalice. He briefly looked around ensuring that no one else was present and as soon as he felt that he was alone he began reciting the words of consecration as written in the Roman Missal. Slightly bowing he lifted the host and while holding it with both hands he said,

"Take this, all of you, and eat of it,
for this is my Body,
which will be given up for you."

He then laid the host back down upon the paten, genuflected, and then grabbed the chalice with the wine inside and slightly bowing he raised the vessel and said,

"Take this, all of you, and drink from it,
for this is the chalice of My Blood,
the Blood of the new and eternal covenant,
which will be poured out for you and for many
for the forgiveness of sins.
Do this in memory of Me."

He then lowered the chalice and set it down upon the corporal. He genuflected and said, "The mystery of faith. When we eat this bread and drink this cup, we proclaim Your death, O Lord, until You come again."

He then grasped the chalice in his left hand, and the host between his thumb and first finger of his right hand, and holding the host above the chalice and raising them both high into the air he said,

"This is the Lamb of God who takes away the sins of the world,
happy are those who are called to His supper."

Instantly, with the host and chalice still raised, Dylan's fingers burned with tremendous heat and a burst of light filled the room. The Host mysteriously began to drip. Originating from within the host itself flowed a sanguineous liquid so profusely that it quickly filled the chalice and then began to overflow on top of the counter and down upon the floor. Dylan was frozen and mesmerized by what was occurring. He was frightened and didn't know what to do. He just stood there while the host continued to flow out blood. He finally blurted out, "Lord, please stop. Please, Lord, stop." Then instantly the flow stopped and all the blood that had been present suddenly evaporated. Dylan gently laid the host and chalice down and then dropped to his knees and began to weep.

Chapter 41

Three weeks had already passed at the camp and although Brook and Carter saw each other daily they had yet to spend any time together away from the others. Feeling quite smitten with her, Carter had yearned to ask Brook if they could go on a walk, or even just hang out and visit, but he was fearful that he would be rejected. He had never asked a girl out on a date and never really considered it before meeting Brook. It wasn't until Brook opened the door to the invitation when she commented to Carter that it was her evening off and that she didn't have any plans that he jumped on the opportunity and asked, "Would you like to hang out?" Coincidently it was also Carter's evening off too. To Carter's surprise, she accepted the invitation and they planned to meet on the porch of the community room after dinner.

Carter arrived early and secured a seat on the porch swing. It was a rather wide swing and there was plenty of room to sit next to each other if she so desired. Now almost a quarter after seven in the evening, Carter saw Brook skipping along the dirt trail and in her hands were two Nalgene bottles. As she approached, she said, "Sorry I am late. I thought I would make us some freshly squeezed lemonade." Without hesitation, she sat down next to Carter on the swing and even though she had ample room to sit further away, she cozied up next to him. The gesture was more friendly than romantic, but it was noticeable by Carter. She had a way about her that was friendly, sincere, kind, and maybe even a little naïve. Carter asked her about her day and she kindly responded but appeared more interested in hearing about his day. She listened attentively as Carter described the adventures he had with the boys that included rock climbing, kayaking, walking while praying the stations of the cross in the forest, and an aggressive game of Frisbee football. There was a natural ease between the two as if they had known each other for years.

After visiting on the porch for almost two hours, Carter began to discern that it wasn't only he who had feelings for her, but that she now appeared to like him as well. Or at least he thought that to be true. He had identified through their visit that she had not dated in the past and like him, she had never had a boyfriend. He found that quite odd, her never having a relationship since she was exceeding beautiful, social, and possessed such a sweet personality. Then as they were taking turns discussing their most embarrassing moments something suddenly came over Carter and he leaned forward and kissed her on her lips. Although surprised by the abrupt move she didn't back away and kissed him back. The kiss was soft, slow, and with their lips only slightly open. It lasted only three to four seconds but during that time it was as if time stood still. As Carter eventually retracted, he felt that her lips were the softest and most sensual thing he had ever experienced. There was a silent pause for just a few moments and then Brook began to cry. She laid her head down upon Carter's chest. He lifted his arm and placed it around her shoulder and began to caress her back as he asked, "What is it, Brook? I am sorry if I offended you." She took a moment to compose herself and to regain control of her emotions and then she slowly sat back up and moved even closer to Carter. She took his hand into hers and shared, "No it isn't you, it's me. I hadn't shared this but up until a few weeks ago I had been Sister Mariam, a Carmelite nun with the Discalced Carmelites of Cristo Rey in San

Francisco and living a cloistered life. I was happy there and I thought everything was going well. I had completed my postulancy after a year and had taken temporary vows and had started the novitiate. One day Mother Superior called me into her office and said that she was concerned that maybe I hadn't adequately discerned my decision to become a nun before coming to the monastery. I was happy and I thought that living there was part of the discernment process. She then said that it wasn't unusual to have postulants and even novices take some time off and return to the secular world for a year or two to deepen their discernment toward their call to religious life." Carter listened intently and deeply identified with Brook, having lived within a religious community and now living back out in the world. She continued, "My tears are emotions of happiness but also of confusion. I want to be a nun. I feel called to be a bride of Christ. I am attracted to you, but maybe the kiss was a mistake. I know it is alright to have feelings for someone, even strong feelings. Even the holiest of women are human, that is what the nuns taught me. I do want to be married to Christ, but what if He doesn't want that? What if He placed you in my life because He wants me to be with you?" Carter's heart ached seeing Brook so confused and torn. She truly was sweet and naïve, but honest and pure. Those qualities made her even more attractive to Carter. She laid her head down upon his chest again and began to softly cry. She was so vulnerable and wounded. Carter continued to comfort her by caressing her back. He then shared, "Brooklyn, I hadn't shared something with you either. Only a few weeks ago I was a seminarian, well I guess I still am, but I had asked for a leave of absence to further discern my calling." She sat back up and looked Carter directly in his eyes. He could see that her eyes had reddened, and her lashes were filled with tears. She asked, "So, you too are like me, but it is you that was questioning your call, and for me, it was my Mother Superior." Carter instantly realized hearing her words that the only thing they had in common was that they both were no longer with their communities.

Brook slowly pulled away and stood up. She graciously took Carter's hand into hers again and thanked him for the nice evening together and added, "Carter, I do possess a special love for you. I just don't know if it is a brotherly/sisterly love or something different. Maybe I can't tell the difference. I need just a little time to think and pray about this. Will you please forgive me?" Carter smiled and gave her a gentle hug and responded, "Brooklyn, your happiness is the most important thing to me. I will pray a special rosary for you tonight and every night that God makes it very clear to you what He wants of you." She smiled a very humble and closed-lip smile and then turned and began her walk back to her cabin.

After Brook departed Carter began to mentally dissect the events of the evening. It was crystal clear to him that Brook was the most special girl he had ever met. He was drawn to her, her beauty, her softness, but mostly her purity of heart. But her words of devotion about wanting to be a bride of Christ stirred an emotion within him that he had not felt so strongly for some time. He also had a desire for an intimate and personal relationship with Christ. A relationship of serving Christ and caring for others in His name. The type of relationship he had always imagined was to be one of priestly life, and one of Christ's priests. His head began to swarm and swirl with mixed thoughts and ideas and for the first time in weeks, he now began to second guess his decision to leave the seminary and thought that maybe God truly wanted him to return. Now quite confused and anxious he decided to return to his cabin and to go to sleep before he made himself crazy with the flood of thoughts racing through his head.

Chapter 42

Jonas found his way to the city of Madera and to Lions Town and Country Park. He spotted a nicely shaded and grassy area next to a stream just off to the side of a small wooden step-bridge where he decided to take a rest. He sat down and reclined his back against the trunk of a large willow tree. The day was hot and dry, but he could feel a delightful cool breeze in the air. Feeling overheated from the many miles he had just walked, he drew towards him the bottom of his cassock and rested the gathered material on top of his upper thighs while exposing his knees and lower legs to the breeze. The air whisked across his skin and as it touched the moist sweat on top of his legs it produced a cooling sensation. The chilling effect although quite enjoyable sent chills across his body. Jonas shivered for a moment and then laughed while saying, “Is that you again Holy Spirit?”

Resting comfortably Jonas fell asleep quite quickly. He began to dream of his older brother, Drew, who in the dream was eight years old and Jonas was six. They were at a park in the playground. Drew was pushing Jonas on the swing and Jonas was yelling, “Faster, faster, I want to go faster.” Each time Jonas would swing back in the direction of Drew, he would use all of his eight-year-old strength to push. Jonas was swinging higher and higher and smiling and laughing. Drew called out, “I think that is enough” worrying that Jonas was swinging much too high for a young boy of six. But Jonas would have none of that and yelled out, "Just a little higher. I want to touch the sky." Drew pushed once again and this time when Jonas swung forward and climaxed at the top of his swing, he let go of the chains and reached into the sky as if trying to touch a cloud. Instantly he lost his balance and fell off the seat. He must have been over ten feet high. Then the dream switched into slow motion as Drew began to run where Jonas was falling. The dream advanced almost like a movie reel in slow-motion inching along. Step-by-step Drew could be seen racing to catch his brother. Inch-by-inch Jonas could be seen falling. Each of the boys had terror on their faces. Then suddenly the dream returned to full speed and just as Drew was about to reach the area where he could catch his brother, Jonas smacked down upon the ground and yelled out a horrifying scream. Jonas suddenly awoke for his sleep and panicked. For a moment he didn't know where he was. He looked to his left and then to his right. He spotted a small playground across the stream with a swing set but there wasn't anyone there. He took in a deep breath and then exhaled. Now somewhat calmer and re-oriented to where he was, he thought, *Wow, that was a crazy dream, well actually a memory.* He was right, the dream was an actual occurrence in his childhood and had played out exactly as he had remembered. He then questioned aloud, "What are you trying to tell me, Lord?" He then pondered the dream and tried to make sense of it. He looked for clues and aspects of the dream that he thought God might be trying to use to convey a message. After a great deal of effort, he thought, *God, I don't get it. I am at a loss. Drew died many years ago. He was a good brother. He loved me and always tried to look out for me. God, I don't get it.*

Somewhat disturbed by the uncomfortable dream and the returning thoughts of not having the brother that he had loved so much, Jonas felt that he needed to move. He stood up, brushed off the grass from his cassock, and started walking in the direction of the baseball field.

While he had been resting, people had started to accumulate at the field and it appeared that a softball game was about to begin. After completing the short walk that it took to reach the baseball park Jonas climbed the bleaches viewing an unoccupied spot five rows up. As he had climbed he excused himself as he bumped a few spectators and then situated himself with a perfect view of the diamond. Now close enough to see the details of the participants he identified that it was an adult women's softball game. The blue uniform team was named with Wildcats, and the red uniformed team was the Panthers. Everyone stood for the singing of the national anthem and afterward a young woman led everyone present in the Pledge of Allegiance while all present directed their gazes toward the erected flag behind center field.

As soon as the pledge was completed the umpire yelled out, "Play Ball!" and the crowd screamed with excitement. The first pitch was thrown with amazing speed and accuracy. The backstop had a mounted monitor screen on each side of the home-plate that was a radar speed detector. It read 98 mph. Another pitch was thrown, and the batter swung and missed. The monitor read 99 mph. Jonas could not believe how fast the pitcher was throwing the large softball. Then came a third pitch and a swing and a miss. The umpire yelled, "You are out!" The crowd roared in excitement. The next batter came to the plate and with the first pitch, there was a connection and a hit. The batter ran and the ball soared to left-field. Just before the outfielder could get under it the ball dropped and bounced. The runner made it safely to first base and the outfielder threw the ball to the infield. Now the game was off and running with a player on first base.

Jonas intently watched the baseball game and each inning there was action and excitement. Both teams had remarkable pitchers that continued to throw the ball at speeds ranging from 78-99 mph and with exceptional accuracy. Jonas had not watched a sporting event in years and found that he was having a wonderful time.

There was a small girl, maybe four or five years of age in the bleachers just two rows below and in front of Jonas and sitting next to what appeared to be her mother. She seemed completely disinterested in the game and more interested in watching Jonas. He had smiled at her a few times as he did notice that she had been staring. Eventually, she climbed the rows that separated her from Jonas and sat down next to him. She carried a large container of popcorn and as she sat down, she offered some to Jonas. Jonas initially declined but she insisted. Jonas had not eaten in over a day and found the buttered popcorn to be especially delicious. The two talked about the birds, the clouds, the flies, and the ant that she identified on the metal bleacher bench. Jonas continued to watch the game while carrying on the conversation with the little girl. Then suddenly and without notice, she climbed up onto Jonas' lap and snuggled in. Instantly Jonas felt very awkward. He was delighted with the degree of comfort the little one had shown but was extremely nervous as to what her mother might think. Just when he was about to ask the little girl to move, her mother looked back and gave Jonas a reassuring smile. She mouthed in a whisper, "She must like you. It's alright." Immediately Jonas' anxiety settled, and he took in a deep breath. The two then continued to visit, she looked at anything that moved in her vision with the exception of the players, and Jonas intently watching the exhilarating game.

After an hour and a half, the game had progressed to the ninth inning. The score was tied at eight to eight and although the pitchers were tiring, they were still able to throw at speeds up to 92 mph. The announcer voiced over the loudspeaker, "Number 26 is now up to bat, relief batter Joanie Mathews." The crowd cheered and the woman sitting to the left of Jonas said, “This girl is amazing. She hits every time she comes to bat and often it is a home run. She is so powerful.” Joanie stood in the batter’s box and overshadowed the catcher and umpire by almost 2 feet. She was a giant of a woman and looked as powerful as her reputation. The pitcher wound up and threw a fastball right down the center of the plate. Joanie with her large bat already cocked back, swung and connected with great force. The ball flew with tremendous speed directly back to the pitcher. With no time to move or duck or react, the ball hit the pitcher directly between the eyes. Instantly the pitcher dropped to the ground. There were gasps in the crowd since everyone there knew this was serious. The players didn’t respond to the hit ball and everyone stood still. A man from the bleachers on the other side from where Jonas was sitting yelled out, “I’m a doctor” as he ran onto the field. He reached the woman pitcher within seconds and began to examine her. He felt for a pulse, listened for respirations, and using his fingers he opened her eyelids and flashed a penlight at her eyes. Jonas could see from where he was sitting that there was blood covering her face. The doctor stood and facing the crowd proclaimed, “I am so sorry, she is dead.” The players immediately ran into their dugouts and the woman who Jonas assumed was the little girl’s mother stood and while erupting in tears ran as fast as she could in toward the pitcher while yelling, “My sister, my sister.” The stands were silent as everyone looked on in disbelief. The little girl caught a glimpse of the woman laying on the pitcher’s mound and commented, “Did my mom fall down?” and pointed toward the pitcher. Jonas instantly picked the young girl up and into his arms and carried her down the bleachers and onto the field. He continued to carry her all the way to her mother. As soon as they had arrived at where the body was, Jonas set the little girl down and then kneeled and placed the palm of his right hand upon her forehead and prayed, “Dear Lord, I know You always hear my prayers and that You encourage us to ask when we are in need, and You promised we shall receive if we do ask. I know Your ways are not always our ways, but I beg of You to restore the life of this woman." Just as Jonas removed his hand the woman opened her eyes and sat up and then stood. She picked up the little girl who started wiping the blood on her mother's face. The spectators erupted in cheers as if they had just witnessed a grand slam.

A reporter who had been in stands covering the game ran to the pitcher to get the scoop of what had just happened. He started asking her questions. After a few minutes and after having asked numerous questions he then turned from the woman and scanned the crowd looking for the man in the black clerical garb who had allegedly saved her. Not seeing Jonas, he yelled out, "Anyone seen the man?" There was no response. He yelled out again, "Has anyone seen the man who laid his hands upon this lady?" Again, no response from anyone. Then the little girl spoke, "After Jesus healed my mom he walked away and then disappeared. He did turn around and wave. I waved back."

Chapter 43

Dylan was quite affected by the miraculous event that had occurred in the sacristy. It had been almost two weeks since the Host had bled in his hands and he had not attended class since. Each day he showered and dressed for class but couldn't find it within himself to make his way to the classrooms. Instead, he drove each day into town, to the Benedictine Brewery, and drank pint after pint of their Black Habit Dark Ale. Dylan hadn't been much of a drinker in the past but ever since the incident he felt so unsettled he was desperately looking for answers and the beer seemed to at least give him the sensation of peacefulness. It was also comforting that the brewery was staffed with retired monks from the abbey and the presence of the religious fostered a level of familiarity for Dylan.

Father Chuck, the brewmaster and one of the non-retired monks oversaw the brewery as the general manager. He was quite older than Dylan, being a priest for twenty years now, but seemed to relate quite well with Dylan. They both had a rather dry sense of humor, but also a very deep contemplative nature. Dylan asked if he could speak to Father Chuck in private. Father Chuck agreed and after leading the way to a room behind the serving area, they rested upon a large oversized couch in the sitting room. After some initial hesitation, Dylan began to share his experience from the sacristy and of the miraculous bleeding of the Host. Father Chuck listened intently discerning if Dylan was attempting to pull his leg or if it was a sincere and honest recollection. It only took a few minutes of listening to Dylan to discern that what he was describing was not a joke, but rather something Dylan deeply believed to be true. Father, who had also studied psychology years ago, held a master's degree in counseling, attempted to evaluate if there was a potential mental illness affecting Dylan's recollection. The more Father listened to Dylan the more he believed him not to be ill, but to have truly participated in something supernatural. The details in which Dylan remembered the incident and how he articulated and recounted the event sent chills down Father's spine.

As Dylan retold the story of the encounter for the second time, he was becoming more and more worked up. Father sensed that he needed to intervene and allow a few moments for Dylan to take in a few deep breaths and to ground himself. He asked Dylan, "Have you heard the story of the miracle of Lanciano?" Dylan shook his head in the negative. Father walked over to a large bookshelf in the rear of the room, retrieved a magazine, and opened it. He shared, "There is an article that I saved from the Denver Catholic, written by Adam Lambert" and then began to read,

"*In roughly 750 A.D., in the town of Lanciano, Italy, a Basilian monk celebrated Mass, but doubted the True Presence of Christ in the Eucharist. During the consecration, the host transformed into live flesh, and the wine, into live blood. The blood coagulated into five walnut-sized globules, irregular and differing in size, while the flesh had the same dimensions as a large host used in Mass and appeared light brown in color. Both the flesh and blood have remained perfectly preserved for twelve centuries and can be viewed in Lanciano to this day. That's not all there is to the story, though. In November 1970, Archbishop Pacifico Perantoni of Lanciano, with authorization from Rome, commissioned Dr. Odoardo Linoli, a professor of anatomy and pathological history and former head of the Laboratory of Pathological Anatomy at the Hospital of Arezzo, to conduct a full scientific analysis of the sacred species. He studied the specimen for five months and presented his findings on March 4, 1971. He confirmed that the flesh and blood were of human origin. The blood was type AB, which he noted was 'particular because it has the characteristics of a man who was born and lived in the Middle East regions.' Perhaps most fascinating of all, though, were Dr. Linoli's discoveries regarding the flesh. He concluded that the piece of flesh consisted of cardiac tissue; that is, the sacred species was, in fact, a piece of a human heart. The tissue contained within was consistent with that of myocardium, endocardium, the vagus nerve and the left ventricle of the heart. Dr. Linoli published his findings in Italian medical publication Quaderni Scalvo di Diagnostica Clinica e di Laboratori in 1971. In 1973, a scientific commission appointed by the Higher Council of the World Health Organization (WHO) was tasked with verifying Dr. Linoli's conclusions. The work was carried out over 15 months, and they confirmed his findings were indeed accurate."*

That was just what Dylan needed to hear. Although he knew that what he had witnessed was real, he had thought that no one would believe him and that if he shared this miracle with anyone he would be thought of as crazy. By Father sharing the story with him it was as if Father was saying, *Yes I believe you, and you have not been the first to experience a Eucharistic miracle.*

Father replaced the magazine to the shelf on the bookcase and then sat back down next to Dylan. With a very somber face, he said, "Now Dylan, sometimes God acts in such special ways that are for a particular purpose. We might not understand why He does what He does, but we must have faith that He knows what He is doing. I have a question for you. Can I ask it?" Dylan nodded his head in agreement. Father asked, "Do you want to become a priest?" Dylan immediately responded, "With all of my heart if it is God's will."

Father smiled and then said, "Well, Dylan, if you share this story with anyone else, I will almost guarantee that you will be kicked out of the seminary faster than you can say heretic." Dylan appeared shocked. Father clarified, "Not that I think that way of you, I actually believe that what you say happened has happened. But, I also believe that your Eucharistic miracle is to be kept private, something between you and God. Others will not think the same way as I do. If shared there will be doubt, jealousy, envy, and all sorts of different reactions, none of which will be supportive and kind." Dylan listened carefully to the words and instructions of the wise and holy priest and as he did his anxiousness diminished and he filled with a sense of peacefulness. Father asked, "Do you understand me, Dylan?" Dylan did, and he thanked Father and decided that it was time to return to the seminary.

The next morning Dylan showered, dressed, and was able to make it to class on time. The professor asked, "We had all been very worried about you, Dylan, is everything alright?" Dylan assured the professor and his peers that although he had been under the weather, he was now quite fine and feeling one hundred percent.

Chapter 44

Carter and Brook had not spoken other than exchanging pleasantries in passing since that emotional night almost a week ago. Each night after ensuring that the boys were in bed Carter would retreat to his bunk and reflect on the events of that special evening. He had such mixed feelings. He was attracted to Brook but questioned what it was about her that was so attractive to him. Yes, it was her beauty, but was it her external beauty or her inner beauty? The more Carter reflected and pondered on that question the more convinced he became that it was her inner beauty, specifically her purity, her innocence, her simplistic way of looking at life, and how she always saw the best in others that brought such joy and comfort to his soul when he spent time with her. He felt a deep love for her but the more he contemplated their relationship he developed a sense that the type of love that he was feeling was not an Eros (Romantic love) type of love, but more of a Philia (Friend-like bond) and an Agape (unconditional "God" love) type of love.

Inspired by his new-found discovery, his discernment of his feelings for Brook, he needed to share them with her as soon as possible. After verifying that all the adolescent boys under his care and supervision were fast asleep, he quietly snuck out of the cabin and under the light of the semi-full moon he made his way to the girl's cabin. Once he arrived, he peeked through the window to ascertain if anyone was awake. He didn't want to scare the young girls or create a perceived situation in which if spoken of the next day by the young girls to the wrong person might lead to the creation of an alleged scandal. He couldn't see anything through the window since the room was completely black. He gently knocked on the window and almost instantly Brook's face appeared. She held a flashlight just under her chin and the light beamed upward. Carter's initial glimpse of her startled him as she appeared to resemble a ghost. She mouthed the words, "What is it, Carter?" He gestured for her to come outside and when she did, they sat on the porch bench. He wasted no time and explained his revelation about how he felt about her and that he was in love with her inner qualities and that it was more than likely her holiness that attracted him the most. Brook was quite confused by Carter's words and couldn't tell where he was going with the conversation. It wasn't until he explained that he felt more of a friendly and brotherly love for her that her face relaxed and she began to smile. It was as if she suddenly experienced great relief. Carter babbled for a few more minutes about his revelation and how he had used the discernment skills that he had learned in the seminary and that he was sure of his conclusion. Brook really couldn't follow what he was trying to explain due to him speaking so quickly and because he wasn't making much sense. However, once Carter finished, Brook shared, "Carter, I have been giving our situation a great deal of thought as well. I am not unhappy with what has transpired. I think God probably willed it to happen the way it did. I can see now why Mother Superior had sent me away. She must have sensed something in me I didn't see in myself. I guess there was a part of me that had a doubt as to if I was meant to be a religious sister or if just maybe I might have had a desire to be married and to have children. It wasn't until I felt feelings for you, and we began to develop an intimate relationship that I knew it didn't matter how great of a man I might meet, or how superficially attracted I might be to him, that I was drastically more attracted to and in love with

Christ. I want to be the bride of Christ and to grow closer and closer in unity with Him. He will give me all the children in the world to love and to care for. They might not be my biological children, but I will love them just the same." Carter watched as Brook's face became lovingly-radiant as she described her profoundly deep desire to be the bride of Christ. He knew that she had without a doubt found her calling and that she would be returning to the convent soon. He reached for her hand, gently picked it up and softly kissed it as he said, "My dear Sister Miriam, please pray for me that I may find my way and know that I will pray for you every day as you have become the light of my soul." He then returned her hand to her lap and stood and walked away.

The next morning Carter helped the boys pack their belongings since it was the end of their weeklong camping experience. After eating breakfast, the parents of the children arrived, and Carter cheerfully turned them back over to their parents and relinquished his responsibility. As soon as all the boys had departed Carter returned to his cabin and retrieved his backpack that he had also packed earlier. He hiked over to the main office and after locating Brook he handed her a letter. She hesitated for a moment and then read it.

To whom it may concern,

I want to thank those involved with allowing me to work at the camp and for the wonderful opportunity to share time with the children and also with the exceptional staff. I have learned a lot about life and myself while working here. I must part from this employment and continue to seek where God might be calling me. Please donate my earned monies to Sister Mariam's order, they will know how to best use it.

Sincerely, Carter

Tears welled up in Brook's eyes and before she could say a word, Carter, using his right hand, held it up to his lips, and then exaggeratedly blew her a departing kiss. He then turned and quickly exited the office. Wasting no time, he jumped into his car and sped away from the camp. While driving he filled with great sadness and while trying to not look back he couldn't withstand the temptation. Taking one last look through his rearview mirror he saw that Brook was standing on the porch and watching him as he drove away.

Chapter 45

Jonas had made his way to the freeway and after only a few minutes of sticking his thumb out like a hitchhiker, he was picked up by a man driving a small pickup truck. The man's name was Perry and he said that he was on his way to the town of Paradise, a town which had just suffered a devastating wildfire that burned almost the entire town down to the ground. He explained that a powerline had fallen and started a fire and the high winds fanned the fire so it quickly grew so massive that it was impossible to extinguish. He complained about the governor, how the State had neglected to care for the forests, and how allowing the downed trees to go untouched for so many years led to this disaster. He further added by having so much fuel on the ground, the downed trees, and by refusing to have the forests logged it was only going to be a matter of time and any small fire would then turn into a massive disaster. Perry was quite serious about his analysis of the timber problem and extremely passionate about his view. Jonas was a great listener and conveyed interest in the conversation without tipping his hand regarding how he felt about the issue.

As the men began to approach the city of Paradise the destruction and devastation became evident. On each side of the road, and for as far back as Jonas could see, there were only remnants of pine trees that had been burned. All the pine needles were gone as well as most of the limbs. The only thing that remained of the thousands of trees were their blackened trunks. It looked as if it had been a war zone but instead of fractured buildings wounded from bombings, the fire had completely burned the buildings down to the ground. There was nothing left standing. One could only see brick chimneys and fireplaces still standing but there was no house surrounding them. Cars were parked alongside the road with most of them half-melted and disfigured. Perry explained the town was once a thriving community with mostly retired people but a vibrant and beautiful mountain town. The sight of what was left was extremely depressing.

Perry continued to drive through the town and just when they were about to reach the end of the once populated area, he turned right onto Redhill road and proceeded for about a mile. He then pulled over at the remains of a home that had been burned. A man was standing amid what appeared to be the rear of the home and he was kicking at the ashes. Perry shared, "That is my best friend in the whole world, Dan." Perry hopped out of the truck and began to walk toward Dan. Jonas followed and allowed Perry to arrive first. Perry asked, "How are you, Dan?" Dan looked up from the ground with his eyes filled with tears and said, "Not well Perry. We lost it all." Perry walked up to Dan and wrapped his arms around him and gave him a tight hug. Dan appeared to hug back for just a moment and then the men separated. Dan immediately returned to kicking at the ashes and it appeared that he was looking for something. Dan hadn't noticed Jonas yet so Perry introduced the two of them. Dan was polite but seemed disinterested. He was consumed with his grief and loss. Perry asked, "How is Barbara?" Dan replied, "She is alright, I guess. Well, not really. She lost all of her pictures. Pictures from when the girls were little. She lost everything." Dan then went on to explain that when they heard that the fire was growing they both left work and raced toward the home to try to save some of the things that they cared for the most, but by the time they arrived at the town it had already been evacuated and the police and firefighters wouldn't allow anyone in stating that it was too dangerous. He added, "We didn't have a chance to grab anything." Still kicking in the ashes Perry finally asked, "What are you looking for?" Dan responded, "The worst is that I had an engagement ring that I was going to give Barbara and I had it hidden in my dresser."

Perry knew that Dan was planning to propose to Barbara soon. Both Dan and Barbara had been separately married in the past for many years, but each of their relationships had deteriorated and had ended in divorce. Dan and Barbara had known each other in high school. After their divorces, they had reconnected through mutual friends. They instantly fell in love and had been inseparable for almost two years now. Dan had finally saved enough money to buy a beautiful engagement ring and had been keeping it hidden until just the right time to propose. The special ring was now lost with the burning of the home and Dan was devastated. He had worked a second job for almost a year to save the money to buy the ring and had just purchased it a few weeks prior.

Jonas had overheard the conversation but not knowing Dan well enough he chose to remain silent. Internally Jonas prayed, *O blessed St. Anthony, the grace of God has made you a powerful advocate in all our needs and the patron for the restoration of things lost or stolen. I turn to you today with childlike love and deep confidence. You have helped countless children of God to find the things they have lost, material things, and, more importantly, the things of the spirit: faith, hope, and love. I come to you with confidence; help me in my present need. I recommend what we have lost to your care, in the hope that God will restore it to us if it is His Holy Will. Amen.*

Just then Dan lit up in excitement and reached down into the ashes and retrieved an object. The object appeared filthy and was black as coal. He spat upon the object and then wiped it across his shirt. He then screamed aloud, "It is perfect. It's perfect. The fire didn't harm it a bit." He began to dance and jump in the air. The finding of the ring enlivened his spirit and provided a sense of hope for the future. He ran over to his friend Perry and hugged him so hard that Perry coughed.

Now full of excitement and enthusiasm, Dan turned to Perry and said, "I have to go. This changes everything. I need to find Barbara and I'm going to ask her to marry me right now. I have to go." He then ran toward his vehicle and within seconds he drove away. Perry then turned to Jonas and said, "Well, I drove here to see how my friend was doing and to see if I could somehow help, but it appears that he is doing alright. Maybe you were our good luck charm. I'm not sure what would have happened if he didn't find that ring. What a blessing that was." Jonas looked at Perry and smiled.

Perry offered to drive Jonas back to where they met, or anywhere else on the way, but Jonas declined and said, "No, thank you anyway. I think I will stay here for a while." Somewhat confused since there didn't seem to be anything to stay for, Perry asked, "Are you sure Jonas?" Jonas smiled and responded, "Yes, Perry, I am sure. Thank you again."

Chapter 46

Father Mateo had been working on dictating his memoir for almost six weeks without a break. His dictated writing was going much faster than he had anticipated and he was already on page 195 of his book. He felt extremely motivated to continue writing until the book was complete, but for some reason, he now felt that he needed a break. He contacted Dylan and asked if he wouldn't mind taking him back to the park as he had done before. Dylan was hesitant. Father had been back to his physician numerous times and had received repeated x-rays to verify how his neck fracture was healing. With each visit, he received an examination from the orthopedist and an x-ray and each time the conclusion was the same. The doctor continued to inform him that the fracture was not healing due to his advanced age and that he wasn't a candidate for bone-fusion surgery due to his numerous health problems. The doctor informed Father that if he went under anesthesia, he would more than likely not wake up. It was at the last visit that the physician shared the prognosis for recovery was at almost zero percent and Father should come to terms with that. He also stated he would need to wear the neck brace for the remainder of his life. The news didn't phase the holy priest a bit. It was if he knew something no one else knew. He continued to smile, remained upbeat, and didn't seem to lose any sleep over it.

Father must have convinced Dylan to drive him to the park because they were already on their way. They left at seven in the morning to allow enough time for Dylan to return to the seminary in time for his first class. As soon as Father sat down Dylan planted the sign firmly into the ground and Katie, the young girl ran and jumped upon Father's lap. She shouted, "Where have you been? I have been waiting for you. I have so much to tell you and what is this thing around your neck, it looks funny?" Father explained that he injured his neck and that it is taking some time to heal and that the doctor wanted him to wear the neck brace for protection so that he didn't harm the bones around the spinal cord. She asked, "What is a spinal cord." Father began to explain in detail and after a minute she interrupted and said, "That isn't that important. I have something much more important than that." and she proceeded to talk about her kitties, the mouse they found under the house, and how many butterflies she could count to now. Katie's energy, innocence, and purity of spirit brought great joy to Father and he was reminded of Jesus' words, *Let the little children come to me, and do not hinder them, for the kingdom of God belongs to such as these. Truly I tell you, anyone who will not receive the kingdom of God like a little child will never enter it.* Then as quickly as she had arrived, but not before leaving Father with her signature peck of a kiss on his cheek, she disappeared.

Father sat in his lawn chair for almost three hours undisturbed until he suddenly noticed the most beautiful fragrance. He could detect the smell of a rose, but it was somewhat different than he had ever smelled before. Then he heard a voice as if it was right upon him. He was shocked and startled by the voice. The voice was delicate, pretty, and almost musical. It was a woman's voice, but he couldn't detect how old the speaker might be. She said, "Dear Father, my Son has been very pleased with you. He knows all that you have become and He forgives you for those things from the years so long ago." Father immediately broke down and began to sob. She opened a wound that had been superficially closed for many years, many decades, but never healed. She continued, "We know that you have never forgiven yourself and that you somehow feel the accident was a punishment. We also know that you have felt so ashamed that you isolated yourself from everyone who had loved you. Father, my Son has never felt anything but love for you. You have punished yourself enough, please stop." Father's emotions had now gotten the best of him and he was sobbing so intensely that he slipped off the lawn chair and was now laying on the ground, wailing in lament, and curled on his side. The woman's voice had disappeared, but he probably would not have noticed if it hadn't due to being so emotionally distraught. His tearful explosion was a purging of his previously trapped guilt and remorse that he had bottled up for so many years. The crying and sobbing were symptoms of being set free, free from a life of bondage due to self-regret. The woman's appearance was a trigger and catalyst that set in-motion the washing and cleansing of a soul so overdue.

Chapter 47

After driving for almost six hours and with the sun now set, Carter could barely keep his eyes open. He knew he needed to find a place to pull over so he could get some rest. He had just entered the small town of Marysville and proceeded down the main street. After almost a mile he came to a stoplight. As he stopped his car he looked to his right and caught a glimpse of a body of water. It looked as if there was a small lake in the middle of the town. He clicked his blinker and turned in the direction of the lake. As he approached, he read a sign ELLIS LAKE. He pulled his car into a parking spot next to the lake and turned off his engine. It hadn't been a full minute and he had already fallen fast asleep.

Carter must have slept the entire night since the sun was now just beginning to peek through the pine trees. With the loud quacking of ducks, Carter blinked his eyes a few times to remove the residue leftover from a hard night's sleep. Within seconds he identified at least twenty extremely large ducks surrounding his car. He honked his horn and that only seemed to irritate them. In response to the honk at least six of them flapped their wings and flew on top of the car. He honked his horn again and they quacked even more fiercely and two of them let loose with a stream of extremely disgusting liquified duck poop that covered his entire front window and hood. He felt trapped by the aggressive waterfowl and just as he was about the honk his horn again a woman knocked on his window and shouted, “Stop that, that will not work.” She then threw pieces of bread into the water and the psycho-ducks quickly raced after it. Instantly they were gone. Carter exited his car and thanked the woman. Following her lead, the two of them strolled over to the park bench. She continued to reach into her bread bag and broke off pieces from the large loaf to throw in the direction of the ducks. They visited and got to know each other.

Carter thought the lady had a delightful personality. She appeared to be in her late forties or maybe fifties and had shared that her name was Mickey. She said that she was raised in Yuba City but now lived in Marysville. She loved the ducks that made their home at the man-made lake and tried to come to visit them every day before she ventured off to feed the homeless at the river bottoms. Carter was intrigued by the idea of feeding the homeless and asked if he could come with her. She immediately agreed.

After exhausting all of her bread supply, the two began their walk across town. Carter had offered to drive but she shared that she was afraid to ride in cars. It wasn’t long, having walked for less than thirty minutes, and they arrived at an old abandoned warehouse on the edge of town, situated next to the levee. Almost instantly they were met by two additional women. Mickey introduced them as her sisters, Colleen and Paddy. All three women had brown hair, brown eyes, and had similar builds. It was obvious that they were sisters.

Paddy and Colleen had already set up the assembly line for the making of the sandwiches and Mickey took her usual spot with the mayonnaise bottle and knife and instructed Carter to assume the position of the cheese layer. Now with everyone in their positions, the process flowed smoothly and in less than twenty minutes there were over seventy sandwiches made. The sandwiches were very simple with just two pieces of bread, mayonnaise, bologna, and cheese. During the creation of the sandwiches the ladies sang songs, visited, and shared jokes as they worked. Paddy shared a joke that her brother Billy had told her just the night before. She said, "Did you hear the story of old Johnnie? Well, Johnnie was at the bar the other day and he was quite upset. He pointed over to the large staircase at the bar and said 'you see that staircase over there? Well, I built it. But does anyone call me Johnnie the staircase builder? Well, no.' He then pointed to the hotel across the street and said, 'Do you see that hotel across the street? Well, I built it. Does anyone call me Johnnie the hotel builder? Well, no'. Then he continued, 'But just one time with a goat and see what they call me'?" Carter burst out in laughter and upon hearing the intensity of his laugh the ladies erupted in laughter as well.

Mickey loaded the sandwiches into a small red wagon and then while pulling the wagon led the group onto a trail that ascended the levee, crossed it, and then took them down into a homeless camp. Carter felt a little nervous and honestly quite frightened. Many of the inhabitants of the camp appeared rough and possibly hostile. Their appearance, however, didn't seem to phase Mickey a bit. She strolled through the camp while speaking out, "Delicious sandwiches, just ask, it is a gift from God who loves you." Some of the homeless were not sure what to think at first but after a few minutes and having watched some of the more aggressive men and women approach her and seeing that she was giving out food while asking for nothing in return, she was quickly swarmed. She passed out the sandwiches as fast as she could and within a few minutes all of her sandwiches were gone. Carter was amazed that not one of the homeless men and women gave her a hard time. Even some who appeared quite unstable, obviously mentally ill and psychotic, were polite and kind to her.

Mickey returned to where Carter, Paddy, and Colleen had been watching, and Carter commented, "That was amazing Mickey. How often do you do this?" Mickey explained that she gives out the sandwiches every Monday, Wednesday, and Friday and that Paddy and Colleen help with the preparation during their lunch breaks. Paddy works as a home health nurse and Colleen works as a teller at the local credit union. Carter asked, "How did you ever get the idea of doing this?" Mickey shared that her aunt, Betty Clare, had started what she called the sandwich shop at the local Catholic Church, Saint Joseph's, years ago and would feed the homeless the same sandwiches almost every day of the week. She stated that Aunt Betty Clare had done that for years until she eventually became too sick and died. Mickey explained that she was so inspired by her kindness shown to the homeless and how they loved her so much for her unconditional love, that she felt that God had put it on her heart to continue the tradition. She added, "But, I wanted to go to where they were instead of waiting for them to come to the church." Carter smiled and knew that he had encountered a living saint.

Chapter 48

Jonas made his way to where the Catholic church of Saint Thomas Moore once stood on the corner of Skyway and Elliot road. The church had been completely burned to the ground and there was absolutely nothing left of the building, only ashes. A small silver airstream trailer was parked on the front of the property and there was a cardboard sign duct-taped to the side of the trailer that read:

Daily Mass at 8:00 a.m.
Confessions anytime.

Jonas walked up to the door of the trailer and knocked. Instantly the door opened and a young priest with a radiant smile said, "I'm glad you're here." and invited Jonas into the trailer. The priest continued talking, quickly and non-stop, describing all the work that he had been doing for the local parishioners and how his daily Mass that was held outside of his trailer with folding lawn chairs, and a plastic picnic table for the altar, was attracting more and more attendees every day. He then said, "Now with you here, we can have double to Masses and double the confessions." Jonas finally understood. It was his cassock. The young priest must have thought that Jonas was another priest who had been sent to help. Jonas took in a deep breath and said, "Father, I think you are mistaken. I am not a priest. I am just a humble man on a mission trying to do God's work. I am not worthy to be one of His holy priests." The young priest looked confused. He stared at Jonas and his black cassock. Jonas added, "These clothes were a gift from Father Avery in Yuba City and before him, Seminarian Carter in Jordan Valley. It was there that I heard God's voice and He told me to go out and change the world, one person, at a time. I have been trying to do so ever since."

The young priest began to cry. His bright and radiant smile instantly evaporated, and his affect became saddened. He then dropped his gaze to the floor. Jonas asked, "What is it, Father? Is it something I said?" After a few moments the young priest lifted his head and responded, "No, it's not that. I had asked the Bishop for extra help. I have been working day and night trying to be a reflection of God to these people who have lost everything, and it has been taking its toll on me physically and spiritually. When I saw you, I thought you were an answer to my prayers and that the Bishop had heard me and believed in what I was doing here enough to send you to help." He paused for a moment and then continued, "Maybe all of this is useless. Maybe there isn't any hope?" Jonas didn't immediately respond. Instead, he directed his thoughts toward God and prayed, *Lord, help me with your wisdom. Help me to say what this holy man needs to hear*. Almost a minute and a half went by before Jonas spoke out, "Father if only Job had suffered as much as you." Father looked up from the ground and then directly into Jonas' eyes and responded, "What do you mean?" Jonas continued, "Well, God allowed Job to suffer almost as much as you. You know, all his friends accused him of sin, he lost his wealth, his children, his crops, his livestock, and even his relationship with his wife. But that doesn't even compare to how much God has allowed you to suffer." Jonas had Father's full attention. Jonas added, "And Job couldn't even stay as positive and faithful as you have been. Boy, Job could have learned a lot from you." By this time Father understood what

Jonas was doing. Using sarcasm, he was pointing out that whatever suffering Father felt that he had been enduring, it was nothing in comparison to what so many others had endured for their faith. Father straightened up and began to hold his head high. He got the message. He needed a swift kick in the butt and Jonas had given it to him. Father responded, "I get it, boy do I get it. Stop being a wuss and be a man." Jonas laughed and then so did Father. Father then asked, "By the way, what is your name? I'm Father Mark." Jonas paused for a moment and then said, "I am Jonas, just simply Jonas."

Father invited Jonas to stay for dinner and he and Jonas visited while Father cooked a large pot of spaghetti noodles. He then microwaved a jar of premade Italian sauce and the men dished up heaping servings of spaghetti and red sauce. The food was hot and delicious, especially delicious for Jonas since it had been some time since he had a full meal. Father shared that he had only been ordained a year and that due to the shortage of priests he was sent to the small town as a parochial administrator. Jonas asked, "What is the difference between a parochial administrator and a pastor?" Father explained that in functionality they are about the same, but since he was such a new priest and the likelihood that he might really screw up, making him a parochial administrator instead of a pastor allowed the Bishop through canon law to more easily remove him from the parish if needed. He also explained that pastors have a lot of rights under Canon Law and when one is assigned as a pastor and starts doing bad things, like stealing money or having relationships with women, it isn't so easy to get rid of them without jumping through a lot of hoops. Father then added, "Really exciting stuff, huh?" Jonas yawned and then laughed.

Father noticed that although Jonas had very good table manners he had consumed the large plate of food rather quickly so he offered, "Would you like a little more to eat?" Jonas looked over toward the pot on the stove and he could tell that there weren't any more noodles. He did notice that the bowl that they had poured the bottles of store-bought sauce into still had some sauce in it so he asked, "Do you happen to have a few slices of bread if it wouldn't be too much trouble?" Father confirmed that he did and retrieved a partially opened loaf from the cabinet. Jonas took out two pieces, the crust, and an inner slice, and then asked, "You mind if I soak up the remaining sauce?" Father laughed, "That is my favorite part as well." Jonas handed Father one of his pieces of bread and then the men took turns wiping the sides of the bowl and eating the sauce covered bread.

After dinner, Father explained that he had a few families coming over at seven o'clock for a vigil service for those who had died in the fire. The bodies were not found but it was assumed that many of the elders were not able to get out in time and burned up in the fire. Jonas asked, "Do you mind if I attend?" Father immediately responded, "I would love it. Maybe you can help me?" Jonas looked at Father and said, "You know I'm not a priest, right?" Father laughed and followed with, "I know, but you're Catholic aren't you?" Jonas nodded in confirmation and laughed.

Just before seven o'clock, a dozen families had arrived at the previous site of the church all with lit candles. They had brought lawn chairs to sit upon since there were no benches that had survived the fire. Father began the service by sharing that since the bodies were not able to be found, he still wanted to give those parishioners a funeral service. He made the sign of the cross and then began,

"Dear friends, we are united with you today in sorrow at the death of our friends.

The reality of death, with all its pain and sense of loss, confronts us at this moment. But as we are united in sorrow, we are also united by something else, our faith.

Forgotten and Lost

Confronted with the reality of death, we must allow ourselves to be confronted with the reality of our faith.

The reality, not a 'maybe' or 'I hope so' or fantasy or wishful thinking, but a reality.

Our Faith opens our minds to the whole picture of life, death, and what happens after death.

Only in the light of our faith can we begin to understand what has happened to our fellow parishioners and how we are to keep going from here.

When in our faith we speak about heaven, and resurrection, and the next life, we do not speak about these things primarily because they give us consolation and strength.

They certainly do that, but the primary reason we speak of these things is because they are true.

God has spoken His Word to us; we hear it in the Scriptures and in the teachings of our Church, and we respond to it by saying, 'Yes, I believe; it is true!'

God has broken the silence about death, and told us that He has conquered it!

Death was not part of God's original plan; it came into the world because of sin. Death is not from God; death is from turning away from God.

Yet God did not leave us in death's power. He sent Christ, who died and rose again and conquered death!

God has spoken to the world through Christ and told us that He wants to give us victory over death in and through Jesus Christ!

Because of this, a Christian is not silent in the face of death! Many people, on coming to a wake or funeral, do not know what to say! Death seems to have the last word. But we who believe are not silent. We speak! Christ is risen! Death has been conquered!

Many people think that the story of human life is, 'Birth, life, and death.'

For a Christian, it's different. The story is not 'Birth, life, and death,' but rather, 'Life, death, and resurrection!'

Death does not have the last word; life does!

Death is not the last period after the last sentence of the last chapter of the human story. There's another chapter to come! Death is not the end of the human story; it's the middle.

The end of the story is resurrection and life that has no end!

The farewell that we give to our friends today is a temporary farewell;

They will live! They will rise!

When our friends were baptized, the life of the Risen Christ was poured into their souls!

They began to share, here on earth, the life of heaven!

At baptism, God rescued them from the power of death; He literally snatched them from the dominion of death and transferred them into the Kingdom of Christ -- a kingdom of eternal life.

Christ said to them on that day, 'You do not belong to death! You belong to me!'

Therefore, a Christian does not merely die. A Christian dies in Christ. Those two words, 'in Christ,' make all the difference in the world!

We belong to Him by baptism, and we live in Him by a life of prayer, obedience to His teachings, and faithfulness to the Sacraments of the Church. If we live in Christ and die in Christ, we will rise in Christ!

In the midst of all this, should we grieve?

Yes, brothers and sisters, it is OK to grieve; it is natural because we love them.

Even Christ wept when His friend Lazarus died, and He wept even though He was about to bring him back to life!

Yes, we as Christians grieve. But we grieve with hope.

It is OK to be sad today that we do not see our friends anymore, but it would be wrong to think we will never see them again.

It is OK to grieve, but it is wrong to despair.

Christ is alive!

We pray today for our friends that they may complete the journey to heaven.

Pray for them every day, and for yourselves.

Look at them with your eyes of faith today and say with faith, 'My dear friends: Bob, Donna, Mary, Chuck, Alex, Ruth, Maria, and all the rest, you do not belong to death. You belong to Christ, and so do we!' Amen."

There wasn't a dry eye held by anyone present. There was sniffling, whimpers, and even some slight moaning expressing the deep emotions held by those seeking some type of closure from the absence of so many whom they had known for so many years.

Chapter 49

Filled with curiosity, Dylan skipped his modern theological exegesis class and snuck into Father Mateo's room knowing Father was still at the park and he could read a few chapters of his book without the fear of being caught. He turned on Father's laptop and when the prompt presented to type in the password, he typed *Purgatory* and he gained access to the computer. He knew the password since he was the one who Father had asked to help him create it in the first place. Searching the desktop folders, he identified a folder named, *The Confession of a Sinful Man – Father Mateo.* He clicked on the folder and then a word document opened. Dylan hesitated for a moment and thought, *I really should not be doing this, I am sure it is a sin.* He then quickly ran through the ten commandments in his mind and coming to the end he quietly whispered to himself, "Better to ask for forgiveness than to ask for permission."

As soon as Dylan began to read, he was drawn deeply into the story. He wasn't sure if it was the writing style that captured his attention so profoundly or if it was his desire to know his spiritual Father more intimately. Nevertheless, by page three he was hooked. He read about Father's childhood, his younger sibling, his father and mother, and living life as poor children on the outskirts of town.

Dylan learned about Father's most inner thoughts, his previous worries and anxieties, and even about his personal struggles.

Not realizing how much time had passed, being so captivated by the information and the story, Dylan had been reading for almost three hours non-stop. He had just come to the section in which Father was describing his time in the special forces' unit, some of the missions that he had partaken in, and the horrific things he had done, that Dylan realized he was already thirty minutes late in picking Father up from the park. Just about when he was ready to power down the computer he read, *I didn't realize what I had done until it was too late. I killed that pregnant woman and her entire family with my grenade...* Dylan felt compelled to keep reading but he knew he had to leave. He pushed the power button and raced out of the room.

Dylan drove as fast as he could without alerting the police and getting a ticket to the park and was expecting that Father would give him a hard time for being so late. Once he arrived Dylan looked at his watch and he was an hour and a half late in picking up Father Mateo. He jumped out of the car and ran toward the elderly priest. Father was sitting comfortably in the lawn chair and as Dylan approached, he apologized for being so late. Father accepted the apology but didn't seem troubled by the tardiness at all. He appeared to be in a somber mood and a little off from his usual self. He was preoccupied. Dylan almost asked if something had occurred but resisted the inquiry. The two drove back to the seminary without speaking a word. Dylan began to feel guilty and wondered if somehow Father knew he had snuck into his room and had been reading his book. He then realized that there was no way Father could have known what he had done unless God somehow intervened.

As soon as the men arrived home, Father wasted no time and made his way to his bedroom and closed the door. Dylan decided to go to the cafeteria to get something to eat since he hadn't eaten in hours. As soon as he entered the cafeteria, he identified a few of his classmates, Alex and Kenny. He helped himself to a tray and then loaded a plate with fried chicken, coleslaw, baked beans, two dinner rolls, and a large piece of corn on the cob. He filled a large glass with iced tea and carried the tray to the table with his friends. As soon as he sat down, he prayed, "Bless us Oh Lord and these Thy gifts which we are about to receive, from Thy bounty, through Christ our Lord. Amen." And instantly began to shovel the food into his mouth as he listened to Alex and Kenny debate which priest faculty would win in a cage fight. Alex kept identifying priests that seemed to be athletic and younger and Kenny seemed to be purposely naming the fattest and most out of shape priests and adamantly argued that they would be the most aggressive and superior in the matches. With each suggestion by Kenny, the mere idea of the absurdity of the choice drove Alex nuts. Dylan knew exactly what Kenny was doing, trying to infuriate Alex, but Alex didn't seem to understand that Kenny was pulling his leg. This banter and arguing continued for the next twenty minutes until Dylan could not contain himself and said, "Alex, you idiot. Don't you see what Kenny is doing? He is identifying the worst possible candidates for your theoretical matchups just to see your reaction." Kenny burst in laughter now that his secret had been revealed. Alex abruptly stood and threw his milk carton at Kenny and stormed away from the table and out of the cafeteria. Still laughing, Kenny commented, "Well, that was a bit of an overreaction." Dylan laughed and began to choke on his food. After a minute of coughing and wheezing, Dylan was able to free the chicken piece from his throat and spit it up and onto his plate. Kenny remarked, "That is gross. I guess I will forgo the apple pie then."

Chapter 50

Carter had been invited to go fishing with Colleen and her husband, Chuck, in the upper Yuba River. They met at the old Linda Mall which was closed after the flood of 1986. Carter parked his car and jumped into the back seat of Chuck's truck where Colleen was already sitting in the front passenger's seat. Chuck drove a well-worn and full-sized Ford pick-up faded green. It seemed to run well but did resemble something from the Beverly Hillbillies television show. Carter found the old truck to be fascinating since everything worked inside and out and that it also appeared to be at least thirty years old. Carter asked, "Chuck, how old is this truck?" Chuck smiled and gave a sly grin as he responded, "That is not the type of question you ask about a man's girl. Who raised you anyway with such manners?" Carter laughed and then noticed that neither Chuck or Colleen were laughing. Carter immediately stopped, silenced himself, and after a brief pause and just about when he was going to apologize for his unthoughtful question, Colleen and Chuck burst out in laughter. Colleen snickered, "Got ya."

The trio drove a few minutes on a frontage road and turned right. They drove up and over a levee and followed the paved road that eventually turned into a dirt path. Chuck guided the rig alongside the river until the dirt path disappeared. He parked the truck, and everyone hopped out. Chuck reached over into the bed of the truck and began handing items to both Colleen and Carter. He passed an ice chest, folding chairs, tackle boxes, and six fishing poles. Chuck scanned all of the items piled on the ground ensuring he had everything he wanted and needed and then directed the others to pick up as much as they could carry and to follow him.

Chuck hoisted the heavy ice chest onto his shoulder and picked up the fishing poles. He led the way through some tall brush while saying, “Trust me, this is my lucky spot.” Colleen and Carter followed and just as Colleen said, “Watch out for gopher holes,” Carter tripped and fell face-first down to the ground. Colleen exploded in laughter and so did Chuck. Humiliated, Carter picked himself up and with his shirt sleeve he wiped the scant amount of blood off of his upper lip. He had struck his nose on the dirt as he fell and created a small nosebleed. As soon as Chuck identified the small injury he asked, “Carter, do you need a tourniquet?” Carter responded speaking slowly, “Ha, Ha, Ha” not finding the joke very funny. Colleen jokingly followed with, “You need a mother’s touch. I know what will help.” She pulled on Chuck's shirt to stop him from walking, reached into the cooler, and pulled out a can of Coors Light. She handed him the can and said, “This is a two-fold cure. First, hold it against your nose for at least three minutes before you drink it.” Chuck laughed and commented, “I think I need to fall down more often if it gets me a beer.” Colleen slapped him on his butt and kicked at him to get him moving again. Carter enjoyed watching Chuck and Colleen bicker at each other, playfully slap at each other, and also compliment each other. They truly were in love and even though they complained almost constantly about the other person and their different traits, it was playful and loving.

Chuck led the group through an opening in the brush to the edge of the river. The bank sloped downward and evened out with a small beach-like area wide enough for all three to spread out. Each of them took a folding chair and placed it on the dirt, approximately ten feet from each other and started to prepare their poles. Chuck handed each two poles and as he gave Carter his he asked, "Do I need to bait it for you, honey?" Carter kicked some of the sandy dirt in Chuck's direction.

Colleen was the first to have her hook baited and launched it far across the water. She inserted her pole into a pole stand that she had positioned to the left of her chair and proceeded to bait the hook of her second pole. She was so quick with the process that she had her second line in the water before either Chuck or Carter had their first rod situated. Chuck didn't seem to be in too much of a hurry, he had popped open a beer and was sitting down in his chair sipping it and looking at the birds in the overhanging trees. Carter, on the other hand, had somehow wrapped the fishing line around a tree branch and accidentally lodged the hook rather deeply into his thumb. Trying not to gain the attention of Chuck, he wiggled the hook back and forth trying to release it, but the barbs on the hook seemed to prevent it from dislodging. Finally, not knowing what else to do, he gained Chuck's attention by raising his hand high into the air and waving it. Chuck immediately laughed and then yelled in Colleen's direction, "He needs another beer, honey." Carter didn't seem to enjoy the joke half as much as Colleen and Chuck had. Chuck did finally get out of his chair and ventured over to the tackle box and retrieved a needle-nose plier. He walked up to Carter and without hesitation grasped the hook with the ends of the plier, quickly yanked it and instantly the hood was freed. Carter yelled out, "Yoooowza." In response, Chuck and Colleen both burst out in laughter.

Luckily the next few hours went without any disasters. Carter seemed to have calmed down after the hook incident and both Chuck and Colleen appeared to be relaxed and content with their ritualistic casting and reeling in of the line. Colleen was the first to catch a rainbow trout, and then Chuck. It didn't take long and each of them had a half dozen on their stringers while Carter was yet to even experience a bite. Finally, Carter asked, "What is it that I am not doing here?" Chuck looked over at Colleen, smiled, and then responded, "Well, did you pee on the bait before you casted?" Carter wasn't quite sure he heard Chuck correctly and asked, "What did you say?" Chuck repeated, "Did you take a wiz on your bait before you casted it out into the deep?" Carter said, "No, is that something we are supposed to do?" Colleen chimed in, "Of course, how do you expect to get the attention of the fish if you don't coat the bait with a little urine. The acid in the urine attracts the fish."

Carter thought for a moment and then questioned, "I didn't see you all pee on your bait. "Chuck quickly responded, "I let loose on our containers at the mall while we were waiting for you. I didn't think it would be polite to pee on your bait being that you would be handling it and we aren't married or anything." The explanation seemed to satisfy Carter and he excused himself, grabbed his container of bait, and strolled into bushes. After a few seconds, Colleen and Chuck could hear the flow of urine. Carter returned after a few minutes and then rebaited his hooks with the freshly urine tainted worms. He then cast his lines into the water and waited for a strike. He waited, and waited, and waited. A whole hour had passed and he hadn't received even one hit. He finally asked, "You guys were pulling my leg again, right?" Colleen and Chuck burst out again in laughter. Chuck laughed so hard and that he even fell out of his chair. Colleen couldn't take it any longer and she walked over to Carter carrying a small bait container and said, "Here are some minnows, the trout here won't hit on worms." Chuck still laughing and rolling on the ground tried to spit out the words between gasps of air, "Don't.... Don't.... forget... to... pee... on... them." Carter took one of the minnows and threw it at Chuck.

Chuck was the first to spot the kayakers paddling down the river. He turned to Colleen and asked, "Is that who I think it is?"

Colleen squinted her eyes and then yelled out, "Hey you guys. Hey you all. Come over here." The kayakers appeared to recognize her, turned toward them, and began to paddle towards the shore. As they approached Colleen said, "Those guys are my cousins, Terrance and Danny." The cousins forcefully drove their kayaks onto the shore and then climbed out from within them. Both men quickly walked to Colleen and hugged her and proceeded to greet Chuck with a handshake. Without hesitation, both friendly men introduced themselves to Carter and asked, "Did he try the urine trick on you?" Carter was speechless. Terrance laughed and said, "Forget about it, he has done that to all of us."

The four visited, drank a few beers, and ate an abundance of turkey sandwiches that Colleen had previously packed for the day-trip. Terrance shared his homemade jerky and Dan pitched in his slightly moist Cheetos that somehow became exposed to the water in the kayak, but they were still edible. Well, edible to the men, Colleen wouldn't touch them.

Chapter 51

After spending almost an entire week with Father Mark in Paradise, Jonas decided he needed to continue his God-inspired journey. He began walking on the mountain road leaving Paradise and was quickly picked up by a Filipino man driving a small SUV. The man introduced himself to Jonas as Felipe and said that he was on his way to Redding for a wedding. Jonas took that as a sign that God wanted him to return to Redding for some reason. The drive took less than ninety minutes and Felipe asked where Jonas wanted to be dropped off. Since Jonas didn't immediately respond, Felipe discerned that maybe Jonas didn't have a place to stay. He offered, "You want to come over to my Auntie Malou's house for some food and maybe stay the night?" Jonas agreed.

Felipe drove to the outskirts of the Redding to an affluent neighborhood. They arrived at a large home with a dozen cars parked outside. Before the engine was even shut off a trail of Filipinos trailed out of the front door led by a classy looking woman to see who had arrived. Felipe jumped out of the car and yelled out, "Auntie Malou, so nice to see you" as he hugged her and kissed her on her cheek. She immediately asked, "Who is this with you?" Felipe explained that the man was Jonas and that he wanted to join them for the night. Without pause, she walked up to Jonas, superficially kissed each of his cheeks, and said, "Welcome, thank you for being our guest." Then the whole group individually introduced themselves to Jonas with a spirit of love and care.

Once inside the house, Jonas immediately saw that every available countertop was covered with plates and containers of food. Auntie Malou escorted Jonas over to a large recliner chair in the corner of the living room as she asked what he would like to drink, another woman had already prepared a large platter-like plate full of food and handed it to Jonas. He felt as if he was being treated like a king and felt a little confused, good, but confused. He accepted the food, it smelled wonderful, and asked, "Why are you treating me so well?" Auntie Malou and the other woman smiled and Auntie Malou responded, "I was hungry, and you gave me food. I was thirsty, and you gave me a drink. I was a stranger and you welcomed me. We are Catholics. We try to see Christ in everyone and try to treat everyone as we would want to treat Christ. Are we treating you alright?" Jonas slightly laughed and humbly said, "More than well, I don't deserve all this." Auntie Malou smiled and responded, "Oh yes you do. We can see just how special you are even if you don't see it right now."

After ensuring Jonas was comfortable and fed, the group of men and women gave him his space and Jonas appeared to be quite content relaxing in the comfortable and plush recliner while he watched everyone interact. Many of the people ate, others visited, and Auntie Malou opened a cabinet that exposed a very large flat screen monitor and as she turned on the device, she also grabbed a microphone from the cabinet. The monitor lit up and instantly there was karaoke. Felipe asked for a turn and after hitting a few buttons he began singing along with the tune. He had a delightful voice and he became very animated as he sang. He danced around the room as his arms moved up and down to the beat of the music. As soon as he finished his song the microphone was handed off and the next person took their turn at singing. Jonas was amazed, after five different singers, it appeared that everyone there had an accomplished singing voice and enjoyed sharing their talents. At the end of each song the entire house of people clapped and encouraged each other lovingly and enthusiastically.

Eventually, Jonas fell asleep in the chair and without being noticed, Auntie Malou covered him with a blanket and she moved the party outside onto the backyard patio so as to not disturb their guest. Jonas must have been extremely tired because the party continued for many hours, well into the early morning, and he had slept through the entire thing. From time to time Auntie Malou would tiptoe into the living room to check on Jonas and each time she did he appeared to be comfortable and resting well. She chose not to disturb him.

Jonas eventually awoke in the early morning and it took a moment to discern where he was. However, almost as soon as he opened his eyes there was Auntie Malou with a cup of coffee asking, "Do you like cream and sugar with your coffee?" Jonas usually drank his coffee black when he had it available, but he felt compelled to ask for cream and sugar thinking if he declined Auntie Malou might think he was just saying no to not be a trouble. He was sure that she wanted him to have the most delicious cup of coffee she could create.

Now the house appeared to be empty and more intimate, Jonas decided to ask again, "Auntie Malou, why have you been so kind to me? You don't know me, and to be honest, I am pretty sure you can tell I am a homeless person." She responded, "Yesterday afternoon I was at Our Lady of Mercy parish, in the adoration room, and during my holy hour I was praying. When I prayed, a scripture verse became very profound in my mind. I knew it was God speaking to me and I meditated on the verse for over an hour. I knew that it had deep meaning and that it had something to do with my big party that I had been preparing for almost an entire week." She then became a little choked up and her eyes slightly teared. She paused for a moment and then said, "The verse was this, '*But when you give a feast, invite the poor, the crippled, the lame, the blind, and you will be blessed because they cannot repay you. For you will be repaid at the resurrection of the just*.' Then you arrived unannounced to my home filled with friends and family. I just knew that you were the one God had prepared me to greet. I knew God was speaking to me through you." Jonas was deeply affected by the sincerity of Auntie Malou's faith and her deep love for Christ. Jonas asked, "Is there anything I can do for you?" She responded, "You have already done it. You are here and you may stay as long as you like. You are our Godly-guest."

Jonas remained at Auntie Malou's house for three days and three nights and was treated like a king. He was embraced by the entire family; Auntie Malou, her husband who is a physician, and their adult son who also is a physician. Each of them visited with Jonas, shared their life stories, catered to his needs, and were truly interested in him as a person. Each evening they all prayed the rosary together as a group, talked about their faith, and reflected upon how wonderful it will be someday in heaven. Malou's husband was a soft-spoken man, fervent in faith, and very articulate with his ideas. He spent long hours with Jonas each afternoon and evening discussing aspects of the faith, doctrines, and how and why the traditions of the faith were so important, especially today. He listened attentively to Jonas' insights and valued his opinions with such degree of reverence it was as if Jonas was helping to reveal some hidden truths that were not recognizable before. Auntie Malou was careful to not allow her husband to exhaust Jonas with his intrigue and often asked him very politely to give Jonas a break.

After the third day of what felt like living in a true paradise, Jonas discerned he needed to move on. After dinner, he shared with the family that he would be leaving in the morning and thanked them all for their hospitality, kindness, and love. They all took turns and hugged Jonas, thanked him for the visit and ensured him that he could return whenever he liked and that he would never have to feel that he was homeless again.

Auntie Malou asked if she could wash his clothing before he left and gave him pajamas to wear. While Jonas slept, she washed and dried his clothing, sewed on two buttons that must have been torn off, and even scrubbed his sandals.

Knowing the whole family would be gone in the morning because they all had to go to work, Auntie Malou prepared a written note and placed it on top of his folded clothes that were carefully placed on the floor just outside of his bedroom door. Her husband also placed three one-hundred-dollar bills in an envelope with a letter. The letter read,

Dear Jonas,

Our Lord has taught us, "Whoever oppresses a poor man insults his Maker, but he who is generous to the needy honors him." You truly have been a blessing to our family, and we feel honored that you chose us to spend time with. You are not a stranger to us, you are now a part of our family. Please stay in touch and come back often. We will include you in our evening rosaries and please pray for us. I know your heart is close to Christ's, and that He has a special ear for your prayers. I look forward to seeing you again soon. Our love to you, now and forever.

Love,

Auntie Malou and family

Forgotten and Lost

Chapter 52

Dylan couldn't stop thinking about Father's book. He felt for the first time he was truly getting to know the man he not only respected so greatly but who also inspired him to be holy and much more than he ever imagined he could become. After dropping Father Mateo off at the park, Dylan skipped his morning theology class and snuck back into Father's bedroom. He wasted no time, accessed the book, and resumed reading. He read,

My little brother didn't realize it, but he possessed something exceptional in his character and in his virtuous soul. He acted with consistent charity and seemed to have a profound love within him much beyond a child of such a young age. I could see it before he ever could. He was going to be a spiritual force in this world if he would ever obtain the confidence to break out of the shackles of vice, immorality, greed, and corruption that the devil, the world, and even the fallen-self tried so hard to enslave us with. I wonder where he is now? I have a deep sense that he is doing God's work. I don't know why I feel this way, but I do. If I wouldn't have dishonored us so badly, and God would not have justly taken my sight away, maybe I would be able to see him. I hope he is alive. If God ultimately forgives me maybe, just maybe, I will see him again in heaven...

Dylan eventually turned off the computer, exited the room, and went for a walk. As he walked, he pondered the written words he had just read for almost two hours. He had such mixed emotions. On one hand, he felt inspired by the love Father had for his younger brother, his parents, and many others he wrote about. On the other hand, he felt such sorrow for Father and how he felt he was being punished by God for his past transgressions and somehow God made him blind. He was also saddened with the idea that although Father had dedicated his life for so many years serving as a priest, a seminary professor, and a spiritual guide to hundreds, that he still felt he might not be allowed entrance into heaven. These thoughts troubled Dylan greatly and now he was struggling with the idea he might not ever be allowed into heaven if a man of such holiness like Father might have doubt for himself.

Dylan continued to walk around the large seminary campus for almost two hours thinking, praying, and trying to discern so many things. He did come to the realization he needed to stop sneaking into Father's room and reading his book since he did not have permission and his action was sinful. Suddenly and intensely he realized those acts of sin were troublesome for his soul and he needed healing. He walked over to the chapel and once inside he noticed Father Victor was praying his breviary in the front pew. Dylan quietly made his way up to Father and asked, "Father, do you have a minute to hear my confession?" Father slowly lowered his breviary, looked up while peering over his reading glasses and responded, "Did you want the confessional, or do you want to do it right here?" Dylan replied, "Right here is fine Father if that is alright with you?" Father nodded and slid over on the pew to make room for Dylan to sit. Dylan sat down next to the priest. Father reached into his pocket and retrieved a small purple stole. He gently kissed it, unfolded it, and wrapped it around his neck. Father quietly mumbled a short prayer and added, "Ok, go ahead my son." Dylan immediately responded and said, "Bless me, Father, it has been at least a month and here are my sins. Father, I know better, I should not have done it, but I snuck into Father Mateo's room, twice, and logged onto his computer to read the book he is writing without his permission." Dylan paused for a moment and the priest asked, "Well, was it any good?" Dylan was shocked by the question and didn't know how to respond. The priest asked again, "Well, was it any good?" Dylan reacted, "Yes, Father, I couldn't put it down. The priest asked, "Tell me more." Dylan took a slow and deep breath and then continued, "It had a lot of his personal life story and so many things I had never heard about, that none of us have ever heard about." Father Victor was well aware of Father Mateo's past. Father Victor was the seminary Abbot, had lived at the seminary/monastery for over forty years, and was the one who received Father Mateo so many years ago before he had any seminary training and had not yet become a priest. Father Victor had listened to Mateo's general confession where he recounted and confessed all the sins of his entire life. The confession took over three hours and to this day it was one of the most heartfelt, contrite, and sorrowful confessions that Father Victor had ever received. He knew everything about Father Mateo and felt great compassion and respect for him.

Father Victor cleared his throat and asked, "Is there anything else that you would like to tell me or to talk about my son?" Dylan's thoughts were racing through his head and he didn't know if he should share any details of the book or just ask for forgiveness. He felt paralyzed. Father must have sensed the inner turmoil and offered, "Let's take a pause for a moment and consider a few things. God never wants us to sin, but He doesn't get in the way when we choose to do so. He uses those times of sin to work in special ways in our hearts and in our heads. He never desired for you to do what you did. You fractured your relationship with Father Mateo, even though he doesn't know what you did, you know. You fractured your relationship with God because you sinned against Him and sinned against one of His children, one of His priests. You harmed your soul in the sense that you allowed sin to enter it. Yet, God will use this act of free-will to somehow bring you closer to Him. Look, you are here, you do have contrition, you do have sorrow, and you are asking for forgiveness. I see that, but you must also see the bigger picture. What was God trying to accomplish allowing you to do what you did? What is the lesson, what is the outcome, what is the meaning to all of this? Don't answer me now, this is between you and God." Father paused for a moment and then asked, "Do you have any further sins that you would like to confess?" Dylan informed the priest that he could not recall any other sins. Father asked Dylan to pray an act of contrition which he did,

"Father of mercy, like the prodigal son I return to You and say: I have sinned against You and am no longer worthy to be called Your child. Christ Jesus, Savior of the world, I pray with the repentant thief to whom You promised Paradise: Lord, remember me in Your kingdom. Holy Spirit, the fountain of love, I call on You with trust: Purify my heart and help me to walk as a child of light."

and then the priest concluded the confession with praying the words of absolution, gently touching his palm upon Dylan's head, and making the sign of the cross over him.

Dylan immediately was relieved and felt as if a ton of weight had been lifted from his soul. He started to stand up and Father gestured for Dylan to sit back down. Father said, "Not quite yet. I still haven't given you your penance." Father paused for almost an entire minute. He was probably praying and trying to discern what the appropriate penance might be. He then said, "Alright my son. You are to never sneak to read that book again, only if Father permits you shall you read it. I want you to pray deep and hard about what you did read and try to discern what it is you are to do with that information that you have gained about Father Mateo." Dylan shook his head agreeing with the penance and then Father said, "Alright, off with you little sheep, now white as snow. Go in peace and be

God's reflection to the world. Off with you." and he shooed him away.

Chapter 53

Carter, Chuck, and Colleen had become much closer friends after spending the entire weekend together. At the end of the weekend, and realizing that Carter had no place to stay, Colleen and Chuck offered Carter one of their vacated children's rooms in their home. Colleen and Chuck enjoyed having Carter around, especially since their children had all moved out of the house and they were struggling with being empty-nesters.

Colleen, who was a supervisor at one of the local credit unions had offered Carter a job working as a teller, but he declined. So then, Chuck, who was a new construction painter, made him an offer to employ him as his apprentice. Carter immediately took Chuck up on his offer.

When Monday morning finally arrived Colleen left for work, and so did the boys. The men loaded up into Chuck's weathered pick-up and began their drive toward Wheatland where there was a new subdivision being built. As soon as they arrived at the construction site Chuck donned his painter's coveralls and handed Carter a set. Carter stepped into the garment and zipped it up. The coveralls were at least three sizes too big and when Chuck looked at him, he laughed and said, "Well, I guess we aren't the same size are we?" Carter laughed then picked up a piece of twine from the ground and made a belt to draw in the excess cloth.

The two men prepared their supplies and after a few instructions, Carter took the paint sprayer hose, climbed the scaffolding, and began to spray the two-story house. During the first hour, Chuck watched Carter closely to ensure that he understood the instructions and that he was coating the stucco correctly. He was quite impressed by Carter's natural ability to paint. He appeared as if he had been doing this type of work for years even though it was the first time he had ever used a professional paint sprayer.

Just to keep things exciting, Chuck would from time-to-time sneak into the garage where the compressor was, and also where the intake hose to the five-gallon paint container was located, and he would pinch the hose. The pinching of the hose set off an extremely loud buzzer at the sprayer end of the hose and would startle Carter. Carter would stop his spraying and climb down the scaffold to check the lines while in the meantime Chuck hid behind the building and out of sight of Carter. Carter traced the line from the sprayer back to the paint supply and didn't find any kinks or abnormalities. He reascended the scaffolding and resumed his painting. Chuck repeated the menacing act every thirty minutes and each time the buzzer went off Carter swore out loud, "Damn it!" Carter's swearing and reaction to the buzzer entertained Chuck tremendously.

At noon Chuck yelled up to Carter who was now almost finished with the upper areas of the house and said, "I'm going to get lunch, I'll be right back." Carter assumed that Chuck was grabbing something for him too but wasn't entirely sure. Chuck returned after an hour and Carter watched as he exited the truck. He was hoping to see bags of food especially since he was now starving from all the physical work. Chuck opened his door and upon exiting the vehicle Carter could only see that Chuck had an extremely large drink container in his hand. Carter internally felt disappointed and his hunger intensified. He spoke out, “Hey Chuck, I’m starving, can I borrow your truck to go get some lunch?” Chuck yelled back, “No, we need to keep working. We have a deadline and we must have this house done by five.” Carter immediately felt irritated and thought that Chuck was not only being unreasonable but was frustrated that Chuck hadn’t done any of the physical work that day at all. Chuck had watched Carter work all morning without doing any physical labor himself. Carter began to wonder if taking the job was a prudent decision or not.

Chuck then yelled at Carter, “Hey, come down here, I need some help with something.” Carter almost yelled back a sarcastic remark but restrained himself and climbed down. When he reached the truck, he said with a slightly irritated tone, “What is it, Chuck?” With an exaggerated flair, Chuck swung the truck door open and revealed numerous take out containers of food. Chuck proclaimed, “Could you help me with my problem? I have all this *El Pollo Loco* to eat. Can you help me take some of this off of my hands?” Instantly Carter knew Chuck had been playing with him and that he truly cared for him. The men blessed the food and they dug in. Chuck had ordered eight pieces of chicken, tortillas, rice, beans, and salsa for each of them. He also had an additional large drink in the cab for Carter.

It was quite difficult, but after consuming the enormous lunch Carter and Chuck resumed the spraying of the house. As Carter continued their work by spraying the lower sections of the house, Chuck climbed the scaffolding and began painting the trim areas by hand. Chuck was extremely quick and precise with his painting skills. It was evident that he was a skilled professional and knew what he was doing. At five minutes before five o’clock the men had finished the entire house and the general contractor, Danny, had just arrived. He was wearing a tan golf shirt and matching khaki shorts. He was extremely tanned and also wore a white golfing hat.

He was a modestly handsome man, in his early fifties, and appeared to be one of wealth. Carter could also see a set of golf clubs in the back of Danny's truck and thought to himself, *What a great gig, playing golf all day while others do the work.* Danny walked around the house inspecting their work and after a few minutes, he walked up to Chuck and said, "Well, as usual, it looks great. I have six more houses for you, are you interested?" Chuck responded, "The same price?" Danny nodded in agreeance. Chuck replied, "Sure." Danny began to walk away and said, "I'll email you the addresses and start dates. I have one ready for tomorrow." Chuck turned to Carter and said, "That was his entire work for the day. I bet ya he is now planning where he will be golfing tomorrow and the next day. He really is a great golfer, but that is beside the point." Carter laughed.

The men initially gathered their supplies, loaded them in the truck, and then cleaned the work site for the next thirty minutes. Upon finishing Chuck turned to Carter and said, "You feel like a beer?' Carter replied, "Just one?" Chuck laughed and responded, "I knew there was something about you I liked." The men hopped into the truck and Chuck drove them to the Red Hen, a small tavern on the outskirts of Wheatland. As soon as Chuck walked inside the tavern, a tiny dark-haired woman yelled out, "Norm, you're back." Chuck turned to Carter and explained in a whisper, "I told her one day my name was Norm like the guy on the old TV show *Cheers* and she has called me that ever since. I thought she would forget, but she has a memory like an elephant." He turned back toward the woman and replied, "Hey Kathy, how's it shaking?" She smiled a huge welcoming smile and asked, "Who is your new friend, well new to me?" Chuck explained that Carter was his new apprentice and that he found him at the river bottoms. He went into great detail about how he found Carter half-dead and after performing mouth to mouth and giving him cardiac resuscitation, he came back to life. He also described how he had fed him through a straw for weeks after the near-death experience and he helped him to recuperate and his life is a miracle. Kathy listened intently and was completely absorbed by the story. In fact, the whole bar quieted down and there were at least twelve other people attentively listening to Chuck as he explained just how bad off Carter was and that he had been in prison for armed robbery but after sixteen years his case was overturned due to new DNA evidence and he had been released without anywhere to go and with no means to support himself. He explained how Carter had begun using heroin and methamphetamine to try to dull the pain of rejection and abandonment. The story became more and more sensational the more Chuck spoke and eventually Kathy looked at Carter's appearance and she knew that Chuck had been pulling her leg. She grabbed a bar towel and flung it at him as she proclaimed, "You are a liar, Norm." Everyone laughed, but not as fervently as Chuck did. He then said, "Two Coors Lights, draft please." Kathy gave a very disapproving look, hesitated, and then poured the beers while the men climbed on top of two stools at the edge of the bar.

Kathy asked the men a variety of questions, she didn't like not knowing everything that was happening in the small farming town and eventually began grilling Carter about who he was and where he had come from. She was quite sweet and sincere about her inquisition, and she truly cared for the eclectic group that filled the bar. As she visited, poured drinks, fetched finger foods, and cleaned the tables, she kept track of everyone and ensured that their glasses didn't empty without asking them if they wanted a refill. She was quite amazing in how efficient she worked and how she made the work look more like socializing than working.

After almost two hours Chuck and Carter had consumed three beers each and had eaten two sides of jalapeno poppers and a large order of onion rings before setting off for home. The sun was now beginning to set and just as Chuck was saying, "I bet Colleen is wondering where we are" he received a text from her that read, "*I bet you are at the Red Hen again. Pick us up a six-pack on your way home. Rough day at the bank. Tell you when you get home. That crazy lady again. Don't get pulled over.*

Chapter 54

After leaving Auntie Malou's place, Jonas decided to head up the mountain. He started the journey by walking alongside highway 44 until a forest ranger pulled over and asked where he was headed. Jonas replied, "I am on a mission. God asked me to climb the mountain. I see that there is a town ahead by the name of Shingletown. I think I'm to go there." The ranger smiled and said, "It's not much of a town, one store, one gas station, are you sure?" Jonas was not deterred. The ranger offered Jonas a ride stating that he was heading to Mount Lassen and the town was on his way. Once inside of the ranger's vehicle Jonas found that the ranger, who by the way was named Sebastian, was quite friendly. They discussed a variety of topics in the twenty-five-minute drive and Jonas felt very comfortable in the man's presence. Sebastian must have also felt quite comfortable because he even began to share intimate details of his life with Jonas. He disclosed he is married and has six children with another one on the way.

Just as the men were entering the city of Shingletown, Ranger Sebastian received a call on his radio. It was the station and they relayed a message for Sebastian to urgently return home. There wasn't any cell service in the area due to the non-existence of cell towers. Receiving an urgent message wasn't common and Sebastian quickly filled with fear. Without thinking about Jonas, Sebastian made an abrupt u-turn and began to speed in the opposite direction of the town. He began to pray aloud, “Hail Mary, full of grace, blessed art thou among women and blessed is the fruit of thy womb, Jesus. Holy Mary, mother of God, pray for us sinners now and at the hour of our death. Amen. And pray for my family.” He prayed the prayer repeatedly until he finally reached his home, a modern large two-story log cabin in the woods. Three of his older children were standing outside of the home waiting. Marcus, the oldest said, “It’s mom, she fell in the shower began bleeding tons and tons of blood from her private place.” Sarah, Sebastian's wife had three previous high-risk pregnancies and had lost the last two children due to miscarriages.

Without thinking Sebastian blurted out, “I knew it, I knew it. The doctor said she couldn’t risk getting pregnant again and the next miscarriage might not only kill the baby but would kill her too.” Sebastian ran into the bedroom and laying on the bed was Sarah and the sheets around her were soaked in blood. He had never seen so much blood before. He froze in a state of panic. She looked lifeless. He thought she might already have died.

The children all made their way into the bedroom and stood around the bed, all remaining silent. They didn’t know what to do. Finally, Sebastian came to his senses and raced out of the room into the kitchen and grabbed the phone that was mounted on the wall to call the emergency number. Unnoticed by Sebastian, Jonas had made his way into the bedroom. He slipped between the children and slowly walked up to Sarah gently laying his hands upon her lower abdomen in the area of her uterus and began to pray. The children watched with great focus as Jonas appeared to be trying to heal their mother. He quietly prayed, “Dear Father, stop the bleeding and repair her wounds. Save the baby and ensure its health. Please hear my prayers, Father.”

Jonas abruptly removed his hands from Sarah's abdomen and began to walk out of the room. The children looked to Jonas for some sort of consolation. Jonas smiled and said, "Your mother is fine. The baby is fine. All is well and all is going to be well. Your father's deep faith has saved her and my father has heard him. You have a very special father and mother and a very special little sister that will be joining you in just a little over two months."

As Jonas made his way out of the bedroom Sarah sat up in the bed. Her facial color had completely returned to normal and she appeared healthy and well. She looked around the room and said, "This is quite the mess, I better get to washing." She then looked at the children and said, "This is too nice of a day to be inside, go outside and play." Seeing that their mother looked as vibrant as ever they obeyed her and scampered out the door out of the house. Seeing the children running, Sebastian dropped the phone and ran into the room. By now, Sarah was standing and changing out of her soiled blood-stained clothing. Sebastian just stood there in shock as he watched his wife, who just a few minutes earlier appeared to be moments away from death, now doing household chores as if nothing had occurred. He ran up to Sarah and hugged her as he said, "I thought I lost you." He began to cry. She hugged him back and said, "I'm not entirely sure what happened but as I was dreaming God came down and touched my womb and said that I was healed and we are going to have a healthy little girl in two months. I feel wonderful, never better. I feel that everything that has been wrong with me has been healed. I can feel the baby moving and kicking. My back doesn't hurt. I am not bleeding." By now Sebastian was sobbing like a baby and the tears were emotions of joy and thankfulness.

After he felt confident that Sarah was alright, he suddenly reacted. Frantically, Sebastian ran outside to check on the children. He first came across Marcus and then little Peete. Sebastian asked,

"Are you all alright kids?" The children smiled and began laughing. Marcus was the first to speak and said, "That was amazing, Dad. That man came into the room and placed his hands on top of Mom's stomach and as he pressed down he prayed and then as he took his hands away he said that everything was going to be alright and that we were going to have another little sister." Little Peete chimed in, "Ya Dad, it was so cool. I need to learn how to do that. Can you do that Dad?" Immediately Sebastian asked, "Where did that man go?" Everyone looked around to spot him, but he wasn't anywhere in sight. Marcus added, "Dad, that man said that Mom was healed because of your faith and that it was your faith that saved her. What did that mean Dad?" Sebastian dropped to his knees and began to cry.

Chapter 55

Dylan had been thinking about his penance for the last three days. He didn't know what to make of the directive to think about what to do with the information he had learned from reading Father's Mateo book. He wasn't sure if he was to do something with the information, or if he was to use the information in some way to help him grow spiritually.

Feeling frustrated, he donned his running shoes and decided to try and clear his head with a run. He circled the seminary grounds a few times and upon beginning to feel quite good he decided to turn his run into a cross-country excursion. He ran out from the seminary grounds onto Abbey drive. He proceeded along the country road until he came to Academy street where he turned left. He continued the run alongside the scant traffic until he reached the cross-road of Hillsboro where he temporarily stopped. On the corner sat Joe's garage and behind it the Community Festhalle. The parking lot of the hall was overflowing with vehicles and even Joe's entire lot was bumper to bumper with parked cars. Dylan began to walk to cool down and to investigate what was happening in the hall. As he approached the gathering of people, he noticed there were signs posted everywhere. The signs didn't appear to be professional and many of them looked as if they were poster boards bought at the local stationery store and that someone used Sharpie markers on them. One of the signs read:

FIND YOUR HERITAGE

FIND YOUR ANCESTORS

FIND YOUR LONG-LOST RELATIVES

Dylan sat down on the curb and prayed, "Lord, is this a message for me? Is this what you are wanting me to do?" He was hoping for some type of confirmation but there was nothing. After a few minutes, he stood up and ventured into the hall. There were dozens and dozens of booths with almost two hundred people inside. He quickly realized researching your heritage and ancestry was quite popular and people were very intrigued by what science could now offer.

Dylan visited each booth and listened to the salesmen's pitches and explanations of what they could offer. He eventually arrived at a large booth and listened to the man with the name tag that read BUTCH. Butch explained that with just a small sample of DNA he could have it processed and scanned through their mega computers to find missing or hard to locate people. He shared that almost everyone has had their DNA taken at some point in their life, although mostly unknown to them. He explained most of the large clinical laboratories that process clinical labs ordered by physicians and hospitals had been selling the left-over blood to research companies for years to do their studies. It wasn't until two years prior that this illegal practice had been discovered and the entire data banks were made available to law enforcement and governmental agencies as part of a nationwide settlement. Butch explained that his company, a private detective firm known as the BINKERTONS, had access to the data bank. Dylan asked, "How much does this cost?" Butch explained that for only $29.99 he could have the DNA sample analyzed and run through the data bank. Dylan asked about the DNA samples and how they collect the sample to be tested. Butch explained, "We give you this specialized kit that is just a small brush-like wand and you can swipe it three times on your inner cheek, place it into the envelope, and mail it off. In three weeks we will send you the report. You will be amazed at how detailed and accurate the results are."

Dylan had an idea. He gave Butch thirty dollars and Butch gave him the kit. Dylan ran back up the hill to the seminary. He changed his clothes and went to visit Father Mateo. As expected, Father was inside his room further dictating his book. Dylan spoke, "Father, I am working on a project and I need a guinea pig." Father responded with a serious tone, "I don't have any of those." Dylan laughed and clarified, "No Father, I just need someone who will let me look into their mouth with this flashlight." Father Mateo responded, "Dylan, I'm an old man. Do you know what shape my mouth and teeth are in? I think you might want someone much younger and with better oral hygiene than an old crotchety priest." Dylan persisted, "No, really Father, it will take just a second."

Father Mateo, being the kind and charitable soul that he is, gave in and said, "Alright, but make it quick. I'm getting to the end of my book and want to finish it." Dylan ripped open the package and said, "Alright Father, open up. I'm going to use this little plastic stick to hold your mouth open while I look around." Dylan then stuck the plastic device inside Father's mouth and quickly and firmly brushed it alongside both cheeks and as he retrieved it he said, "That's it, Father, I saw all I needed to see." Father responded, "Well that's good, cause I can't see a thing." Dylan raced out of the room and back to his bedroom. Once inside, he followed the directions for the care of the swab and followed the packaging and mailing instructions. Once the container-envelope was secured and sealed he then ran to the seminary mail office and placed the package into the outgoing mail slot.

Chapter 56

The weekend had finally arrived and both Carter and Chuck were exhausted. They had knocked out five houses at work, one house per day. Danny had offered the men a twenty percent bonus if they could paint all five houses by the end of the week so Carter and Chuck agreed they would work each day, no matter how long it took, to finish each house. Their typical day began at five in the morning and often lasted until ten at night. There were no Red Hen stops after work that week.

Chuck had completely forgotten about the invitation he had agreed to regarding a weekend on the lake. He was still sleeping when Colleen's sister Paddy began knocking on the door. Colleen would have reminded him, but she had stayed at her other sister's house, Mickey, all week to help with the preparation for the annual Homelessness Festival. Mickey, along with almost one hundred other local business leaders and individuals planned a festival each year at the end of the summer. The festival was in honor of all the homeless. California now possessed over half of the homeless population in the United States and their needs were clearly visible to most in the State. At the festival, there were booths for haircuts, clothes washing, medical booths for shots and medications, and even dental booths for the pulling of teeth. Everything was free. However, the most popular booths were the needle exchange booth, the free clothing and blanket booth, the free tent booth, and not to mention the over fifty food booths.

Chuck finally responded to the relentless knocking of Paddy at the door and opened the door while standing in his boxers. As soon as Paddy realized that Chuck was in his underwear, she reached for the doorknob and while forcefully pulling it shut, she yelled out, "Chuck, put some clothes on." Chuck walked over to the living room window, cracked it open, and asked, "What are you doing here so early Paddy?" Then it struck him. Two weeks ago, he committed to a lake weekend and to tow the patio boat to the lake. Chuck offered, "I am so sorry Paddy, I am running late..." Paddy interrupted and with a slightly agitated attitude, she commented, "Running late? You liar, Chuck. You totally forgot about me." Chuck felt embarrassed but stuck to his story, "No way Paddy, you're my favorite sister-in-law. I am just running late. Carter kept me up too late last night at the store getting our supplies for the weekend. I bought beer, snacks, and even Bar-B-Que meat." Paddy seemed to believe Chuck's explanation and her mood calmed. Realizing that Paddy's SUV was parked outside with her ski boat attached, he added, "You go along to the lake. I'll finish packing the ice chests and will swing by your house and pick up the patio boat. Carter can help me. I'll see you all there in an hour or so. I'll even gas up the boat." Paddy smiled and agreed to Chuck's plan.

As soon as Paddy left Chuck walked into Carter's room and threw a glass of water on his face. Carter jumped up from a deep sleep yelling, "What is it? What is going on?" Chuck proclaimed, "You totally forgot about the lake, didn't you?" Chuck had never mentioned it to Carter before. Carter looked puzzled. Chuck continued, "Carter, we need to get going. We must stop by the store and buy a ton of beer, snacks, and meat. How much cash do you have on you?" Carter wasn't fully awake yet and responded, "I have cash, remember you paid me yesterday." Chuck smiled and said,

"Great, bring your cash. You can buy the groceries and I'll get the gas." Carter was now able to focus a little better, and he inquired, "What is it that we are doing?" Chuck explained that every year they have a huge family gathering at Camp Far West Lake where all the cousins, nieces, and nephews get together, and Paddy brings her patio boat and ski boat, and everyone has a great time.

After Chuck and Carter ran through the shower at record speed, they grabbed what they needed and were on their way to Paddy's house to hook up and tow the boat to the lake. Chuck was speeding while attempting to make up some time. He remembered that he told Paddy that he would meet them in an hour, however, buying the groceries and filling the boat with gas took longer than expected. Just as they were entering the town of Wheatland, Carter commented, "Better slow down, there is always a cop with a radar gun. This town is totally a speed trap." Just then they passed a parked police car and instantly the lights and siren were activated. Chuck knew he was caught. He pulled the rig over and in his rearview mirror, he could see the police car began following him and parked behind him along the side of the road. Chuck rolled down his window and waited for the officer to make his way up to the car. As soon as the officer approached, he heard, "License and registration, please. You know you were doing fifty in a thirty-five, right?" Chuck had just passed the three-year mark without getting a ticket and their insurance rates had dropped to almost half. The only thing he could think of was how angry Colleen was going to be when she found out he got another ticket. Chuck then looked out his window at the officer and said, "Officer, I am aware I was speeding. It's my friend here." Pointing to Carter, "He ate some bad Asian food this morning and he said he was going to poop his pants. He was screaming and panting and holding his butt. I was trying all I could to make it to the Frosty Freeze before he exploded in my truck. I would have never been able to get the smell out. I was being a very careful officer. I knew I was speeding but I related this to the like of a woman having a baby. He needed to give birth and I was just being thoughtful and generous." During the explanation, Chuck had elbowed Carter who began playing along and he began to moan, pant, and hyperventilate. He reached back and made a fist he sat upon it as if it was some sort of butt plug. By now the officer was laughing so hard he dismissed them and said, "You better get him to the bathroom or you will never get the smell out." Chuck immediately started his truck and sped to the Frosty Freeze knowing that office was trailing them and watching, Carter jumped out of the truck, and while holding his butt with his left hand still in a fist, he skipped on his toes all the way to the bathroom.

Chapter 57

After leaving the Shingletown area Jonas was picked up on the highway by an elderly man and woman driving a Subaru wagon. The couple had been visiting their son in Yuba City and spent a weekend on retreat at the Vina Monastery. They were now on their way back home to Westwood, near Lake Almanor. They were quite delightful and enjoyed talking, especially Maribeth, Darnel's wife. They were both self-professed fervent Catholics. Darnel was a retired professor and Maribeth was an artist, specifically an iconographer. They both were raised in San Francisco and even though they spent many years in the ultra-liberal and progressive heart of America, they seemed to be quite balanced. Maybe it was their belief in the faith that kept them from swaying too far in the liberal and conservative directions.

Jonas was intrigued by Maribeth's claim of being an iconographer, especially when she stated that she wrote icons and didn't paint them, and since he knew very little about it he asked if Maribeth could elaborate on the subject while they were driving. She explained that she started with a panel of seasoned wood, sanded it, sealed it with natural glue, and covered the wood with fine linen. She then applied several layers of gesso (Gesso is whitening or alabaster mixed with heated rabbit-skin glue.) She then sanded it down to an ivory smoothness to receive the lightly incised drawing, the gold, and the colors which are raw pigments mixed with white of egg. She further explained that the icon differs from Western art in many other ways by stating, “It is normal for a Western painting to be recognized by the artist’s distinctive style and brushwork. Iconographers, however, regard their work as a prayer, where style is irrelevant, and where the real author is the Holy Spirit, so iconographers do not sign their work. They submit their talents in obedience to Holy Tradition and rules with as much care and accuracy as a medieval monk transcribing the words of Holy Scripture. There is no place for personal interpretation. An icon does not reflect the author’s personality: it is a mirror in which the Divine is reflected.” Jonas instantly discerned that Maribeth was passionate about her writing of icons and after he heard she had a studio at her home, filled with icons she had created, he hoped he would be able to see them. Jonas asked, “May I take just a moment and see your studio?” Maribeth lit up and immediately responded, “Yes.”

After a few hours of driving which seemed to pass very quickly, they arrived at the mountain home. Walking around to the rear of the home the studio was just as Jonas had envisioned. It was a large room built onto the house with large windows on all three sides allowing copious amounts of natural light to fill the room. Once inside, Jonas was breath taken with the views of the forest through the windows. One could gaze in every direction at God’s delightful creation of nature from anywhere inside the room. Jonas felt inspired by just being in the room. It possessed a type of holiness, peacefulness that was usually only felt by Jonas inside of Catholic churches, but it was present there as well.

Maribeth toured Jonas through the room and explained each of the over thirty icons that she had recently worked on. There were icons of Mary, Christ, and almost every saint you could think of. They were beautifully done and wonderful to look at. Maribeth then took Jonas over to the center area of her studio and uncovered her most recent work. It was an extremely large icon, standing almost six feet tall and it was an icon of Mary of Perpetual Help.

Jonas was mesmerized by the beauty of the icon and especially the eyes of Mary. He stared into her eyes and it was as if her eyes were looking right back at him. Maribeth noticed Jonas' reaction and she commented. "It's the prayer that goes into the writing of the icons that you are experiencing. It isn't just a painting, it is so much more. This icon is filled with prayer, love, and devotion. It has been infused with our faith. It is sacramental." She asked Jonas to walk around the room while keeping his eyes fixed on Mary's eyes. As he walked, he began to cry. The emotions inside of him burst out and he couldn't contain himself. Finally, he belted out, "Her eyes are following me everywhere I go. It's as if she is alive and she is following me while speaking to me through her eyes." Maribeth explained she had been commissioned to write this special icon for the Mount Angel Seminary in Oregon and she was waiting for the paint to cure so she and Darnel could drive it there. Jonas returned to the icon and sat down on a chair positioned in front of it. Maribeth and Darnel could see that the icon was having a profound effect on Jonas and they decided to back away and have a cup of tea while Jonas took as much time as he needed in her presence.

After spending almost an hour in meditation and reflection in front of Maribeth's icon creation, Jonas caught a view through the window of what appeared to be a small cabin or shed situated a few hundred yards away. It was almost unrecognizable by the cover of the trees. Jonas looked back to the corner of the studio where Maribeth and Darnel looked quite comfortable relaxing in the studio chairs drinking their tea and asked, "What is that room over there?" Darnel immediately stood and responded, "It is my prayer shed. I haven't used it for some time. You want to see it?" Jonas replied, "Yes, I'd love to." Darnel led the way and the men ventured through the woods and came upon a much smaller structure than it originally appeared. It couldn't have been more than eight feet by eight feet. Darnel opened the door and inside there was a small window, a desk, chair, wood stove, and a simple wooden bed with a three-inch mattress laid on top of it. It looked like a hermit's shed. There were no amenities other than three books sitting on the table: a bible, The Imitation of Christ, and Saint Augustin's Confession as well as three of Maribeth's icons mounted on the wall. There was also a simple crucifix on the wall opposite the head of the bed. Tucked in the corner there was a prayer kneeler. Jonas asked, "What do you use this room for?" Darnel explained that he had spent various days in the room for silent personal retreats, fasting, and praying, but since he had aged, and now had some health issues, he hadn't used it for some time. Jonas loved the room. He carefully scanned every inch taking it all in. Darnel could see how intrigued Jonas was and offered, "Would you like to make a retreat here?" Jonas asked, "What do you mean?" Darnel clarified, "You could make a silent retreat here if you have the time. It could be a day, a week, or maybe even 40 days if you like. I could bring you a small meal each day, once a day, and it could be a wonderful Spirit-filled retreat if you so like." Jonas questioned, "You would do that for me?" Darnel responded, "Sure, it wouldn't be much at all. Maribeth and I are not going anywhere, except to Mount Angel." Darnel hesitated, looked at the calendar on his watch and then calculated in his head. He then said with enthusiasm, "We are not going anywhere for exactly 40 days. I think this is a sign. Why don't you start right now? I will bring a simple meal, maybe a small piece of fruit, bread, and water each day and leave it outside the door. Maybe 500-700 calories, just enough to keep you from starving. You want to make this a little difficult to gain the graces." Jonas immediately responded, "Yes, I can start right now. You and Maribeth are so kind. I will be praying for you both as well; for your health, your happiness, and your souls." Darnel's eyes filled with tears as he reached out and shook Jonas's hand with a firm but sincere shake.

Darnel returned to the house while leaving Jonas behind. Jonas looked around the room and instantly he realized that there was no bathroom. He laid down on the bed and was pleasantly surprised that it was quite comfortable even though the mattress was thin and sat on top of a plywood frame.

He must have fallen asleep because when he opened his eyes the sun was setting and it was already getting dark and cool outside. He walked over to the door, opened it, and sitting on the ground was a plate covered with a napkin, a container of wooden matches, an envelope, a blanket, sheets, pillow, toilet paper, a small plastic hand shovel, a pencil, pad of paper, three jugs of water, and a dozen large candles all sitting in a wooden box. He lifted the box and brought it inside. He took one of the fresh candles from the box, lit it with one of the matches, and then opened the envelope. The letter read:

I've taken the liberty to stack firewood behind the shed. Please use it, the nights can be very cold. Here is everything you need. I will replenish the supplies as you need them, just leave me a note. The bathroom is anywhere outside of the shed. Just dig a hole, do your business, and then bury it. Please bury it. I don't want any surprises on my hikes. Hahaha

Jonas uncovered the plate and laid there were three fresh strawberries, a half of a large French bread loaf, three small squares of butter, a plastic knife, and an apple.

Chapter 58

Dylan had been waiting for weeks for the results of the DNA testing to arrive. Even though he knew it would be too soon he began checking the mailroom for the letter every day after he had mailed the sample. Finally, today when he went to check the mailroom, the envelope had arrived. He grabbed it from the cubby with his name on it and ran back to the privacy of his room to read the results. He knew that something special was going to be inside the envelope and then he would know exactly what he was to do with the information he had obtained, although sinfully, from sneaking and reading most of Father Mateo's book. He knew that his confession would not be complete until he had accomplished his penance. The idea of not having his sins forgiven weighed on him greatly. Secretly he cursed the priest for not giving him a simple penance like most priests did, like five Hail Mary's, or ten Our Fathers. He thought, *Why did my penance have to have some action attached that I don't know how to fulfill?*

Once inside his room, he sat down at his desk and quickly opened the letter and proceeded to read it.

Dear Participant in the DNA mega data search. We are always grateful for our supporters and are still shocked at how many people believe what we say about having a mega computer with everyone's

DNA. This was a total hoax, a scam, and you fell for it. We did make a killing in your area and your $29.99 helped quite a bit. Go ahead and report us to law enforcement, there will be plenty of reports along with our descriptions of middle-aged men all named Butch. We are long gone now and please know that we have delightfully left the country.

Thanks again.

Sincerely, Butch.

Dylan suddenly felt quite sick. He had such high hopes and now he had nothing. He couldn't believe that he had been so gullible. He should have known better than to believe such nonsense. He laid down upon his bed and closed his eyes. He prayed, *Dearest Mother Mary, I am such a loser. Why do I always do these types of things? I don't feel worthy to be here any longer. I think I should pack my bags and leave. Please give me a sign if I am to remain at the seminary and become a priest*. He then opened his eyes and awaited his sign of confirmation, but there was nothing. He looked around the room and still nothing. He waited, and waited, and waited. Yet, nothing, no sign. He finally spoke out, "See Mary, you are just like all the other women that I have counted on in my life. Never there, never any help, never any support, always nothing."

He then glanced at the three-foot-tall statue of Mary that sat on the end table next to his bed. A tear rolled down from her eye. He couldn't believe what he was witnessing. He grabbed a tissue and wiped it dry. But, another tear appeared, then another, and another. He then prayed *I'm so sorry Mary, please stop crying. I didn't mean it. I was just tired, scared, and afraid. I'm so sorry, please stop. I love you, Mary. I know I can count on you to be my advocate, my mother here on earth and in heaven. I know you will always present me in the best of light to your son. I am so sorry, please forgive me.* Suddenly the tears stopped and Dylan wasn't quite sure, but it appeared that the semi-smile that the statue of Mary had previously possessed might have grown just a tiny bit.

Forgotten and Lost

Chapter 59

Carter had a wonderful time at the family reunion. He met the six brother-cousins, Kevin, Tim, Terrance, Patrick, Mike, and Dan, as well as their numerous children. He met other cousins from Michigan, North Dakota, Florida, Texas, Maine, and North Carolina. There were many from so many different states he couldn't keep track. They were all nice, well, except for the half-nephew from Oakland, which Carter was pretty sure wasn't even really related. His name was Bartholomew but he wanted to be called Betty-Benjamin. Carter wasn't quite sure if he was a male transitioning to be a female, or a female transitioning to be a male, but he was quite sure that the person was quite weird. He/She sat by themselves for most of the reunion and threw rocks at everyone.

During the reunion for the first time in a long time, Carter felt extremely out of place. It wasn't because the families were uninviting or unfriendly. They were quite the opposite. Almost everyone went out of their way to include him in discussions and in playful events, treating him just like everyone else. There was just something inside that felt at odds. He felt that maybe he had been spinning his wheels and living like everyone else wasn't quite enough. He began to think about the seminary again and a life of service and devotion to the Church. He identified a deep longing inside of him to possibly want to return to the seminary. He needed to talk to someone, but he didn't know who to turn to. He had been away from the religious life for so long now that he felt isolated. He had overheard Paddy talking about her pastor and her parish, maybe he could ask her?

Carter walked to the living room where Colleen and Chuck were watching television and he asked Colleen, "Could I possibly have Paddy's phone number?" Chuck immediately replied, "You know she is almost twenty years older than you?" Colleen threw a pillow at him and looked at Carter as if she wanted to ask why, but before she could Carter shared, "No, it isn't anything like that. She had said something about her priest and I wanted to see if I could meet with him." Chuck chimed in again, "You're not thinking of killing yourself, are you?" This time Colleen threw her empty soda can at him and it struck him squarely across his forehead. He reacted, "Damn it, sweetheart. That hurt. Next time could you at least throw a can of beer so I would have something to dull the pain." Colleen laughed and Chuck followed with a bellowing laugh that made Colleen laugh even more fervently.

Colleen had Paddy's phone number memorized so she asked, "Are you ready?" Carter pulled out his smartphone and as she dictated the number he punched it into the phone. After a few rings, Paddy answered and Carter reintroduced himself and explained he had overheard her at the reunion speak about her parish priest and was wondering if it would be alright to get his number and maybe use her as a reference so he wouldn't think that he was some crazy guy calling him out of the blue. She shared in response, "I can do better than that. I am going to Mass tonight at six-thirty and why don't you join me? I can call ahead and see if he can meet with you after Mass?" Carter agreed.

Carter drove to Saint Isidore's parish in Yuba City and met Paddy outside of the church a few minutes before the Mass was about to begin. They both entered the church together and Paddy informed Carter she was able to get ahold of Father Avery and Father suggested that they grab something to eat after Mass unless he wanted a confession. Carter thanked her and said the plan sounded perfect. He said he just needed some spiritual direction.

The Mass began in the usual way and after the initial readings, Father proclaimed from the Gospel of John.

"I am the bread of life. Your fathers ate the manna in the wilderness, and they died. This is the bread which comes down from heaven, that a man may eat of it and not die. I am the living bread which came down from heaven; if anyone eats of this bread, he will live forever; and the bread which I shall give for the life of the world is my flesh." The Jews then disputed among themselves, saying, "How can this man give us his flesh to eat?" So Jesus said to them, "Truly, truly, I say to you, unless you eat the flesh of the Son of Man and drink his blood, you have no life in you; he who eats my flesh and drinks my blood has eternal life, and I will raise him up at the last day. For my flesh is food indeed, and my blood is drink indeed. He who eats my flesh and drinks my blood abides in me, and I in him. As the living Father sent me, and I live because of the Father, so he who eats me will live because of me. This is the bread which came down from heaven, not such as the fathers ate and died; he who eats this bread will live forever."

The words of the Gospel pierced Carter's soul. His mind filled again with thoughts of becoming a priest and being able to stand In Persona Christi, to be in the person of Christ during the Holy Mass, and to participate in the miracle of transubstantiation, the changing of ordinary bread and wine into the Precious Body and Blood of the Lord, Jesus Christ. He thought to himself, *What am I doing? What was I thinking? What else in life could compare to being one of God's priests? But what about marriage? What about those feelings I felt for Brook? I am so confused.*

Before he knew it, it was communion time. He stood and followed the parishioners up to the steps of the altar where Father was standing and he received the Precious Host onto his tongue. He took a few steps and received the Precious Blood from the deacon and proceeded to return to his pew. Once back at his pew he kneeled, closed his eyes, and let Christ's Body and Blood become absorbed inside of him. As he meditated, he felt as if he was being consumed by Christ and his entire body began to tingle. It was a delightful feeling and the only thing that came to Carter's mind was that he didn't want it to stop. Yet, the tingling did stop after a few moments and now without the sensation, he resumed his meditation.

He prayed internally, *Dear Lord, please help me with my discernment. I know both choices would be alright, but I do feel called to be your servant. I also think about what life would be like with a sweet wife and children. Please help me, Lord*. Just then he heard, "Let us pray." Father was already praying the concluding prayers. Carter stood to join the rest of the parishioners listening and responding to the prayers.

After Mass Carter waited with Paddy outside of the church and when Father finally finished greeting his parishioners, he devested and joined them. As Father approached Paddy and Carter he said, "You must be Carter. Nice to meet you. I'm Father Avery, but you can just call me Father Avery." He then cracked up at his own joke. He continued, "Let's go get something to eat, I'm starving. Are you alright going to the Waffle Barn? I have been craving their Bacon Pecan Waffle and biscuits and gravy." Carter didn't care where they were going so he said, "Sure." Father quickly said, "I'll drive" and walked at a quick pace around the church to the rectory and jumped into his Jeep Wrangler. Carter hopped into the passenger seat and they quickly sped away.

Once inside the Waffle Barn the waitress took Father's order and Carter chose to only have coffee. He had no appetite due to his troubled emotional state. Father downed a full glass of water and said, "So what is it Carter that you wanted to talk about? It doesn't have anything to do with sheep, does it? Just kidding. I have been hanging out way too much with those high school football guys. Seriously, how may I help you?" Father's demeanor quickly changed and he became serious and focused. Carter shared, "Father, I had been a seminarian, well I guess I still am officially, but I asked to take some time off to discern if I was really called to be a priest. For many months I felt that I had made the right choice leaving but over the last few days I have begun to reconsider. Now I can't stop thinking about becoming a priest and what a wonderful honor and beautiful life that would be. The problem is, from time to time, I also think about the possibility of maybe wanting to get married too. I am so confused." Just then Father's waffles arrived. They paused to bless the food and as Father began shoveling food into his mouth while still chewing he responded, "What percentage of priests do you think also have thoughts of what it would be like to have a family?" Before Carter could respond Father continued, "How about ninety-five percent? I'll leave out five percent for the weirdos that somehow slipped through. I think the diocese is doing a much better job of that now. It is normal for those called to the priesthood to think about and desire a family. What you need to do is to think and pray about what it is that you feel called to do. When you make your decision, then that is your decision. It is like a man who chooses to marry a woman. He should discern quite well and not make a hasty decision, but once he makes his decision then he needs to stay faithful to that decision. It has more to do with his will, his dedication, his word, his honor, his commitment. A man can't just say that I thought I made the right choice but now I am choosing to divorce you. Well, I guess many do, but that is not the point. They shouldn't. The same is true for a priest. If a person chooses to become a priest, takes vows, and accepts ordination, he is married to the Church. This means in sickness and in health, in good times and in bad. Stop being wishy-washy, make a well-informed and well-thought-out decision, and then live with it for the rest of your life. That is what a man does. Be a man." Father's words were direct and to the point. They were not mean or meant to be mean, they were honest and true. That's exactly what Carter needed to hear.

The waitress arrived with Father's biscuits and gravy and suddenly Carter's appetite returned. He turned to the waitress and asked, "Can I get a meat-lovers omelet?" She responded in the affirmative and walked away. Carter spoke, "Father, thanks for your wisdom and your directness. Most priests are afraid to talk to people like that. I think I can be a good priest and that is what I am going to do." Father lifted his head from his plate of food and smiled. Carter noticed that Father had a huge glob of syrup and a pretty good size piece of waffle on his collar. He contemplated telling him but chose to keep that bit of information to himself. He wanted to see how long it would take Father to notice it.

Father continued to eat his meal and as soon as Carter's omelet arrived, he dug in as well. The two men visited and talked about a variety of things ranging from cigars to weight lifting to alternate-day fasting and the football season. When the bill came Carter reached for it but Father quickly grabbed it and said, "No, I'll get this. Seminarians are usually broke and if you're not, you will be soon." Carter thanked him and after paying the bill Father drove Carter back to his car and they parted each going their own separate way.

Chapter 60

Jonas had been on his silent retreat for almost 3 weeks. Except for relieving himself outdoors he rarely left the shed. Every three days or so he did a quick armpit, groin and backend wipe down with a washcloth, a little water, and the tiny bar of soap Darnel had left for him.

Jonas had already read through the Imitation of Christ and he was rereading it for the second time. He was surprised that he had never heard of the book before, especially when he read in the introduction that it was the most widely read book in the world next to the Holy Bible. He developed a routine of reading a chapter and setting the book down to meditate upon what he had read for anywhere from ten minutes to the entire day depending on how the Spirit moved him. One night he read non-stop, rereading each chapter seven times before he moved on to the next. He especially enjoyed the section on the interior life, probably because he saw himself as a type of contemplative. The section contained chapters on meditation, humility, and purity of mind, not to mention many other interesting topics.

For some reason, Jonas was unusually hungry, much more than all the previous days. Maybe it was because he had been severely constipated and that morning he had evacuated a painfully large bowel movement that was so large he couldn't believe it came out from inside of him. Before burying it, he measured it against his foot. It was three inches longer than his foot and half as wide. He guessed that he has lost at least ten pounds in the defecation event.

As had been the routine, without notice and without making a noise, Darnel had come to the shed and left a wooden box at the foot of the door. Jonas had been checking frequently for it that day and now it had finally arrived. Since Jonas didn't have a watch or a clock, he was not aware that Darnel brought the box each afternoon at the same time, three o'clock.

After carrying the box inside, Jonas uncovered it and to his surprise, it was quite different than the usual delivery. Sitting on top there was a one-sided card that simply read, *Congratulations, you have reached the halfway mark, 20 days!* Sitting below the card was a medium-sized steak, sizzling hot, with sautéed mushrooms, and a little gravy. There were green beans, mashed potatoes, and a piece of pumpkin pie. Instead of the usual plasticware, Darnel had included real metal eating utensils and a steak knife. Also, instead of the jug filled with well water, there was a store-bought tall bottle of mineral water. Jonas began to cry thinking of the kindness of Darnel taking the time to so carefully plan a halfway-mark feast.

As he gently removed the food items from the wooden box he eventually discovered that there was something else hidden below the plate wrapped in what looked like a paper shopping bag. He carefully unfolded the edges and the object was revealed. The mere sight of it made Jonas' heart fill with emotion. Tears began to stream down his face even more plentiful than before after seeing what Darnel had done for him. This was much more than a charitable gift, it appeared to be prophetic. Maribeth had created a special icon just for him. On a small piece of artistically colored paper and attached to the icon it read,

Forgotten and Lost

Here is Saint Jonas for you Jonas. May he bring you peace and consolation as you have and will to so many on your earthly journey.

Jonas was so moved by the appearance of the icon that he completely forgot about the delicious-looking food. He stared deeply into the icon until he fell asleep.

Suddenly in the middle of the night, Jonas awoke with a terrible pain in his lower abdomen. He was experiencing a cramp and he didn't know how to relieve it. He tried to twist and turn but the pain was unbearable. He finally was able to stand up and as soon as he did, he experienced a tremendous intestinal rumble that started at his breast bone and traveled somewhere deep down by his pelvis. It was as if a snake or monster was wiggling inside of him. It frightened him greatly and his mind filled with thoughts of having demons inside of him. He even pictured a huge tapeworm with the head of a devil. He began to panic thinking he had become possessed and started to yell out, “Lord, help me. I have been invaded by the devil. Help me, Help me, Lord.” Suddenly he opened his eyes and woke up. He had been having a nightmare. After taking a few deep breaths and wiping the sweat from his brow he relaxed. He reached over to the side table and feeling around in the dark he eventually located the matches and lit one by striking in on the top of the wooden table. He used it to light the candle and in the illumination, he could see the food he had neglected to earlier eat. He realized that he was having extreme hunger pangs and he needed to eat. He blessed the food and began slowly by first tasting the potatoes, then the green beans, and then started in with the streak. Even cold, the flavor of the food enlivened his taste buds. Not being used to eating such heavy food he took his time and after a few bites, he took a break. This process of eating a few bites of each item and then resting continued for almost two hours until every morsel of food had been consumed, even the pumpkin pie. Now completely stuffed, Jonas laid back down, closed his eyes, and fell back asleep.

Chapter 61

Dylan had been feeling better since the miraculous event with the Mary statue a few weeks prior. The negative self-talk that had filled his mind had disappeared and he was feeling quite optimistic about the future. He was attending class again, completing his homework assignments, and even leading most of the evening liturgy prayers with his fellow seminarians. He was exercising again and going for long daily runs. He was feeling balanced and well adjusted.

Dylan was scheduled for a presentation in the morning theology class and he was excited to use the PowerPoint slides he had created. He had spent almost a week preparing specific slides for each of the following areas:

Prolegomena (first principles)

Theology Proper. The existence of God. The attributes of God.

The doctrine of Man (theological anthropology)

Christology

Soteriology. Justification. Sanctification.

Pneumatology (doctrine of the Holy Spirit)

Forgotten and Lost

Ecclesiology (doctrine of the Church)

Eschatology and the afterlife.

He had almost entered the classroom building when he realized that he had forgotten his flash drive back in his room. Looking at his watch he realized that class started in less than four minutes and he was scheduled to be the first presenter. He knew if he was late, he would be passed over and might not get a chance to present it. The professor, Father Arnold, was a stickler for proper procedure and accountability. He often said that if something is important you should plan appropriately for it, even if that means showing up five hours early.

Dylan took off running as fast as his feet would carry him. He was jumping over benches, grabbing walls as he swung around them, and making remarkably great time. As soon as he arrived at the dorms, he threw the door open and raced down the hall. He only had to make two more turns until he would reach his room. Finally reaching the end of the first hallway he sped around the corner and briefly lost his balance. He didn't even see Father Mateo opening his door and the two crashed into each other. Father flew backward and Dylan rolled in the opposite direction. Dylan heard a loud pop and it sent a cringe throughout his body. He quickly rose to his feet and shook each extremity and identified that he was unharmed. He then looked over toward Father and immediately realized that he wasn't wearing his protective neck brace. His neck looked bent and Father appeared unconscious. Dylan wanted to try and sit him up but remembered what Father had said before when he had initially broken his neck. He didn't want to be moved. Dylan raced back to the lobby and used the reception phone to call 911. He explained what had happened and didn't hang up until they permitted him. He returned to Father's side and began to pray.

Dear Lord, You Lord are our medicine.

Forgotten and Lost

Your Words Lord are Truth and Life.
Help us put our trust in You.
You, Lord, are the greatest physician.
You heal,
You protect,
You care,
You love,
You are kind,
You are patient,
You are thoughtful,
You are strong.
You, Lord, are our Creator.
You know our thoughts,
our sighs and our cries
and every hair on our head.
You are wonderful and make all good things for us.
Heal Father Mateo Lord,
if it be Your will.
Amen

Dylan prayed the prayer over and over until the paramedics and the firemen arrived. They asked Dylan if he knew what had happened and if the man had any medical conditions. Dylan explained how he had run into him, knocked him down, and that he had always worn a neck brace due to his broken neck that would never heal and that he must have forgotten to put it back on after his shower. The paramedics carefully positioned Father onto his back and while supporting his neck and keeping it aligned placed a trauma collar around his neck. They started an intravenous line and shared that his vital signs were stable, but that he was unconscious.

Suddenly Father's breathing began diminishing and then the paramedics grabbed an Ambu bag and placed the mask over Father's mouth and then began squeezing it pushing air into Father's lungs.

One of the paramedics yelled out, “Let's get him to the hospital, something is wrong, he stopped breathing. I think it is his neck.” They quickly lifted him onto the gurney, loaded him into the ambulance, and then raced away.

Dylan followed the ambulance to the emergency room and by the time he arrived and inquired as to where Father was, he was informed they had already rushed him off for emergency surgery. Dylan made his way over to the surgery waiting area and sat down in one of the chairs. There was no one else in the entire room. He felt very alone and scared. His mind filled with thoughts of Father dying. He opened his Divine Liturgy and began to pray evening prayer. He was hoping the prayers would take his mind off of the negative thoughts, but he was unable to keep focused long enough to get through even one of the psalms without losing his place in the book.

It seemed like an eternity had gone by and finally, an extremely fatigued-looking doctor came out from behind the double doors wearing scrubs and a mask draped down around his neck who asked, “Are you from the monastery?” Dylan immediately answered “Yes.” The doctor continued, “I don’t have very good news.” Dylan’s heart sank. The doctor added, “The monk is stable for the moment, but he severely twisted his injured neck and it severed most of the spinal cord at the vertebrae level C-4. He is not able to breathe on his own and although I was able to stabilize the vertebrae, the damage done to the cord is not repairable. He is on a respirator and still unconscious. With his age, the degree of injury, and so many other factors, his prognosis is very grave. There is a chance that he might not make it through the night. If there is anyone to call, please do so now.” The doctor apologized that he couldn’t do more and then turned and walked back into the surgery room. Dylan stood motionless. He was in shock.

After standing in the middle of the waiting room for almost twenty minutes not knowing what to do or who to call, he finally thought of calling the Abbot. He made his way back to the lobby and asked the receptionist if he could use the phone. He dialed the monastery and after identifying who he was he asked for the Abbot. After holding for almost eight minutes the Abbot finally came to the phone and asked, “Is everything alright Dylan?” Tears instantly filled Dylan’s eyes and he became choked-up. He almost couldn’t speak but he pushed his trembling words out, “Father Abbot, it is Father Mateo. He is at the hospital and they think he isn’t going to make it through the night. They asked me to call whoever I needed to call and to let them know his condition. I am so sorry.” The Abbot reassured Dylan and informed him to stay right where he was and that he and a few of the other monks would be there in a few minutes.

Dylan felt better. It was as if he had called his own father and his father had told him that everything was going to be alright and he was on his way to make everything all better. Dylan knew the feeling he was experiencing wasn’t based in reality, but for the moment, it felt comforting. He returned to the surgery waiting area and sat back down in one of the chairs waiting for the monks to arrive.

Chapter 62

Carter had made up his mind that he was going to return to the seminary and resume his studies. He felt extremely grateful for the opportunity the Bishop had given him to further discern his vocation but now he felt with unshakable faith and conviction he was making the right decision. All he needed to do was break the news to Chuck and Colleen, pack up his gear, and make the long drive back to Oregon.

With it being Saturday Carter felt it was the perfect day to break the news. Chuck would have enough time to find another laborer before Monday if he felt he needed help and he could miss most of the city traffic on interstate 5 since most people were off work on the weekends.

Carter had cleaned his room, stripped the sheets from the bed, and even cleaned the bathroom toilet and shower. He packed his backpack as well as two plastic shopping bags full of his personal items and clothing that he had acquired over the last few months. After washing the coveralls that Chuck had loaned him, he carefully folded them and laid them on top of the dresser.

He heard Colleen yell out, “Time for breakfast.” Following the voice, he made his way to the kitchen and sat at the kitchen table.

Colleen was in a better than usual mood and she joyfully whistled as she finished scooping the scrambled egg and sausage mix onto three plates. She picked up two of them and after delivering one to Carter, she took the other one and sat down across the table from him. Carter said his blessing over the food, Colleen joined in, and they both wasted no time beginning to eat. Colleen asked, "You want some Tapatio sauce, it is a little bland?" Carter shook his head in the affirmative and she immediately stood to grab it from the counter. After handing it to Carter she returned to eating and he smothered his eggs with the spicy sauce. Carter was waiting for Chuck to arrive before he delivered the news, but Chuck was taking too long and he felt terrible keeping a secret. The anticipation finally got to him and he blurted out, "I'm returning to the seminary." Colleen dropped her fork and said, "What did you say?" Carter repeated, "I'm going back to the seminary." She replied, "That is what I thought you said. Well, this is out of the blue. Are you sure?" Carter shared he had been discerning for some time what he thought God's call for him was and over the past few days he felt surer than ever that he was being called to be a Catholic priest." Colleen smiled and said, "I can see that in you. I don't see you turning into a Chuck, your spirit is different. Don't take me wrong, I love Chuck. I think he is the moon's pie. I just eat him up, I love him so much. But you are different. I am happy for you." She then stood up, walked around the table, wrapped her arms around him, and gave him a huge motherly hug. Instantly Carter felt supported and loved. He wasn't sure how she would react, especially since they had taken him in as a son and made him a part of the family. Chuck finally arrived just as Colleen was finishing her hug and commented, "Hey, what you are doing with my wife?" He laughed and added, "No, really, what are you doing with my eggs and sitting in my seat? First my wife, now my seat and my eggs. What's next? The thing that gets me the most is my eggs, the wife thing and the seat thing, well, not so much." Colleen threw her fork at him and it poked him on his shoulder. Totally overreacting he dropped to the floor and began to roll from side to side yelling, "My eye, my eye. She poked out my eye." Colleen kicked him with a soft kick on his butt and said, "Get up you silly man. I'll heat your eggs while Carter tells you why he is quitting you." Chuck instantly became serious, sat up, and asked, "You are leaving us, son?" Carter explained that he truly loved living with them both and enjoyed working with him very much. He described how he had been thinking about returning to the seminary for some time and he finally received confirmation the previous night that he needed to return. Chuck asked, "Confirmation, you sure it wasn't just gas? You know I get gas sometimes and it makes me feel not only weird, maybe it is the fumes, but I even start to have dream-visions." Colleen shouted, "Knock it off Chuck. Not everything is a joke." Chuck finished laughing and then in a much more serious tone thanked Carter for their time together and getting a little choked up said, "I will miss you. It was like I had a son and we not only worked together but we're friends too. I will truly miss you." He stood up and with a firm handshake shook Carter's hand. He said, "You probably want your pay then too?" Colleen dropped the frying pan and screamed, "Chuck, you are the worst."

After finishing breakfast and repeating their good-byes he loaded his things into his car and drove away from the house. He programmed the seminary address into his GPS device and it estimated a little over an eight-hour drive and 510 miles. Looking at his watch and reading it aloud he said, "Eight o'clock, so eight plus eight is sixteen, minus two, then four, so I could be there at four o'clock." Planning to arrive in the afternoon before the sunset made the long drive seem very doable. He turned on the Spotify app on his phone, linked it through his BlueTooth in the car stereo and rocked out to a song from the '80s.

The drive up the 5 interstate was unremarkable except for having two gas breaks to refuel, two McDonalds stops that included buying and consuming food and copious amounts of coffee, and six times of pulling the car over on the side of the freeway to get out and pee. Arriving back at the seminary felt as if he was returning home. It was a comforting and familiar feeling.

Carter parked his car in the seminarian parking lot and made his way to the dorms. He passed by numerous rooms but didn't see anyone there. He wondered if they were all still in class, or if there was some type of special event happening. He had been away from the seminary for a while, even before his discernment sabbatical, since he was completing his pastoral year in Jordan Valley. He finally decided to venture over to the administration office to see if he could meet with the Abbot.

Luckily the administration office was still open. He requested to have a few minutes with the Abbot and surprisingly he was granted permission even without having an appointment. The Abbot greeted Carter in the lobby and Carter immediately noticed that the Abbot had aged quite a bit since he had seen him last. He looked tired and distracted. Carter asked, "Is everything alright, Father Abbot?" The Abbot all but dismissed the question and led Carter back to his office. The abrupt and rude behavior was not typical for the Abbot and Carter began to second-guess the timing of his visit. He started thinking the Abbot might not be in the best of spirits and feared that welcoming him back at the level of the Prodigal Son might not be as high of odds as he anticipated. As soon as the Abbot sat down behind his massive desk he asked, "What is it that I can do for you?" Carter noticed that his tone was much nicer now and he figured the Abbot must just be tired. Carter explained that he had been away discerning his call to the priesthood with the Bishop's permission and that he is returning feeling confident that he is making the right choice and is excited to resume his formation. The Abbot reacted in a very reserved and matter-of-fact manner as he said, "My son, it is not up to me to say if you can return or not.

Your situation was decided by the Bishop and it is the Bishop that can either grant your return or deny it. You need to go and see the Bishop." Instantly Carter's heart dropped and he felt fear building inside. He mentally reminded himself of just how kind and supportive the Bishop had been and planned that he would go visit him in the morning to straighten all of this out.

After leaving the Abbot's office he stopped at the receptionist's desk and quietly asked Lupita, "I'm going to see the Bishop tomorrow about returning to the seminary, but for now, I just drove over 500 miles to get here and I am exhausted. Is there a room where I could rest for just tonight?" Lupita carefully looked behind her to see if anyone was listening and when she discerned that there wasn't, she replied, "Yes, Father Mateo is in the hospital and he will not be back for some time, at least that was what I heard the Abbot saying on the phone. Go ahead and use Father's room. No one will know and by the way, you know Father, he wouldn't mind. Just put everything back the way it was so he doesn't trip on it." Carter thanked her and after verifying specifically where the room was, he exited the building.

Carter returned to his car and gathered just the supplies, toiletries, and clothing he would need for the night. He then located Father's room and made himself comfortable. There weren't any locks on the doors so there wasn't a need for a key. Exhausted from the journey, as soon as his head hit the pillow, he fell asleep.

Chapter 63

Jonas has now reached day thirty-three of his silent retreat and he had grown more and more fond of the isolation. In the beginning, he had some difficulty with the extended silence, but now he often had multi-hour conversations with himself, debating theological topics, playing both the good theologian and the bad theologian. He had developed the ability to empty his mind of almost all thought and then in prayer asked God to fill it. He meditated and reflected on singular words such as 'Father' or 'Lord' or 'Heaven' or 'Hell' one at a time and using just the one word he would be consumed deeply in contemplation. This contemplation, although beginning as a purposeful and directed act, quickly changed to where Jonas was taken over by Divine grace and it captivated his soul. These almost hypnotic-like states carried him directly to the mysteries of Christ. Mysteriously and miraculously, Jonas frequently found himself in the presence of the pre-resurrected Christ and he was able to speak to him as easily and clearly as the apostles and the early disciples had done so many centuries ago. With each encounter, Jonas was filled with Christ's teachings and His love and it was transforming him significantly. Every time Jonas had returned from one of these deep meditative states, he was not entirely the same person he had been before. Christ was progressively changing him from the inside into a deeply spiritual being.

Jonas had changed his eating pattern to now only eating every other day and he felt that his days of fasting helped him with his prayer. He found he could easily live on the word of God alone and that it satisfied him more than earthly food. Darnel had become concerned as he noticed that every other day the wooden box was not being picked up. One day, a few days prior, Darnel was so consumed with the fear that maybe Jonas had fallen ill that he snuck up to the shack's window and looked inside. What he witnessed gave him consolation. Jonas looked quite well. He was sitting on his bed, legs crossed in a meditative pose, and his facial expression was as if he was experiencing some sort of ecstasy. He looked healthy, much thinner, radiant, vibrant, and without any observable sign of concern.

With just one week left in his planned silent retreat, Jonas had left a note for Darnel requesting a piece of sketching paper and some charcoal pencils. He assumed that Maribeth would have some. The very next day they were included in his wooden box delivered to the step of his door. Jonas decided that with each of his meditative encounters he would pay close attention to how Jesus looked and would try to capture His image as specifically as he could and draw it for a gift to Darnel and Maribeth for their hospitality and friendship.

Each day Jonas worked on his sketch and meticulously drew to the best of his ability, Christ, as He appeared to him. Jonas was confident that who he was encountering in these miraculous events was Jesus of Nazareth before his resurrection. His appearance did not seem to be that of the resurrected Christ. His body did not appear to have been glorified and he didn't see the wounds in his hands.

The most magnificent feature that Jonas recognized in his encounters was Jesus' eyes. They were pure but powerful. They seemed to be able to see right inside of Jonas and penetrated with such ease all the way to his core, his soul. It was as if Jesus could see directly into his soul and read his most intimate thoughts and feelings. He also felt that as Jesus looked at him, just his gaze had the power to modify his soul, actually writing upon it with indelible marks, changing who he was as a person. One encounter he specifically recalled the feeling that Jesus looked at him and saw written on his soul was a stain of pridefulness, He erased it and wrote upon it a mark of humility, and when he separated from Jesus at the end of the encounter his being had been altered. He was literally a different person from the action of Jesus. It wasn't just a theological thought, but an actual occurrence and physical transformation.

Jonas continued to pray, draw, fast, and reflect upon his life and his vocation. Finally, on day 39 of the retreat, he completed the drawing. Although he never thought of himself as having artistic abilities in the past, the drawing was simple but quite good. He attributed it to God's grace and the supernatural aspects of the encounters that allowed him to produce something beyond his innate capabilities.

Chapter 64

The Abbot and six of the monks arrived at the hospital and after locating Dylan, they patiently waited until Father was transferred to the ICU. Taking turns, two by two they visited Father although he remained unconscious throughout the evening. Surprisingly his condition did not worsen as the surgeon had anticipated and by eight in the morning it appeared he had stabilized. He still had not awakened from the coma and he was reliant on the ventilator, but his vital signs were stable. After speaking to the intensivist and receiving confirmation that it appeared Father's condition did not appear to be as critical as the night before, the monastic group along with the Abbot chose to return to the monastery. Dylan, however, had received permission to remain at the bedside of Father Mateo.

Dylan kept occupied at Father's bedside by praying the full Liturgy of the Hours at each traditional time:

- Matins at 3 a.m.
- Lauds at 5 a.m.
- Prime at 6 a.m.
- Terce at 9 a.m.
- Sext at noon
- None at 3 p.m.

- Vespers at 6 p.m.
- Compline at 8 p.m.

As a seminarian he had become accustomed to praying Lauds when he rose in the morning and Vespers after school in the late afternoon, that was what was required of them, but with so much time on his hands, he felt there was no excuse not to pray as the monks did.

It had been four full days since they arrived at the hospital and Father had shown no signs of waking up from the coma. Dylan had overheard the surgeon and the hospitalist talking about Father earlier in the day. They were standing outside of the room and didn't seem to notice that their voices carried quite so far. They were discussing the possibility that Father might have suffered significant brain damage and there was a good chance he might never wake up. The men also discussed the possibility of harvesting some of his organs but they both agreed he was too old and the organs were not worth the trouble. Then the hospitalist said something that shocked Dylan. He commented on the need to start talking to the next of kin, if there were any, about making the humane decision to pull him off the ventilator and to let him die peacefully. Although Dylan knew the situation was quite serious, he never really thought that Father would be dead.

In a panic, Dylan called the Abbot and told him everything he had overheard. The Abbot comforted him and reassured him that no drastic decision would be made about Father's care without a great deal of discernment and prayer.

The next morning a social worker entered the room and introduced herself as Brianna. She spoke in a child-like way, high-pitched and unconvincingly sweet. Dylan instantly felt a dislike for her even though he was trying to be charitable. She spoke indirectly and Dylan got the sense that she had some bad news but was trying her best to deliver it in a roundabout way. Dylan finally interrupted her and said, "Just spit it out please, you are killing me." She was totally offended by his remark and she instantly replied, "I do not have to put up with your violence. I feel that I have been assaulted and this is to be a safe space. I am pretty sure I can sue you for that act of misogyny and as a hate crime due to my sexual preference." Dylan laughed out loud, he couldn't help himself. The laughter further enraged her, and she stormed out of the room.

Dylan turned to Father and began speaking to him, "Father I am not sure if you can hear me or not, but I am going to take my chances and let you know how much I love you. You probably didn't even realize it but I have a lot of little quirks and often I feel that people don't always understand where I am coming from. I did visit a counselor once, but the counselor told me I was more normal than anyone he had ever treated and said I was just overthinking things. Well, anyway, maybe he was right. What I am trying to say is that you always treated me with such great care and attention and you always made me feel relaxed and confident. I am a little worried that if God chooses to take you now, I might not be able to get by so good. Do you think you could ask God to allow you to hang out for a while longer?" Dylan paused for a moment and then added, "I guess I am just being selfish. Your dying would be a great reward for you. I am pretty sure you would go directly to heaven and not need any more than a pitstop in purgatory. Who wouldn't want to be in heaven? Your neck wouldn't be broken. Your eyes would be fixed. Wait, you won't have any eyes, you won't have a neck. I am so confused." He then stopped talking and just sat there and stared at Father's face until a very large man, meaning rotund, entered the room. He introduced himself as Doctor Alphonsus. He spoke in a condescending tone. He began by stating, "I was informed that you harassed one of my social workers and made her cry. This type of behavior is not tolerated here and I would ask that you do not repeat that abusive behavior or I will have to contact security and request to have you removed from the hospital." Dylan was shocked by the accusation and by the threat. He asked, "Now who are you?" He instantly replied in a firm tone, "I am Doctor Alphonsus." Dylan waited for additional explanation, but none followed so he asked, "No, really who are you. I get it, you're a doctor, but what type of doctor are you and why are you here? You really have no idea what occurred between me and that nutty woman. I think she needs serious mental help. By laughing at her I am being accused of assault, being threatened with a lawsuit, and being evicted from the hospital. This is just nuts. Again, who are you?" The morbidly obese man, who was now perspiring profusely retrieved a handkerchief from his pocket and wiped the sweat from across his brow and dabbed the rag numerous times under his chin catching the liquid that had run down his face. He replied, "I am Doctor Alphonsus, chief social worker, and discharge planner." Dylan laughed and then replied, "You're not even a real doctor." The man yelled back, "Yes I am. I am so tired of hearing I am not a doctor. I went to many years of school, have degrees, and deserve your respect. I demand your respect. I am not going to take this anymore. Wait until I tell my therapist about how you treated me. I'll show you, he will agree with me and that will serve you right. Now I see what Brianna was talking about. You are horrible. You are intolerant. You are a racist and a homophobe. I bet you are even a republican and voted for Trump. I should have stayed in academia where people understand what this world is about." He then turned and waddled out of the room. Instantly the hospitalist entered the room with a smirk on his face. He said, "I'm sorry, I overheard fatso chastising you. Oh, I'm sorry, chief doctor fatso. Don't give him another thought. His whole department is ultra-liberal looney tunes. I'm even a democrat but they take the cake. I don't even know what they are, socialists, communists, Martians, I don't know." Dylan liked the physician despite what he overheard him saying earlier. He seemed sincere and spoke to him like a real person. The hospitalist politely asked,

"Can I sit down and talk with you?" Dylan said, "Yes." The middle-aged physician sat down and said, "Dylan, that is your name, right?" Dylan nodded. He continued, "I just got off the phone with Father Abbot and I also wanted to talk to you. Father Mateo appears to be stable and he doesn't need hospital-level care any further. He does need special care however to make sure his basic needs are met and he doesn't develop bedsores or other complications. I think the best place for him would be in a good skilled nursing facility where the staff is specially trained to care for people just like Father."

Dylan didn't know what to say. He wanted to say *no, that is a bad idea. I want you to fix him and make him like he was before*, but he knew that wasn't reasonable. So instead he just listened. The physician continued, "I have already taken the liberty of asking the social workers to make arrangements to transfer Father Mateo to Orchard Meadows in the morning. They have a really good reputation and an excellent palliative care program." Dylan shook his head, gesturing that he understood. His eyes were now filled with tears and he really couldn't speak. The physician stood and shook Dylan's hand and proceeded out through the door. Dylan wanted to ask what palliative care was but didn't have the opportunity due to being overwhelmed with emotion.

Chapter 65

Carter awoke early before the sun had even risen, packed his belongings, and started driving toward the pastoral center in Boise. He wanted to catch the Bishop and get his permission to return to the seminary, get back to his life, his formation, and become what he now realized without a doubt he was called to be, a priest.

The day was going to be a long day. The drive alone was a seven-hour drive and he was hoping to catch the Bishop before he left for the day at five in the afternoon. He had texted his friend the day before, Ignacio, who was the diocesan youth director at the pastoral center and had asked him to check with the Bishop's secretary to see if the Bishop was scheduled to be at the office. Ignacio had confirmed the Bishop would be there all day and relayed that information back to Carter via text message.

Carter was making good time. He had already driven through Portland and had just gassed up his vehicle in Hood River and still, the sun had not yet risen. He planned to keep driving to Baker City before resting and getting something to eat. He had learned a few years ago that having sunflower seeds while driving not only helped to ward off hunger, but the act of putting seeds in the mouth, cracking them open one by one, swallowing the seed, and then spitting out the shell was enough to keep him occupied and awake.

He had purchased an extra-large bag just as he was leaving Mount Angel.

Carter turned the radio to the AM frequency and scanning the channels he finally stopped on a Catholic talk radio station. The reporter was describing an event in which two unnamed individuals videotaped themselves, faces hidden, going into a cathedral in Rome, stealing what they called pagan idol statues that were replicas of the ones being used at the African Synod, and threw them in the Tabor river in an act of protest at the liberal members of the Church. The reporter explained the statues were what the African people considered fertility goddesses and they prayed to them for fertility favors. The reporter said, "What on earth they were doing in a Catholic Cathedral made absolutely no sense and I am glad someone had the guts to purify the Sacred Temple." Carter laughed and hit the scan button to see what else was on the radio. The station digits on the radio screen continued to scroll until it stopped on 1240 am. The voice of the host caught Carter's attention. It was Mike Roberts from Caldwell and his podcast. Carter listened attentively to Mike's words,

"Currently, in our modern culture, the word 'Authentic' is in vogue. Everywhere you turn you hear just how authentic that person is and how we should all strive to be our authentic selves. But what does that mean, and is that truly a good thing? It appears that being authentic means that you are transparent, that what you see is what you get. That you are not putting up a facade, but rather exposing who you truly are without disguises or gimmicks. Being authentic doesn't mean you are a good person, it just means that you are aware of what you are and that you are alright with that. So, in theory, if you are a liar, a thief, an adulterer, and you don't try to hide it, you are authentic. Being authentic has nothing to do with having integrity. Integrity means you are a person with the quality of being honest and have strong moral principles and those

principles guide your life. As Christians, we acquire our understanding of morality from the Creator of the world, the Creator of humanity, and the Creator of us. That person is God. God has revealed Himself in the most perfect way through his Son Jesus Christ, but even before He sent His Son, He gave us the ten commandments for our guide of what is moral and just:

- *I am the Lord thy God, thou shalt not have any strange gods before Me.*
- *Thou shalt not take the name of the Lord thy God in vain.*
- *Remember to keep holy the Sabbath day.*
- *Honor thy father and mother.*
- *Thou shalt not kill.*
- *Thou shalt not commit adultery.*
- *Thou shalt not steal.*
- *Thou shalt not bear false witness against thy neighbor.*
- *Thou shalt not covet thy neighbor's wife.*
- *Thou shalt not covet thy neighbor's goods.*

Take a minute and reflect upon these commandments and discern if you are an authentic person, an authentic person with integrity, or neither."

Carter turned off the radio and pondered Mike's words. They appeared to make a great deal of sense, but he had never thought about integrity and authenticity in the way that Mike had described it.

Carter coughed and realized he had almost eaten the entire two-pound-bag of sunflower seeds and his tongue and internal cheeks were so dry that there was no saliva to be found. It was a desert of dry mucous membranes. He needed some sort of fluid. He grabbed his smartphone and keyed in the word STORE in the search engine and waited for the results to show him where the nearest store would be. Instantly the internet provided a list with the first reading 68 miles away. Carter yelled out, “Dang it.” then coughed again due to his dry mouth. Suddenly he remembered a trick he had learned in the Troops of Saint George (A Catholic version of Boy Scouts) when he was young. He searched his floorboard with his hand, keeping his eyes on the road until he felt what he thought was a small pebble. He quickly placed it into his mouth and began sucking on it. He recalled that when a person places an object in the mouth, even if it is a rock, and starts sucking on it, the digestive juices in a person’s mouth are activated and released. He sucked as hard as he could, and the taste was horrifying. He picked the rock out of his mouth and examined it closely. It wasn’t a rock that he picked up but instead a brownish looking crusted clump of who knows what. His imagination immediately went to ‘poop’ and he began to cough and gag thinking that he might have placed a piece of poop into his mouth and began to suck on it. He eventually couldn’t stand it and pulled his car over to the side of the road and then jumped out and opened his truck. He dug around until he found an old Gatorade bottle with just a swig’s worth of juice left in it. He quickly opened the cap and consumed the small amount of residual drink. It was quite stale but a much-appreciated improvement from the other taste lingering in his mouth.

Carter finally arrived in Baker City and he saw McDonald's was open. He swung around to the drive-through. He ordered a sausage biscuit, hash browns, and a large coffee with six creams and six sugars. He was starving and couldn’t wait to get the food. Almost as soon as he approached the pick-up window his food was already bagged and waiting for him.

He looked at his watch and discerned he was not traveling as quickly as he had anticipated. He quickly drove to the gas station, filled up, and was back on the freeway in record time. Now cruising at eighty-five miles an hour, he set the cruise control and felt ready to open his food bag. He reached into the bag and retrieved from it what appeared to be a happy meal carton. He opened the carton and it contained three plastic toys and a salt and sugar packet. He dug back into the bag and after feeling around a bit he pulled out a small fry, just one fry that must have mistakenly fallen into the bag. He couldn't believe they had messed up his order. He was looking forward to the sausage biscuit and the hash browns. Now reaching for his coffee he flicked off the lid and noticed that the coffee was black, no cream to be seen. He took a sip and it was immediately noticeable that there wasn't any sugar either. He lowered the cup and he identified that written on the side of the cup were the words DECAF. He yelled out, "You gotta be kidding me."

Chapter 66

Day 40 of the silent retreat had finally arrived and Jonas opened the shed door. For the first time in almost a month and a half, he exited the shed without the plastic shovel in hand. He raised his eyes toward the sky and drew in a slow deep breath. He slowly released his air and said, “God has been so good to me.” He walked toward the house. Maribeth must have caught a glimpse of him through her studio window and yelled out, “Darnel, he has finished. He has finished.” She ran out of the house and quickly came upon him and hugged Jonas with all her strength. She immediately withdrew and said, “Jonas, you stink so badly.” He was oblivious to the stench probably desensitized from the extended exposure. Darnel had joined them and commented, “I think I smelled you from the house. The soap wasn’t that useful?” Maribeth firmly directed, “You get in the tub right now and give me those clothes. I’ll wash them, fumigate them, and see if they still need to be burned or not.”

Jonas did as asked and followed Maribeth into their home and into the bathroom. It was a small bathroom that couldn’t have been more than four feet by six feet, but it did have a full-size bathtub. Not a modern full-size, but full-size for the sixties. He closed the door, disrobed, and carefully set his clothing outside the bathroom on the hallway floor. His clothing consisted of a one-piece cassock and that was it. No socks and no underwear.

Before getting in the tub he looked at himself in the mirror. He initially didn't recognize his reflection. His beard had grown almost five inches and he must have lost fifty pounds. He looked as if he was ninety years old, malnourished, dehydrated, atrophied muscles, and what the medical community would have to call cachectic. Yet, his external appearance didn't match how he felt physically and mentally. He felt as if he was twenty again and hopeful for the future.

He reached for the scissors that were laying on the back of the toilet tank and began cutting away at his beard. He had initially planned to just trim a few inches and to try to get some of the natty hair, but the more he trimmed the better it felt to be rid of that coarse and scratchy hair. He cut and cut and in no time, there was a mound of hair that had accumulated in the sink almost a foot high. He trimmed his beard until there was just a quarter of an inch left.

He climbed into the tub and with the water almost too hot he slowly lowered himself down. Instantly the water turned brown and it looked as if he was sitting in a sewer. He pulled the plug and allowed the water to drain. He then turned the faucet on and filled the tub, but it too became grotesquely brown. He repeated the process six times of filling the tub and then draining it until the water remained semi-clear. He then took the bar of homemade soap that Maribeth created and lathered his entire body including his head, neck, torso, legs, and the private areas. He allowed the soap suds to sink in thinking it had some chemical properties that would dissolve the filmy build-up of sweat and oil that layered his skin. He submerged his body under the water and rolled side to side. The water had turned light brown so he drained it and refilled the tub. This time there wasn't any hot water so the tub was filling with ice-cold water and he began to shiver. He took the bar of soap and lathered himself again but instead of submerging his body, he splashed water onto his skin to rinse it off. After a few minutes he had enough and still partially soaped up, he stood and climbed out of the tube. He dried off with the towel hanging on the rod and quietly opened the door. There laying on the ground was a perfectly folded cassock. He reached for it and saw that under it was a pair of underwear, socks, and a new pair of sandals. The items looked new. He quickly dressed and walked to the dining room and asked, "Where did the clothing come from and what happened to my old clothes?" Maribeth smiled and said, "Darnel knew you would be needing new clothes so a few days ago he drove to Yuba City and asked Father Avery if he would help with obtaining clothing for you." Darnel chimed in, "He was more than willing to help, and he said he knew exactly what size you needed, his size." Jonas's eyes filled with tears and he commented, "You have been so nice to me, I don't know how I will ever repay you." In reaction, Darnel and Maribeth were now also crying. Finally, after a long period of silence, Maribeth responded, "I know how you can repay us. Tomorrow, come with us to the monastery and help us deliver the icon. We will need some help lifting it onto the trailer, tying it down, and making sure it doesn't get damaged on the drive." Jonas immediately replied, "It would be my honor." Maribeth yelled out, "That's wonderful! We get to spend more time with you."

While Maribeth was celebrating, Darnel had retrieved a casserole dish from the oven and began setting the table with dishes and food. He set place settings for three and in a matter of two minutes, the table was set with dishes and utensils, the casserole dish, a bowl of stuffing, bread and butter, yams, green beans, and corn on the cob. He also opened a bottle of red table wine from the Trappist monastery in Vina.

The three individuals visited, ate, and enjoyed each other's company and not once did Darnel or Maribeth ask Jonas about his time in the shed. They assumed that whatever he encountered while on his silent retreat was not only personal but that he would need some time to process the significance of it as well.

Jonas asked again, "What did you do with my old cassock?" Darnel looked at Maribeth, she looked right back at him. Without speaking words, they were communicating. She finally blurted out, "He burned it."

Chapter 67

Dylan had helped with ensuring the transfer of Father Mateo to Orchard Meadows went as scheduled despite the social workers' attitudes and behavior. The morbidly obese snowflake, Doctor Alphonsus fatso, had filed a restraining order against Dylan and had him served an hour before Father was to be transferred. Dylan was escorted out of the hospital by the security staff and he was forced to watch the ambulance arrive and load Father into it, all from 250 feet away and off the official hospital grounds. He followed the ambulance over to the skilled nursing facility.

Upon arrival at the skilled nursing facility, Dylan was greeted by Henrietta, the administrator, who spent almost an hour talking to Dylan and asking questions about his relationship with Father Mateo. She asked how long they had known each other, if they were officially related in any way, and if he (Dylan) had been previously arrested for any crimes of theft or aggression. The woman was very nice, but she asked such probing questions that it seemed extremely unusual. He finally asked, "I don't mean to be rude, but are these questions part of the normal admitting process?" She laughed a huge bellowing laugh and after catching her breath she replied, "No, not at all." I can now see that what we were told has nothing to do with the truth." Dylan was confused and the look on his face must have shown it. She continued, "We received a call initially from a social worker by the name of Brianna. She stated that we needed to be cautious of a man named Dylan who would be dressed in clerical clothing, but that he was actually the devil himself. She said she had been assaulted by this man and if we allowed him to enter the facility, he would torment the staff and could possibly be a child molester. We then received a call from Doctor Alphonsus who reported he had filed charges against this same man by the name of Dylan and he was quite sure that Dylan was trying to steal all of Father Mateo's money. He said he had already filed a report with adult protective services for elder abuse and that he was so frightened for his life that he had to take out a restraining order against the man." Dylan exploded in laughter and trying to compose himself he stated, "Not one bit of that is true, and what is the most hilarious thing is that Father Mateo had taken a vow of poverty over thirty years ago. How much wealth do you think an elderly monk has hidden under his mattress? He doesn't even own a pair of socks or underwear without holes in them." By now she was laughing even harder than Dylan.

Henrietta shared with Dylan that after the first minute of meeting him she sensed what type of man he was and dismissed all that nonsense from those quaky social workers. The two hit it off from the start and quickly developed a friendship bond.

Father was treated quite well by the staff at the facility and they ensured his ventilator was oxygenating his body, that his skin remained clean and intact, and that he received his tube feedings as prescribed. The hospitalist was right when he said the facility had a good reputation and they not only knew what they were doing but also gave a superior quality of care.

Initially, Dylan had hoped Father would somehow miraculously wake up but with each day and no observable change in status, Dylan was starting to lose some hope. Yet, he remained at the bedside for at least 18 hours of each day, only leaving to sleep at night and to get fresh clothes and a shower. He would return and spend the rest of the day with his most beloved friend. He would talk to Father, read him stories of the saints, and the early Church Fathers, especially John Cassian. He would tell jokes, and they even prayed together. Well, Dylan was doing all the talking, reading, and praying, since Father seemed to just lay there. Father remained in a chronic coma-state.

Chapter 68

Carter finally arrived in Boise and made his way to Federal Avenue and to the pastoral center. Looking at his watch he noticed that it was five minutes to five and he had been told he would be able to meet with the Bishop if he arrived by five o'clock.

Carter began to run as quickly as he could but sitting in the car for so many hours, he had developed a few cramps in his legs and the spasms slowed him down. Pressing through the pain he raced into the building and ran to the reception desk and blurted out, "I have permission to see the Bishop. I'm seminarian Carter." The receptionist immediately called upstairs, and Carter could overhear parts of the conversation. He heard, "The Bishop is leaving in three minutes." Carter spoke out, "I only need one minute." The receptionist waved her hand authorizing Carter to get on the elevator and head to the Bishop's office. Carter moved as fast as he could. He had anticipated when the Bishop saw him he would be greeted with a warm reception, maybe a hug, and then have a pleasant conversation. However, when the Bishop did see him, he didn't seem too excited. The Bishop said, "I was just walking out the door, Carter, what is it?" The Bishop removed his jacket, walked back into his office, and sat down behind his large desk. Carter followed and began to explain all he had done during his discernment sabbatical and even before he got to the good stuff, the Bishop cut him off and said, "Carter, I don't think religious life is cut out for you. I think you should give it a try in the secular world. When a man gets cold feet and walks away, that usually is a sign that he wasn't ever really invested in the first place." He stood up, donned his jacket, and as he walked out of the room he said, "Sorry, but I have an urgent matter I must attend to. Good luck Carter." He disappeared into a back room and Carter could hear footsteps resembling a man walking down a flight of stairs.

Carter was speechless. The encounter did not go as planned. He just knew the Bishop would welcome him back and he would be back at the seminary just like before. This was like a nightmare. He would never have guessed that he would be denied the opportunity to become a priest. Yet, in a flash of a few seconds, it had all been taken away. It was as if the Bishop didn't even listen to him. It seemed like the Bishop had already made up his mind before he had arrived. Something wasn't right. He questioned, "Did someone say something from the seminary about me that made the Bishop act like that?" This just doesn't make any sense. He then said aloud, "I'm not going to roll over so fast. I'm going back to Mount Angel to find out what happened. I know God wants me to be a priest. I am as sure as a man can be sure. I am going to get to the bottom of this." He then rushed out of the building and back to his car. He started the engine and then began in the direction back to Oregon. He looked at the rosary hanging from his rearview mirror and said, "We can do this Jesus, hold onto your chain, we are going to make record time back to the seminary." He pressed his gas pedal down to the floor and the car launched forward.

Carter began to calculate how long it would take to return to Mount Angel. It was at least a seven-hour drive and he left Boise at five-forty in the afternoon. Counting on his fingers he came up with arriving close to 1 am if he didn't stop except for gas. He immediately knew that he would not be able to drive all those hours without falling asleep at the wheel. So, he adjusted his plan and was hoping to make it at least to Baker City where he could sleep at the rest stop and resume driving early the next morning. Now knowing he wasn't going to do the ultimate driving marathon, he felt more relaxed and comfortable. He turned the radio back on and started to scan the stations. He stopped on the Salt and Light Catholic radio station and began listening to the Mancave show. The show was hosted by Brian and the co-host was Pat King. Their guest was the newly ordained Deacon Toby Green. Toby was describing his recent ordination and how he was now being assigned to Our Lady of the Valley parish in Caldwell. Toby described his first attempt at preaching and stated, "I prepared all week for my turn at preaching. I wrote my notes and rewrote them. I practiced my presentation at least twenty times and I was about as prepared as I could be. After proclaiming the Gospel, I took out my notes and feeling comfortable I was just about to begin when Father Mike whispered, "that was the wrong reading." I immediately looked at the book of the Gospels and verified that Father was right. I not only had read the wrong gospel, but I had based my entire homily on the wrong gospel. I was petrified. I began to sweat. I had never given a homily before and now I needed to re-read the correct Gospel and then preach for at least ten minutes on something I was not prepared for." Pat asked, "What did you do?" Toby stated, "I said a quick prayer in my head, proclaimed the correct Gospel and then prayed again internally that God would send his grace down upon me and help me say something not entirely stupid." Brian asked, "You must have been ready to pee your pants?" Toby smiled and said, "That is an understatement. Well, I just started talking and glancing down at the Gospel reading from time to time. I let the Holy Spirit guide me and before I knew it my timer said twelve minutes and I ended the homily. I have no idea what I said. I think the nerves blocked it all out. But at least twenty people came up to me after Mass and thanked me for the homily. Two people said that they felt that God was speaking to them directly in the homily." Pat asked, "So, no more preparing for homilies?" The men laughed. Toby responded, "That is not the case. From now on I will double-check to make sure what I am planning includes the proper readings."

Carter turned off the radio and decided to stop even a little earlier. He was starting to fall asleep and upon identifying a trucker's rest stop he pulled in, parked, and quickly fell asleep.

Chapter 69

Dylan had just arrived at the skilled nursing facility and was surprised to see the Abbot standing in the lobby talking with Henrietta. As soon as she saw Dylan she called him over and said, "We have been waiting for you, you have a minute?" Dylan confirmed that he did, and she then led the men into a conference room down the hall. Inside the conference room were three other gentlemen sitting down. Henrietta gestured toward the Abbot and then to Dylan to have a seat. Once everyone was situated Henrietta began, "Thank you all for coming. This is our medical ethics review meeting and at the request of Father Abbot, we have gathered today. Father Abbot, would you like to begin?" He nodded and then spoke, "Thank you all for coming. We have a very difficult decision to make regarding Father Mateo. Our Catholic belief is that when one is sick, we are to ensure that they are provided the basics like food and water and if they have an infection then the proper medication is given. As you know Father has been on a respirator for some time and it appears that he is dependent on it. Many would say that a respirator is an extraordinary measure and not just the basic food and water needed to live. Just yesterday when I was looking for something in our seminary files, I came across a Living Will I didn't know that we had for Father Mateo. Apparently, he filled it out almost ten years ago and it was co-signed by the Vice Abbot who is now deceased. The Will states that if he becomes in such a state that he cannot sustain life on his own he requests that no extraordinary measure be given to sustain his life. So that is where we are today." Dylan was completely surprised by what Father Abbot was sharing and was listening intently. The other men introduced themselves as the Medical Director of the facility and the other as the Chief Nursing Officer. The third was the lawyer for the facility. Each of them concurred the Will was quite clear and it was apparent Father Mateo did not want his life continued in the way it was currently being sustained.

Father Abbot stated he would like to have the Bishop anoint him and then they would want to have the tube removed for Father to be able to pass peacefully. The three men and Henrietta agreed. Internally Dylan wanted to shout out that there must be some other option, but he felt quite intimidated by all those in the room so he remained quiet. Father Abbot stated he had anticipated everyone would be in agreement and he had already reached out to the Bishop who was expected to arrive later around noon. After a brief discussion, it was agreed that anticipating the Bishop would arrive as expected and the anointing could be done at that time, then the ventilator could be turned off afterward and the intubation tube removed.

The meeting broke up quite suddenly and within a minute the room cleared and all had left except for Dylan. He felt as if he was in shock. He could not believe that in just a few hours his best friend would be dead. He began to hyperventilate. His head became light and as he stood, he immediately collapsed and hit his head on the edge of the table on the way down. It tore open the skin and he bled copiously. He regained his senses, crawled over to the sink in the corner of the room, and grabbed a few of the paper towels from the dispenser. He pressed the towels against the wound on his forehead to stop the bleeding. By palpating his skin at the wound site he assessed that the wound was not serious, more of a deep scrape than a gashing laceration. He did identify that he must not have been quick enough with the towel because the entire front of his white shirt was now stained in fresh red blood. He didn't want to look so disheveled on Father's last day on earth and knew that if he left right then he would have enough time to drive back to his room, change clothing, bandage his would, and return in time and spend a few hours with Father before his spirit left this world.

Chapter 70

Darnel, Maribeth, and Jonas finally arrived at the seminary towing the U-Haul rental trailer behind their Subaru wagon. Luckily it was an enclosed trailer because it had begun to rain just as they entered Oregon from California and the icon would have been damaged significantly if it had been exposed to the downpour. The journey could have been completed in much less time but Maribeth repeatedly asked to stop for bathroom breaks about every hour. She also wasn't the quickest with using the restroom and returning to the vehicle. She liked to browse in the gas station convenience stores for a few minutes and completed a set of leg stretches at each stop. She also wanted to stop at Crater Lake to do a little sketching and have a picnic meal. She remembered how beautiful the lake had been years ago when she and Darnel visited it. She packed a delightful meal for all of them to share, complete with fried chicken, watermelon, and freshly baked bread with local honey.

Darnel knew the seminary complex well, having studied there himself many years ago. He initially thought he would become a priest, but like so many good men he left the seminary to fight in the war and he met his wife to be. Then the vocation turned from a life of holy orders to a life of matrimony and marriage. Darnel drove the vehicle and the trailer up next to the monastic chapter house and informed Jonas he wouldn't be able to help lift the heavy icon due to having a back condition that just flared up in the last few minutes. Jonas, not phased by the notification, decided to stroll around the area and look for a strong seminarian who could help him lift, carry, and deliver the larger-than-life icon of Mary to its reserved resting place. He first looked inside the chapter house, but it was empty of humans. He then looked in the adjacent building but also didn't see anyone. Standing on the edge of the walkway he patiently waited and prayed that God would send him a young strong man to help him.

After waiting for almost twenty minutes Dylan arrived in the seminary vehicle. He jumped out of the car right in front of Jonas and Jonas asked, "You have a minute to help me?" Dylan, in a rush to change his clothes and do the few tasks he had to do, completely ignored Jonas and kept running in the direction of the dorms. It wasn't until he reached the doors of the dorm that his conscience got the best of him. He thought, *Why did I ignore that man? I was the furthest thing from Christ to him.* He quickly turned around and ran back toward Jonas. Jonas was still standing on the walkway when Dylan arrived and said, "I'm sorry sir, I was so preoccupied. How can I help you?" Jonas explained he needed some help just for a minute to unload and carry the icon. Dylan smiled and confirmed he would be happy to help. The men untied the icon and together began to carry it. While carefully walking with the large icon in their hands, Dylan realized that he had not introduced himself to Jonas and did so. Jonas responded, "Nice to meet you, Dylan, I'm Jonas." For some reason, the name Jonas struck him as familiar. He thought and thought where he had recently heard that name and it wasn't until they walked into the chapter house that he realized he had read that name in Father Mateo's book. Dylan playfully asked, "You didn't grow up on Jeffrey Court in Olivehurst, California, did you?" Jonas look surprised by the question but answered, "Why yes, how did you know that?" Dylan almost dropped the icon and stopped dead in his tracks. He sat the icon down on the ground and looked

Jonas right in the eyes and asked, "Do you know Father Mateo?" Jonas replied, "I don't think so, should I?" Darry was confused and tried to remember all that he had learned about Father and what he had read. Then it came to him, Father had changed his name when he became a monk. Dylan asked, "What about a man by the name of Andrew or Drew Kline?" Jonas' eyes filled with tears and he slowly responded, "That was my brother's name. He died many years ago serving in the military." Dylan responded immediately, "No, he didn't. He is a monk here at the seminary. He was my teacher. He is like a father to me." Jonas was confused. His brother had been dead for many years. Jonas commented, "You must be mistaken, son." Dylan then recited numerous things he had read about Father's childhood from the book, as well as details about their parents, their friends, how he went off to war, and how he walked away from everyone and everything after he had murdered those innocent people. The tears began to stream down Jonas' face. Dylan said, "Let's go, I will take you to him." Then he suddenly remembered Father Mateo was about to die. That at three o'clock they were going to disconnect him from the ventilator. He shared, "Jonas, he is very ill. He is on a ventilator and they are going to allow him to die this afternoon. We need to get you there as soon as possible." Jonas was overwhelmed with the news. He needed to think and time to take this all in. He hadn't seen his brother for so long. He didn't know what to think. Dylan said again, "Jonas, they are going to disconnect him from the ventilator at three o'clock, we need to get there right away. I need to get there right away." Jonas asked, "Where is the chapel here? I need to see Jesus." Dylan pointed in the direction of the chapel, it was just a few hundred feet away. Jonas asked, "Where is my brother?" Dylan explained that he was in a skilled nursing facility and what the name of it was. Jonas thanked Dylan and said, "I'll be there. I just need some time with Jesus first. I'll meet you there." Dylan felt he had finally conveyed the urgency to Jonas and he understood. He also understood that

Jonas needed a few minutes to recollect himself now knowing that his brother was alive. He said, “alright, but please be there well before three o’clock.” Jonas stated that he understood and began walking in the direction of the chapel.

Chapter 71

Dylan drove as fast as he could and arrived back at the skilled nursing facility a little after noon. Bishop Kerry had already arrived and had started the anointing ritual. He began by giving a greeting to all who had gathered and then directly to Father Mateo. He took the aspergillum, dunked it into the holy water vessel, and then as he sprinkled holy water onto Father in the form of a cross, he blessed him and brought attention to the water being a reminder of Father's baptism which gained him status as a Christian and also the opportunity for life everlasting in the kingdom of heaven. He asked for all present and Father to also recall their sins and to ask for forgiveness and led everyone in the penitential right:

I confess to almighty God and to you, my brothers and sisters, that I have greatly sinned in my thoughts and in my words, in what I have done and in what I have failed to do, through my fault, through my fault, through my most grievous fault; therefore I ask blessed Mary ever-Virgin, all the Angels and Saints, and you, my brothers and sisters, to pray for me to the Lord our God.

He prayed over Father Mateo in silence while gently laying his hands upon his forehead. Father Mateo had not moved, blinked, or made any noise that would suggest that he was aware of what was occurring. The Bishop then took the anointing oil and rubbed it upon Father's forehead and upon his hands.

The Bishop removed a small golden Pyx from a burse that hung around his neck and rested against his breast, slowly opened it, and took a host out from within the container. Grasping it between his thumb and first finger, he raised it high into the air and said,

"Agnus Dei, qui tollis peccata mundi, miserere nobis.
Agnus Dei, qui tollis peccata mundi, miserere nobis.
Agnus Dei, qui tollis peccata mundi, dona nobis pacem."

Which means,

Lamb of God, who takes away the sins of the world,
have mercy upon us.
Lamb of God, who takes away the sins of the world,
have mercy upon us.
Lamb of God, who takes away the sins of the world,
grant us peace.

The Bishop said and all joined in,
"Lord I am not worthy that you should enter under my roof, but only say the word and I shall be healed."

He lowered the host and broke a small piece from it. He gently laid a tiny morsel upon Father's parched tongue, and then consumed the remainder. There was a long period of silence and silent prayer that lasted for almost fifteen minutes. Dylan watched as the Bishop appeared to be fervently praying for his priest. Suddenly the Bishop spoke, "My dear Father Mateo until I see you again, God willing, may you rest in peace and be held closely in Christ's arms today. Amen." He then made the sign of the cross with his right hand over Father. The Bishop removed his stole and placed it along with his supplies back into his bag. He then sat down next to Father Abbot.

The medical director, Doctor Philips walked into the room and asked, “Everything going as planned?” The Bishop and Father Abbot both said in unison, “Yes, as planned.” Dylan began to cough loudly and so forcefully that he started to choke. Doctor Philips looked at him and seeing that he wasn’t in any real distress, just reacting to saliva going down the wrong pipe, encouraged him to get a glass of water from the nurses’ station. Dylan, still coughing, did as was suggested and left the room for water. The Doctor looked at his watch and said, “So, I’ll be back in about an hour and a half?” The Bishop looked at the Abbot and then said, “There really isn’t a need to wait is there? The Abbot replied, “Not really.” The doctor explained that it was quite a simple process. He would turn off the machine and extubate the patient. He stated the whole process would take about thirty seconds and he didn’t expect the patient to take in any breaths since the brain had been so damaged. Father Abbot confirmed they should proceed but asked to wait just a moment so Dylan could be present.

Doctor Philips prepped the patient, Father Mateo, by removing the air from the internal balloon that kept the intubation tube from slipping out, and as soon as Dylan walked back into the room, the doctor turned the ventilator switch off and slipped the tube out of Father’s mouth. Suddenly realizing what was occurring Dylan dropped the water glass and as it shattered on the floor he yelled out, “What are you doing? His brother Jonas hasn’t arrived yet. I told him to be here before three o’clock.” Everyone looked at Father Mateo. There was no movement of the chest. There was no sound of air. Dylan looked to the doctor and said frantically, “Can you put the tube back in and turn on the machine?” The doctor with a very saddened face replied, “It doesn’t work that way, son. It isn’t that simple. I am so sorry.” Dylan began to cry and moan loudly, “But his brother isn’t here.” The Bishop tried to console Dylan but at the moment it was impossible.

Chapter 72

Jonas was sitting in the front pew closest to the tabernacle and while praying a young man walked into the chapel. Jonas didn't look back to see who it was, but the man stared at Jonas and kept walking towards him until he was upon him. Jonas then turned to look at the man whose presence he now felt, and he instantly recognized him. It was Carter. He immediately stood and hugged him with all his strength. Carter said, "I have missed you. I thought about you almost every day since you came into the church and took off all your clothes." The men laughed. Jonas said in reply, "I have thought about you too. Are you alright?" Carter explained what had occurred and that he needed to speak to the Abbot to see if he would help change the mind of the Bishop. Jonas pointed his finger toward the tabernacle and said, "He knows what to do, just trust in Him." Carter acknowledged that he believed the statement to be true and then sat down next to Jonas.

The men sat in silent adoration for almost an hour, and then Jonas broke the silence by saying, "My dead brother isn't dead." Carter was confused and asked, "What do you mean?" He explained that he had ridden to the seminary with friends to help deliver a large icon for the chapter house and he met a young seminarian by the name of Dylan and Dylan had informed him that his dead brother was not dead, but he would be dead at three o'clock. Carter was still quite confused but did ask, "Where is your brother?" Jonas explained that he was at a skilled nursing facility, and mentioned the name. Carter stated that he knew where that was. Carter offered, "You want me to take you there?" Jonas agreed so the two men rose from the pew, genuflected toward the tabernacle, and walked out of the chapel. Carter's car was parked just outside and they hopped in it and drove to the nursing home.

Upon arrival, Carter parked his car and led the way into the lobby. The receptionist saw Jonas' cassock and assumed he was there to meet with the other religious men and directed them to room 304, Father Mateo's room.

As soon as Jonas entered the room, he saw his brother lying there lifeless. Dylan yelled out, "Jonas why did you not come? They turned off the machine and he died almost 30 minutes ago. Why did you not come?" Dylan was crying forcefully. Jonas didn't respond. His eyes were fixed upon his brother. He walked up to him and taking in a deep breath he then released it upon his brother's face. Suddenly Father Mateo gasped for air. Now the Doctor, the Bishop, and the Abbot were all still in the room and the gasp caught everyone's attention. There was another gasp, then another, and then Father began to breathe on his own and in a regular fashion. Jonas then took his own hands and wrapped them around the back of Father's neck and squeezed while he prayed, *Heal the brokenness of this man's bones. Dust to Dust, and light to light, heal him, papa, heal him.* He then removed his hand from his brother's neck and then spat upon his palm. He rubbed the spittle together and then wiped it across his brother's eyes while saying, *Dear Lord, you can make the blind see and you can bring the dead back to life. Papa, please do this for me, heal my brother.* Suddenly Father Mateo opened his eyes and sat up. It was miraculous. The dead man had risen from the dead. He looked directly at Jonas and said, "I can see you, my brother. I have missed you greatly. I love you so much." He then turned to Dylan and said, “I heard everything you said to me while I was asleep. I love you too Dylan. To me, you are my son.” Father Mateo then stood, walked a few steps toward his brother, and wrapped his arms around him. Jonas did the same, hugging him closely with such deep emotion and the men stood embraced for a long time. Everyone in the room watched in amazement of what was occurring, it was surreal. The doctor kept pinching himself to make sure he wasn’t dreaming. Father released his grip, looked directly toward the Bishop, and asked him to approach. The Bishop immediately did as asked and Father Mateo asked him to lean forward and he said, “I was in the arms of Jesus just a moment ago and He shared with me a message for you.” Father then leaned in even closer and whispered into the Bishop’s ear. The Bishop listened for a moment and collapsed to the ground. He began to sob violently. After a few seconds, Father placed his hand upon his shoulder to help calm his emotions. The Bishop still down on his knees turned his head toward Carter and said, “Carter, will you please return to the seminary. I have made a grave mistake. Please forgive me.” Carter burst in emotion and as tears washed across his face he said, “Of course Bishop, of course Bishop.”

Chapter 73

One year later

Father Mateo had not only awakened from the dead but was miraculously healed of his broken neck and blindness. He seemed younger than ever and full of life. He returned to teaching at the seminary full-time and was the most inspirational and beloved professor at the seminary. He now drove himself to the park weekly and Katie still visited him every time he was there. He hosted a weekly seminary podcast with the help of the seminarians and broadcasted it live over the internet and he named it "Alive Again." It had become the number one spiritual podcast in the nation in less than three months after its origination.

Jonas was last seen walking through New Mexico and there were reports he continues to change lives one encounter at a time. There were now a handful of investigative reporters aggressively trying to track him down and locate him for an interview to find out if what the people were saying about him was true or if he had become an urban legend. Every time they thought they were about to corner him he would vanish. Every report and sighting identified him as still wearing the black thirty-three button priestly cassock and barefoot.

Forgotten and Lost

Carter had returned to his studies at the seminary, was helping Father Mateo with the weekly podcast, and had been ordained a transitional Deacon in the late spring. He stayed in contact with Brooklyn (Sister Mariam) as pen pals and spent all his school breaks with Colleen and Chuck. Excited to finish his final year, he would be ordained to the holy priesthood in less than eleven months, God willing.

Dylan was sent off for his pastoral year to a parish and was assigned to Saint Bernard's parish in Jordan Valley with Father Clemens who had returned from his sabbatical in Rome.

About the Author

Deacon Pat Kearns and his wife, Liz, live in Northern California. They have three grown children. Deacon Pat is a U.S. Navy/Marine veteran, an ordained Catholic cleric, and a psychiatric nurse. He holds a master's degree in nursing leadership and management, is board certified in psychiatric and mental health nursing, and is a certified public health nurse. He is currently the Nursing Director of a large psychiatric hospital in Northern California and ministers at parishes in the Sacramento diocese. He is also the founder of Catholic *Men-In-Motion* Retreats and Host of The Catholic Journey Podcast.

Deacon Pat and Liz have also lived in Southern California, Western Idaho, and the mountains of Guatemala while serving as full-time Catholic missionaries and developing nutritional and health care programs for the local Mayan people. Deacon Pat walked the Camino de Santiago (The Way of Saint James) across Northern Spain during the summer of 2017 with his brother Tim (one of the six brothers) and is planning a similar walking journey again for 2021.

As an author of numerous novels, spiritual guides, and bilingual children's books, Deacon Pat uses his life experiences, as well as his imagination, to create wonderful stories grounded in the faith. He has become a popular novelist due to his easy-to-read writing style, thrilling adventures, relatable and life-like characters, and for the messages of hope, redemption, love, forgiveness, and joy, that so many of the stories possess. He is also a spiritual director, gifted preacher, and a popular spiritual retreat leader.

Books by Deacon Pat Kearns

Available through Amazon.com and other outlets.

Adventure / Spiritual Novels

Forgotten & Lost

Climbing Out of the Darkness

Breaking Away

C.S.F.
Catholic Special Forces

The Hermit's Word

The Hidden Journey

Church
More Than Just a Building

Spiritual Guides

100 Days to Freedom

Health, Happiness,
and Holiness

Children's' Books

(Bilingual - Spanish/English)

I am Nene
Yo Soy Nene

I am Isabelita
Yo Soy Isabelita

My Greatest Treasure
"The Kearns Family"

Saint Patrick,
Pray for Us!

Made in the USA
Columbia, SC
30 May 2020